ien Assassin

"...ly are things high octane, but the story is twisty and clever and ...me it seemed like I knew where things were going, there was ... surprise."

—Joyfully Jay

"...uspense and mystery mixed with romance and characters that are so well written, you feel like you've known them for years."

—Diverse Reader

Tramps and Thieves

"Rhys Ford is just amazing with the written word and storytelling. There are quite a few parts in this novel where the writing is just poetic and is very emotional. It's a must read!"

—The Novel Approach

"Rhys Ford has a knack for drawing a reader in and then leaving them on the edge of their seats."

—Gay Book Reviews

Hellion

"An author with a broad scope of genres under her belt, Ms. Ford dazzles the reader with descriptions that satisfy the soul."

—Paranormal Romance Guild

"Rhys Ford somehow makes every emotion…every bit of anger and love and fear and happiness seem so real by painting this amazing picture with their words."

—Love Bytes

By RHYS FORD

Published by DREAMSPINNER PRESS
www.dreamspinnerpress.com

RHYS FORD

BACK IN BLACK

Published by
DREAMSPINNER PRESS

5032 Capital Circle SW, Suite 2, PMB# 279, Tallahassee, FL 32305-7886 USA
www.dreamspinnerpress.com

Cover Art
© 2020 Reece Notley
reece@vitaenoir.com
Cover content is for illustrative purposes only and any person depicted on the cover is a model.

Trade Paperback ISBN: 978-1-64405-827-5
Digital ISBN: 978-1-64405-826-8
Library of Congress Control Number: 2019951828
Trade Paperback published February 2020
v. 1.0

Printed in the United States of America

This paper meets the requirements of
ANSI/NISO Z39.48-1992 (Permanence of Paper).

This is for the Five. Because it always starts with all of you.

For Lisa, sorry about the mess, and to Mary, sorry but you've got to give them back now.

Also to Greg, because once more into the breach, baby.

And to Elizabeth, thank you for taking a chance on the first one and letting me take Cole back out again.

ACKNOWLEDGMENTS

To my wonderous Five—Penn, Tamm, Lea, and Jenn. I love you all.

And to my other sisters—Lisa, Ree, Ren, and Mary—much love.

Thanks will always go to Dreamspinner—Elizabeth, Lynn, Liz and her team, Naomi (who I bribe with cookies and tea), and everyone there who polishes what I send them. Thank you for being there.

And to all of the readers who have wondered what happened to Cole and Jae. Here you go. Saranghae.

ONE

I SPENT most of my formative years in Chicago, faithfully cheering on the Cubs and looking down at people who put ketchup on their hot dogs. My older brother, Mike, was—and still is—a hard-core White Sox fan. This doesn't explain anything about us as brothers other than he's always on the wrong side of the fence when picking teams.

Always.

For example, at some far-off point in our childhood, back when he was actually taller than me, we played an imaginary game we called Cows and Sheep. I'm not sure where we got the idea, probably from some old movie, because it was pretty much an excuse for all-out warfare with dirt clods and water balloons under the guise of me as a cattle rancher and Mike as a sheep wrangler battling it out for control of the land's only water source for our herds.

Namely, the garden hose attached to the faucet on the side of the house.

Now, while we didn't actually have any cattle or sheep, I knew enough about the woolly ungulates to know they weren't bipedal, six feet tall, with a flap in the front of their bodies for easy access to their dangly bits.

Nor did they have a loaded Desert Eagle and a pair of Dobermans intent on running me to ground.

"I'm supposed to be here!" Shouting over my shoulder didn't seem to help. Maybe the costume's head was too thick for him to hear me screaming at him, or perhaps he couldn't make anything out except the dogs' vicious, frenzied barking. I dodged a thick bush, but its branches slapped at my face with a withering sting as I went by. "I'm doing a security—"

The sheep answered me with a bullet, blowing away the overgrown trellis I'd ducked through to get some distance between us. Its wood frame shattered, showering me with a tidal wave of leaves and splinters, probably adding to the welts already on my face and hands.

This was supposed to be a quick recon—me testing the perimeter of a Brentwood estate not far from the Craftsman I shared with my husband, Jae, and where I ran my investigation business out of what used to be the massive sprawl's front rooms. I'd taken the job as a favor for Dante Montoya, a detective my best friend, Bobby, used to work with. His boyfriend owned an elite security firm and needed someone who knew the area to scope out the grounds of an overgrown château. He'd been hired by the guy who recently bought it and discovered it was not only missing a perimeter wall but also was in Mother Nature's firm, hard grip. But since he was being paid to break into the place on another night to test its defenses, he wanted someone who had no dog in the fight to give him a sketch of what the jungle around the battered château looked like but keep him clueless of the interior to better assess the situation.

If I survived the culling, I was going to find Montoya's boyfriend and punch him right in his pretty, funky-ass-eyed face.

"I'm going to fucking kill you!" the sheep screamed from somewhere behind me.

I couldn't hear the dogs anymore, but I did kind of hope the man in the full-body costume took the time to Velcro the front flap closed. From what I had seen, it wasn't much protection against the thorny hedges around us, but at least it would save some of his skin.

I hadn't gotten a good look at the man wearing it, but as costumes went, it was spectacular. Probably custom-made, it was a hair too cute for my tastes, but then I also couldn't imagine myself dressed up as an ungulate complete with a pink bow and enormous round tinkling bell tied around my neck or somehow shoving my feet and hands into what looked like hard hooves.

The place should have been empty. I'd been told no one lived there yet and it would be a month or two before renovations began to restore the old, creaking mansion. But when I discovered a light on in the small guesthouse a few yards from the garage I'd parked in front of, I went to investigate.

I expected maybe a few teenagers drinking beer and smoking pot they'd taken from their mom's stash, or even a transient who'd found a way into the fairly large single-room structure, planning on keeping safe and warm inside its thick walls.

Instead I'd found Psycho Lamb Chop playing blanket mambo with an elegant socialite in pearls and ruffled bloomers, a slit worked into the pantaloons' seams to allow Brave Sir Baa Baa easy access to her worldly treasures.

I probably could have sneaked off without either one of them being the wiser except for one thing—well, two actually. The damned dogs.

I'd seen this movie before. Hell, I'd been a recurring guest star in that particular strain of disasters through most of my career as a private investigator. But the sheep was new, and the dogs were really damned determined to take a chunk out of my ass.

Seeing as I liked my ass where it was—and I had a husband who seemed pretty fond of it—I bolted.

Shocked the hell out of me that Lamb Chop not only had the presence of mind to grab a weapon but also had the dexterity and stamina to run in those damned hooves.

The lawn's overgrowth made it easier to avoid the dogs, but they weren't too far behind me. I knew the left side of the property shared a fairly solid wall with the next estate, but the original twelve-foot-tall wrought iron fence surrounding the enormous plot had fallen into such disrepair that there were gaping stretches along the back and right boundaries. It was a contentious point with the property owners, or so I'd been told. Rather than erect their own fencing, they battled and sniped about the château's falling metal spires and left the rusting iron segments to molder instead of securing their own homes.

It was kind of ironic being chased by a man in a sheep costume after catching him in a nefarious act with a woman who had a few years on him and obviously was way out of his league, but honestly, I wasn't all that surprised. Shit like this always seemed to happen to me. This wasn't the first time I'd come across a couple of people having sex—make that kind of weird sex—only to have them spot me, nor the first time I had to run for my life while someone tried to blow my head off. It was kind of an occupational hazard. Private investigators usually didn't get to pick and choose the cases that came through their front door, and since most of society's problems revolved around sex or money, it made sense that most of our business at McGinnis Investigations dealt with spouses wanting to catch their significant others doing the nasty with someone other than themselves.

This job wasn't supposed to be like that. I was just to go in, take a recon of the buildings, and leave. I shouldn't be on the run, although I had some serious questions about why the woman and Lamb Chop had two Dobermans with them in the guesthouse.

"Where the fuck am I going?" It was difficult to make heads or tails of where I was. The paths through the greenery were vague at best, and the thickets were practically opaque, making it difficult to see beyond what was right in front of my face. "I don't even know which way I'm facing."

There was a myth about moss growing only on the north side of a tree. Since I could barely remember if the Hollywood sign was north of me at any given moment, that wasn't going to get me out of the jungle I'd stumbled into. The hard stone paths were littered with leaves, and every once in a while, I caught the hard clop of the sheep's hooves striking rock, but the dogs were now oddly silent.

"Where the hell are you guys?" I slowed my run down and crouched behind a stand of bushes and an oddly posed statue that could have been a woman with six arms or an aroused cuttlefish looking for a good time. Cloaked in shadows and a thick layer of tangled vines, it was difficult to tell what the carving was, but it gave me enough cover to catch my breath. "Shit, I've got to work on my conditioning."

The cuttlefish exploded in front of my face, its massive weave disintegrated by whatever high-powered piece of lead Mr. Flappy Sheep had loaded in his Eagle. Needless to say, it was enough of an incentive to get me moving again.

Not knowing the grounds, I was at a severe disadvantage, and apparently I was being chased by an ex-Olympian or something. I couldn't shake the sheep. He kept up with me pace for pace. Maybe he knew how the damned bushes and trees were laid out around the complicated multilevel stone terraces and hills that some idiot decided would be great to put down as landscaping for the château. It was an Escher vomit of leaves, rocks, and the occasional naked statue missing an arm or a head but still sporting raging cock-stands or pert breasts. Perhaps both. I wasn't stopping long enough to admire the art when I could still hear the random movement of a Doberman somewhere behind me.

While I couldn't see the garage anymore, I was hoping it was behind me. Then I found out one of the dogs wasn't.

It came at me from the right, a slavering beast with a mouthful of shark teeth and glowing eyes. I love dogs. I have a dog—a small, slightly rotund mop of a dog named Honey who'd come back into my life after she was taken by my boyfriend Rick's family when he was murdered. Honey was now a spoiled princess who spent her day toddling after Jae while he cooked or lounging in one of several dog beds in our house. Her biggest aggressive act to date had been a particularly virulent gaseous attack following the ingestion of a bag of frozen brussels sprouts she liberated from a shopping bag while we were putting away groceries.

This Doberman was definitely *not* Honey.

I couldn't comment on its gas issues, but it sure as hell didn't resemble the furry lump that slept at the end of our bed every night.

It launched itself from a thin-leafed row of bushes I'd been about to run through and grabbed at my forearm. Up close, the dog looked even more massive than I remembered, but then the brain does funny things when it's running on pure fear.

Teeth longer than a scorned woman's memory sank through the arm of my leather jacket, raking over the skin beneath. My heart stopped, picking up an erratic beat on my next panicked breath, but by then physics took over where my panic abandoned any logic and my jacket sleeve tore away, split apart by the dog's sharp teeth, leaving leather shreds filling its mouth. Enraged, the Doberman shook its head, and I pulled hard, yanking my scraped-up arm out of the remains of my sleeve and leaving the dog to its impotent kill.

I broke back into a hard run, leaving the Doberman to play with its best toy ever and hopefully distracted enough not to notice I'd left it behind.

"Okay, McGinnis." I started to give myself a pep talk because it didn't seem like Lamb Chop had any intention of letting me get away without looking like a colander. "Just find a wall. That'll either lead to the back or the front, but either way, you'll at least be off the property."

My arm stung where the dog bit, but it wasn't like I had a first aid kit in my back pocket. Jae was used to me coming home with all kinds of scrapes and bruises, but a dog bite, even one as shallow as this one, meant I was probably going to face his raised eyebrows and a skeptical snort. He never seemed to believe me when I said I never intended to get into any trouble. It was almost as if he hadn't known me for several years and picked various bits of glass, metal, and the occasional thorn out of my skin. But I wanted to avoid having someone from the LAPD knock on our front door to tell him I'd been gunned down by a six-foot-tall sheep. There's only so much humiliation a man can take, and that's sure as hell not what I want written on my headstone.

"Died having sex with his husband at the age of ninety-five" was more my style. But if I didn't get my ass moving, Sir Flappy Bits would have my head mounted to his wall above a roaring fireplace and spend his cold wintry evenings regaling his animal-costumed friends of his hunt through the jungle on his own personal Wild Human Safari.

Calming my breathing down, I listened for signs of the other dog and the rat-tat-tat of hooves on the uneven paths. The sounds of the Doberman working its way through my jacket sleeve were faint but distinct. It seemed happy, almost gleeful. So long as it was entertained and not coming after me, I was okay with it. I was less concerned about the other dog and deeply worried about the Desert Eagle.

I didn't know a lot about gardening, but I knew enough to recognize the bramble of rosebushes in front of me were about one foot shy of having a giant purple-and-black dragon fighting off a prince so he didn't take away her kidnapped victim. There were a few faded, withered blooms clinging valiantly to the nest of neglected, spindly branches, but even in the sparse light from Los Angeles's ever-present gloam, the thorns were abundant.

There was a comment about life there. In the most horrific neglect, beauty fought to survive while violence thrived.

It could've been just that the rosebushes had a lot of thorns. Bacon and Hobbes definitely weren't threatened by my entry into philosophy. I would rather while away the evening with a hot pastrami sandwich and a cold beer than spend a couple of hours discussing whether or not we were made out of paper.

The tinkle of Lamb Chop's bell told me he was nearby. I had to get moving. I needed to find a way out, and I needed to find it fast.

An aggressive bark growing louder spurred me on. The bushes suddenly didn't appear so daunting, and if Prince Charming could hack through them to rescue a comatose woman he'd never met but intended to marry, I sure as hell could at least give it a try.

Fuck. The rosebushes hurt like hell.

They tore at my bare arm, digging into my already split-open skin. It seemed like every thorn grew an additional six inches simply to rip me open. My jeans protected my legs, and I pulled up the arm still encased in a sleeve to protect my face. I couldn't see an end to the thicket, and searching for a way around didn't seem like the smartest use of time. I didn't know how long the Doberman would be enthralled with my jacket arm, and there was no telling how close the sheep was.

To be fair, he didn't need to get very close. He just needed a clear line of sight to blow my head off. I didn't understand his rage, but then I didn't know the story behind him in the sheep costume or anything about the woman he was with. Something back there was important enough for him to kill someone over, and I would rather that someone not be me.

It seemed to take me forever before I was through the rosebushes, and when I stumbled free of the spindly branches, I found myself facing the fallen remains of a wrought iron fence. I almost kissed its rusty corpse with glee, but I wasn't quite out of the woods yet. Literally.

The château's rear neighbor seemed to be resigned to the overgrowth, allowing at least a few yards of thick bushes and untrimmed trees to encroach the property line. They probably let it run rampant solely to hide the eyesore going stagnant behind them. A five-foot-tall decorative wall of stucco and tile jutted up from a strip of well-manicured lawn, offering me the promise of an oasis on the other side.

I broke into a run as soon as I heard the bell chiming behind me.

It felt like I was suffering from a thousand paper cuts, minute slashes from leaves and thorns with an ooze of blood turning my skin sticky. A warm trickle ran down my forehead, getting into my eyes, turning my vision blurry, but I was focused on the wall. I was tall enough to get my hands over the top of it and had enough faith in my abdominal muscles to pull myself over it, but I knew from unfortunate experience that the same could be said about a motivated Doberman.

I was worried less about the dog now. Still kind of worried about the guy with the gun, but I had an intense hope that the neighbors kept their lawn clipped and I would be able to sprint up to the back of their house while screaming my head off for help.

It wasn't much of a plan.

But it *was* a plan.

I took the wall with ease, but the scar tissue along my ribs and chest chose that moment to seize up. Healed-over bullet wounds are the worst. They leave a guy with a tangle of keloids wrapped around nerves and muscles that sometimes fire off conflicting messages. In my case it was like being struck with a handful of charley horses knitted through my ribs and down toward my spine.

Getting up onto the wall was easy. Going over the wall was less than ideal. Seized up by spasms and pain, I went down hard, rolled up like an armadillo trying to avoid being roadkill stew. I landed with a grunt loud enough to wake the dead.

Or at least I thought I was loud enough to wake the dead.

Unfortunately, the dead woman I landed on didn't seem to share that opinion.

I was having a hard time breathing. Some of it was from my twisting scar tissue, but a lot of it was from shock. I *knew* this woman. Surprised breathless, I scrambled from her lifeless body and planted my ass in the middle of a stretch of wet lawn.

The irony of finding her dead on this job didn't escape me.

Lying on her back, her arms and legs flung brokenly away from her torso, Mrs. Adele Brinkerhoff was dressed much like she'd been when I was first hired to catch her cheating on her husband. When I'd taken that job, I couldn't imagine the grandmotherly woman whose photo I'd been given was into leather corsets, braided whips, and a lesbian love affair with a woman much younger than herself. But as I found out then, looks can be deceiving.

She chased me that night, much like Lamb Chop did just a few moments ago, but she'd been armed with a shotgun and had a hell of a lot better aim than the guy in the sheep costume. I dodged her through a topiary sprinkled with bushes shaped like animals. She nearly took my head off with a powerful blast but took out a leafy elephant instead.

Judging by the hole in her chest and her bloodless, sagging face, Mrs. Brinkerhoff wasn't going to be cheating on her husband any longer.

She was a doughy-soft woman, but she'd tucked those curves and fleshy thighs into a black leather jumpsuit. Her feet were bare, and the expression on her face was one of deep surprise. I tried fumbling for my phone, my fingers cold and unresponsive as I reached into my back pocket. The gore of her chest wound was immense, and even in the faint light, I could nearly see through her to the lawn… or at least my imagination could.

That's when I spotted the handful of sparkling gems in her partially closed right hand.

It wasn't like I'd kept up with her and her husband. They'd reconciled or at least come to some sort of agreement after I caught her, because both of them showed up in my office, paid the bill, and thanked me for my time. In a lot of ways, she had actually been the beginning point of my new life. I came home to find my older brother, Mike, sitting in my living room with a job that would eventually lead me to cross paths with Jae-Min Kim, the love of my life and the man who was stupid enough to agree to marry me.

In a lot of ways, Adele Brinkerhoff was the leather-wearing BDSM godmother who'd made our lives possible. Sort of. And now she lay dead at my feet, holding a handful of diamonds that looked expensive even to my uneducated eye.

"Oh, Adele," I whispered, finally getting my phone out of my pocket. "What the fuck have you gotten yourself into?"

I had just hit the last number for LAPD's emergency dispatch when the second damned Doberman came over the wall and took me down.

TWO

ODDLY ENOUGH, the Doberman who tackled me kept me company. His attack consisted of a fierce bathing with a damp tongue and then trying to climb up the front of my body to be held when the man in the sheep costume flung himself over the wall. I'm not sure if the costume's hooves did him in or if he just wasn't that athletic, but even from ten feet away, I heard both of his legs snap as he landed. He dropped down into the lawn face-first, and the Eagle went flying, discharging a bullet when it bounced on the ground. The shot hit the wall, and the Doberman probably decided it had located the spider monkey part of its genetic thread and scrambled up my body to quiver on my shoulder.

He weighed a lot less than Jae and smelled a hell of a lot worse, but I would take the claw marks over his teeth into my jugular any day.

I coaxed the Doberman down and left Lamb Chop where he landed after I kicked the gun as far away from him as possible. I ignored his screaming while I limped up toward the house, dialing 9-1-1 as I went. No one was home at the estate, but the cops assured me they would be there in a few seconds, drawn by the barrage of calls from outraged residents at the sounds of shots being fired in their safe, elite neighborhood. The dog fell into step behind me, and I trudged out to discover Central Dispatch hadn't been wrong. A few minutes later, two cop cars screeched to a halt after I'd made it out the side gate.

The enormous black-and-tan Doberman promptly pissed on the sidewalk, then rolled over on his back when the cops began shouting for me to put my hands up. All in all, it was the shitty beginning of what was probably going to be a long night, and I still hadn't done any recon on the estate I'd been sent to scope out.

An aurora borealis of red-and-blue swirls churned above the formerly dim street, courtesy of the phalanx of cop cars crowding the tree-lined sidewalk. Their bright, saturated lights pushed away the milky orange-yellow coming from the streetlamps that sparsely dotted the side of the road. This part of Brentwood was very much old-school Los Angeles, clinging to the outdated opinion that their intimate, cloistered neighborhood was kept safer by darkened streets and heightened security. Because of the area's proximity to the observatory, the local lighting was subdued to prevent the ambient glow from bleeding into the already not-so-dark night sky that hugged the city. But I could have used a little bit of light. Until the cops arrived, I could barely see my hand while standing in front of the estate where I'd found Mrs. Brinkerhoff's body.

"Now, let me get this straight, you were hired to check out a property for a security firm owned by Montoya's boyfriend, when you were pursued and shot at by Ralph Branigan." Lieutenant Dell O'Byrne stood silhouetted against the floodlights, her pen furiously dancing across the page in the notebook she was using to document the scene.

"Is Ralph Branigan the guy in the sheep costume?" I asked. "I've just been calling him Lamb Chop and other names in my head. He had a gun. And was shooting at me. I didn't stop and ask him his name."

"Yes, the man you're calling Lamb Chop is Mister Branigan." O'Byrne's dark eyes flicked up the page, their depths filled with an annoyance that I could see through the shadows clinging to her strong face. "Help me out, McGinnis. Just give me the facts first. Then you can give me all the commentary you like. What were you doing that prompted Branigan to come after you with a gun?"

"I don't know. Could have been me looking through the window and getting a good look at him schtupping that blond lady." I shrugged as nonchalantly as I could, but my brain was still having a hard time wrapping around the details of what happened. "You know, the former nun. Mother Mary Stigmata or whatever her name is."

"I'm trying to be serious here, McGinnis." Another glance up, but this time there was a hint of a smile tugging at the corner of her mouth.

"O'Byrne, I just spent the last half hour of my life running away from a gun-toting crazy man in a sheep costume with his dick waggling around through a flap in the front because I caught him having kinky sex with a former nun who is now a powerful California lobbyist for faith-based charities. He was trying to kill me. Sicced the ex-nun's dogs on me, who thankfully thought it was all just a game of tag, apparently, but the damned bullets were real." I held my hand up, pinching at the air with my thumb and index finger. "He missed me by this much. And just when I thought I'd gotten away from him, I stumble across a former client's dead wife. If I can't laugh at any of this, I'm going to lose my mind."

O'Byrne was a whipcord-lean Latinx with a beautiful face, a serious demeanor, and a scowl fierce enough to stop a herd of rampaging toddlers dead in their tracks. We hadn't seen eye to eye when she first rolled into her position with the LAPD as a senior detective, but over the years, I must've done something right, because she eventually retained me as a consultant with the department. I'd been a detective with the LAPD when I was shot by my partner and best friend, Ben, who'd somehow gotten into his head he was in love with my boyfriend, Rick. Rick didn't survive the shooting, and I wasn't so sure I had.

I did. And I'd grown a lot since then. Fell in love. Got married. And now stood over the corpse of a case I'd left behind me a long time ago.

O'Byrne took shots of her own a few years ago while working on a case with me, and she'd pulled out of the wreckage of her body a lot better than I had. She went back to wearing a badge, while I was rolled out, too devastated and scarred up to be any good. I didn't know a lot about Dell or her personal life. We weren't the kind of "get together on a Sunday and have a beer while watching a football game" friends, but it was safe to say we respected each other. Or at least I was willing to admit I respected the hell out of her.

I just hadn't planned on having one of the craziest evenings of my life when I kissed Jae goodbye that afternoon and walked out our front door.

"Tell me what you know about Adele Brinkerhoff," O'Byrne said, nodding to a passing uniform who'd wrangled the Dobermans into the back of his police car to wait for the ex-nun's husband to arrive and take them home. "You say her husband hired you a few years back to catch her cheating?"

"They came to an understanding, paid off my bill, and thanked me for my time," I replied. "I haven't really had much contact with either one of them since then. It seemed like they were going through a rough patch and worked it out. Or he just decided he could live with a bisexual, leather-wearing dominatrix who had torrid love affairs on the side. I didn't really ask, because it was none of my business. The check cleared. That was the only thing that counted."

"She was wearing leather when she was killed. Was it like what you saw her in the last time?" She cast a quick glance around the neighborhood, probably scanning the high walls and tall hedges blocking any commoners from peering at the sprawling estates tucked in above Koreatown. "If we start knocking on a few of these doors, do you think we'll find she had a thing going with someone around here?"

I hadn't spent a lot of time staring at Adele. There'd been other concerns, like the dog and then the guy with the gun, not to mention dealing with the shock of seeing her grandmotherly face slack with death. Thinking back on what I could remember of that moment, I shook my head.

"This is going to sound crazy, but it seemed to me like what she was wearing wasn't sexual in nature. I mean, the first time I saw her, there wasn't any question that she was dressed for a good time and to deliver a firm spanking. She looked more like… I don't know, like she was going to a party?" I realized at the bite of a breeze against my arm that I was still wearing my tattered jacket. I shrugged it off and left it on the hood of the police car, assuming someone would come gather it as evidence for the dog attack at some point. "The woman kind of led two lives. When she and her husband showed up at my office, she was bordering on frumpy. I really can't tell you much about her."

"What about the diamonds she had in her hand? Know anything about those?"

That question rocked me back. My brain had decided they were gems the first time I spotted them, but the idea didn't fit into the narrative I'd conjured up to have the evening make some kind of sense. It was already crazy enough without discovering Adele Brinkerhoff dead, and tossing a handful of diamonds into the mix only tipped things over into the land of grinning cats and talking playing cards.

"So they're real? I wasn't sure."

"I'm going to assume they're real, because I don't have any explanation for why I have a little old lady shoehorned into a black leather jumpsuit and found dead in the middle of a neighborhood where it costs five dollars just to take a whiff of fresh air," O'Byrne drawled, a faint sneer on her face.

"I'm feeling attacked," I shot back. "I live in this neighborhood. Okay, not on the huge-mansion side of things but still in this neighborhood."

"Yeah, I've seen where you live. So it only costs four bucks." The sneer grew, but the humor in her face did as well. Jollity looked good on her. I didn't see it very often. Usually my presence brought annoyance or slight ridicule to her expressions. "I'd like to see your case notes from back then if you still got them."

"It's been five or six years, but all of my case notes are kept digitally, so I'll be able to send over everything I've got. I've got a contact number for her husband, but it's been a while, and he seemed a lot older than she was. I don't even know if he's still alive." I was beginning to regret taking off my jacket, because the wind began to carry a bit of ice in it. "Did you consider that Branigan might have killed her? I mean, it would be kind of cold-blooded of him to blow a hole through her and then go back to the ex-nun for a bit more fun, but that Desert Eagle of his would sure as hell explain the crater in her chest."

"I'd considered it, but from the looks of things, it seems like Adele Brinkerhoff's been lying there for more than a couple of days. Branigan and his *associate* were in Sacramento until early this afternoon. She lives down the street and knew the place was empty and on the market." O'Byrne closed her notebook, tucking her pen away into her jacket pocket. "She told her husband she was going to take the dogs for a walk, then scooted down here to hook up with Branigan."

"Well that explains the dogs but not the sheep." Whenever I closed my eyes, I still could see Branigan's pale fleshy bits swinging back and forth as he ran, framed by tufts of woolly white fur. "I mean, I guess when she was a nun, her old job was pretty much tending to her flock, but that's just going way too far."

There wasn't enough bleach in the universe for me to get that out of my memory. With any luck I would get bashed on the head on the way home somehow, giving me a bit of amnesia. At the very worst, I would totally lose every memory of my past, but I had a lot of faith that I would fall back in love with Jae as soon as I saw him. He would understand. He'd understood much worse.

"He connected to the lobbying she does in Sacramento?" I was curious, because somehow coming after me with a gun powerful enough to take down a giraffe seemed like a bit of an overreaction to being discovered having sex as a sheep. "Because I've got to tell you, he seems like the kind of guy who would gun down an old lady."

"See, that's where this gets very sticky," O'Byrne said, making a sour face. "She's been punching at the government to get more religious programs into California's prisons, and two days ago, Branigan became the deputy director for one of the Corrections and Rehabilitation departments. So, once news of all of this spreads around, something tells me he's going to be losing that corner office and she's going to be out a connection to the state's purse strings."

I contemplated what O'Byrne laid out. Then I turned to her, crossed my arms over my chest, and said, "I get all that, but it still doesn't explain the fucking sheep suit."

IT WAS three in the morning by the time I fit my key into the front-door lock. I'd sent Jae a text telling him I was okay but some shit had hit the fan so he might as well go to bed without me. I was surprised to find the living room lights were on and my husband curled up in the middle of one of our couches, our black cat, Neko, stretched out alongside his thigh, her tiny body extended as far as she could and taking up as much of the cushion as she could, mostly to prevent Honey, our poof of a dog, from taking up residence.

I'd bought the Craftsman following Rick's death. Without him and Ben in my life, I'd been left adrift, riddled with scars and brain groggy from a coma. Back then, I didn't know which keloids hurt more, the ones on my body or the ones in my heart. Weak, exhausted, and soul sick, I attacked the decrepit sprawling two-story house with an intense fervor, working to resurrect it as if somehow bringing it back to its former glory would also fix me.

A couple of years later, the house was restored to its showcase prime, and I'd opened up my private investigation business after converting the formal dining room and front parlor into an office and conference room. Along the way I picked up Claudia, a sharp-tongued, Southern-born black woman who'd retired from driving a school bus and decided to not only manage my office but also my life. She'd become my mother of sorts and was the first person who realized I'd fallen in love.

Way before I did.

Kim Jae-Min was everything I wasn't looking for in a man but really needed. A photographer by trade and a former dancer at a gay Korean gentlemen's club called Dorthi Ki Seu, he'd been at the center of a murder case I stumbled into, then wormed his way into the center of my heart. We'd been through a lot—fights, broken hearts, hurt feelings, and cultural conflicts—but those were in our past, and now I wore his ring on my finger.

Or at least I thought it was on my finger. There were some days I was pretty sure it was actually threaded through my nose. On those days, I just kept my mouth shut and answered yes to anything I was asked.

Who said I didn't know how to be married?

"You didn't have to wait up," I said, padding barefoot into our living room. Carefully I moved the six pounds of fury and black chinchilla fur we laughingly called *our* cat and sat down next to him, sighing contentedly when Jae leaned against me. "Not that I'm complaining, because you are exactly who I need to see at the end of this day."

I didn't need to see the bowl of orange-dusted fruit strips sitting on the table next to the couch to know he'd been eating *li hing mui* mango. Jae's kiss tasted of it. Its sweet licorice-sugar stung my tongue, reminiscent of tamarind with a punch of Jae behind it. I was dead tired, scraped up to hell, but my body responded as it always did, flaring to life whenever he was near. My desire for him became incendiary whenever we touched, and there were moments when I was convinced I would one day be found as a pile of ash at the side of our bed. I would be the happiest pile of ash ever.

He was almost my height, skimming six feet, but we were built so very differently. For all of my being half Japanese, very little of it settled in my bones and musculature. My face wore ghosts of my mother's Asian blood, but my personality and body were purely descended from the McGinnis side of the family—a long line of Irish brawlers with a nose for trouble and a thirst for adventure. I kept fit by boxing and running, usually accompanied by Bobby Dawson, my best friend and a former LAPD detective, and lately I'd tried to keep up with Jae doing yoga, hoping it would help ease the scar tissue knotting up my body.

Jae was a sleek, beautiful Korean man with a pretty face it almost hurt to look at and a flexibility that almost guaranteed my destiny as that pile of ash. His black hair framed his sculpted face, falling almost down to his shoulders and long enough to pull back into a ponytail, something he did when he went all mad scientist in the kitchen. As much as I loved his mouth, I loved his eyes even more. They were a smoky honey-rye silken brown mixed with burnt gold, and I loved seeing the world through them when he told me about his day. He was graceful in a way I could never compete with and seemed to possess a fondness for spicy things that even amazed other Koreans. He'd come to me guarded and hating his attraction to other men, but to be fair, I'd come to him broken and hating myself.

Along the way, we kept each other company as we patched up our wounds even as life injured us further. But we'd still found each other, still climbed over rigid walls to admit our love, to embrace our connection and eventually exchange rings.

I regretted nothing of the pain we'd gone through to reach this point in our lives, but I would have to say I wished I had brought more smiles to Jae's full lips. Since we were both in our thirties, we had a lot more years ahead of us, and I looked forward to teasing those smiles out of him for a long time.

"I'm glad you're home, Cole-ah." Even his voice held a hint of the chilis he loved, scorching a fusion of lust and desire down my spine and across my belly. The kiss ended way too soon, and I went in for seconds, but Jae pinched the end of my nose, stopping me in midswoop. "Hold on to that thought, because I planned on waking up when you came home, but something dragged me out of bed."

"I'm guessing that something has to do with me," I mumbled as if suffering a tremendous cold, unable to speak clearly with my nose held firmly between his fingers. "Could you let go? I sound as if I'm going to go take a job as a nanny for a man named Sheffield with three kids and a butler."

He let go, leaving me with a kiss on my injured nose tip. Reaching across of me, he dislodged Neko, who'd settled against me on the other side, and snagged a piece of paper I'd not seen tucked in under the bowl of mango.

"I wasn't asleep, because I was worried about you, even though you told me you were fine. I was still worried," Jae admitted in a soft whisper. Neko, however, voiced her opinion at being ruffled with a loud strident meow at odds with her tiny body. Honey, probably sensing the cat's impending rampage across the room, wisely picked herself up off of the floor and shuffled over to one of the dog beds where she would be safe.

"I was fine." I could see he didn't believe me, and since I'd left out the part about being shot at, Jae probably suspected I was lying. Actually it was probably more than suspicion, because he could always tell when I was lying. "It was a little hairy at times—and remind me to tell you about the sheep—but I was okay. What woke you up?"

"The phone." Jae held up the piece of paper so I could see the numbers he'd written down. "A man named Arthur Brinkerhoff called about an hour ago. He'd like you to find out who killed his wife and why the cops are accusing her of stealing two million dollars in diamonds."

THREE

"WAIT. BRINKERHOFF." Claudia hovered at the edge of my desk, holding my coffee cup hostage, just out of my reach. "We know that name, right? Wasn't that the name of the spanking dominatrix grandma who nearly popped your head off with a shotgun a few years back?"

"I don't know about dominatrix," I grumbled, grabbing at my cup as it wove closer. "Okay, maybe."

"She sure as hell beat your ass," my alleged surrogate mother shot back as she set my coffee down with a firm thump. "And now she's dead, and somehow it's your problem?"

"Well, I did kind of find her." The coffee was strong. At some point in Claudia's past, someone taught her how to make paint thinner out of coffee beans, and she's been perfecting her toxic brew ever since. I was surprised I still had nostril hairs, but I was grateful for the punch to my heart, since I'd gotten so little sleep the night before. "I feel like I owe this guy. I haven't thought about them in years, but it's the case I was working on when Mike dropped Hyun-Shik's case into my lap."

The look I got from Claudia was a stern reminder of how she raised eight sons to a steady, responsible adulthood where they all made a good living and treated their significant others with love and respect. We'd both come a long way since the day she walked into my office, resplendent in her Sunday-go-to-church best, and subsequently took over my life. She became the mother I never had, a strong, bighearted Southern woman who told me when to pull up my socks and when to shut my mouth. Unfortunately for Jae and me, Claudia was also now best friends with Jae's adopted aunt, a Filipino kathoey lounge singer named Scarlet who spent most of her life as a woman and a voice of reason alongside of Claudia's already brimming sea of knowledge. The two of them together kept us wrapped up tight, doted on and loved but also subjected to their extremely strong opinions about practically everything under the sun.

I got a lot of sympathy from Claudia's sons and their children, but mostly I believed they were just happy to have someone else take the occasional hit.

Judging by the contemplative expression on Claudia's face, I was about to take one helluva hit.

I just didn't know when.

My neighborhood in Brentwood wasn't filled with châteaus, castles, and McMansions, but rather with vintage Craftsman- and Victorian-style buildings. The homes here were large, some nearly big enough to serve as small hotels, except zoning regulations frowned on that kind of thing. I'd barely gotten permission from the city to run my business out of the bottom front of my restored Craftsman, but since a few people had already converted smaller carriage houses across the street from me to a coffee shop run by hippies and a couple of other storefronts, I'd been able to leverage my way in. There were other little cottage industries half a block down the street from us, including a pizza parlor with pies so delectable angels wept every time one was pulled out of the oven.

Sipping my coffee, I stared out of the large wooden-sash windows looking out onto the street and watched the odd foot traffic flow in and out of the tree-hugging, otter-scrubber coffee shop that had once been the bane of my existence. Its owners and I had come to an agreement. They would make sure their customers didn't dump their trash onto my lawn or piss in the hedges along the side of my property, and I wouldn't shoot the next person I found watering the stunted bush at the front of my house. It already suffered from almost being blown up and had become almost a pet of mine. I'd fought hard for it to survive and didn't appreciate the golden showers it occasionally had to suffer through. I didn't care if the coffee shop was pretty much an illegal pot dispensary or that they committed an act against all humanity by serving a rock-hard vegan carrot cake I could've used to build a brick wall, but disrespecting my poor blast-victim bush had been my breaking point.

The coffee shop settled down into the neighborhood, its customers skewing as much soccer mom as Coachella attendees. Floridly painted Schwinn bicycles were now kept company by strollers large enough to transport a baby yak, and the outside patio usually sported a healthy canine population—one that was sometimes gifted with the angelic presence of Honey and her favorite caretaker, Jae. She'd been Rick's dog and subsequently dumped by his family, but she did remember me when I came to get her. While she adored me, she fell in love with Jae, and I didn't blame her one bit.

I was about to head across the street to grab some of the dog biscuits the coffee shop bakers whipped up for their canine customers when Claudia cleared her throat.

I sat my ass back in my chair before it rose more than two inches off its padded cushion. Judgment Day was coming, and I was going to have a front-row seat.

"Seems to me that getting involved in that woman's death is only going to give you a headache. Probably the stupidest things you've ever considered doing, and boy, you don't need me to tell you how many really stupid things you've already gotten into so far in your life." Claudia's rich voice was soft, but its steely point was made. "It's been a long time since you ended up getting shot at, and I don't know if my blood pressure can take sitting vigil for you at the hospital chapel again."

"Actually I got shot at last night." There were times when I swear to God, my mouth was installed by a pack of demons, because I never seem to be able to swallow words that would get me into trouble. If I thought the look Claudia gave me earlier was glaring, the one she gave me now was hot enough to cook my skin off my flesh.

"Best start talking, boy," she murmured.

It was a gentle, sweet rejoinder, but I'm sure many a child riding her bus over the years pissed in their pants when they heard her say it. The only thing more terrifying would have been if she pulled the bus over to the side of the road, turned around in her seat, and said it. Since the office wasn't moving and she was already facing me, I was probably experiencing a nightmare more than a few full-grown adults still dreamed about, even after leaving Claudia's bus for the very last time.

She was a large woman, built to have large children, and with a personality big enough to rest the world's weight on. I briefly thought about telling her it was nothing, but one did not lie to Claudia Dubois. So I gave her the whole story, not leaving out one thing, including the flappy man bits poking out of the sheep costume.

"Huh," she finally said when my story ran down. "I'm not saying people don't have the God-given right to do anything they want in their bedroom or with who they want, so long as no animal or child is hurt, but you'd think they'd have the common sense to not get caught flying their perversions out in the open."

"That's funny," Bobby said as he came through the office's wooden screen door. "People still say that about guys like me and Cole."

"Tell Bobby about the sheep thing and see what he says then." Claudia sniffed, patting a stray curl down. "I've got some billing to do. You figure out if you're going to go meet that man about his dead wife, but mark my words, Cole, you take that case and this nice quiet life that you've had over the past couple of years is going to blow up into a mess of trouble like you haven't seen in a long time."

"So you haven't heard a damned whisper from this guy since… he and his wife came tucked tail into your office after she tried to blow your head off?" Bobby whistled a low, keening note. Then he chuckled when a woman being dragged by a trio of yappy long-haired Dachshunds walked past and gave him a filthy look. "Trust me, lady, as cute as your dogs are, I'm whistling at my friend here."

The woman hurried past, ignoring my apologies for Bobby's brashness.

"Swear to God, one day someone's going to punch you in the nose for being an asshole," I muttered, closing the Rover's driver-side door. "Or maybe just punch you in general. Quit being a dick."

"It's kind of what I'm known for, Princess," he jabbed back, giving me a wicked, disarming smile.

I didn't know what my half brother, Ichi, saw in him. Despite being older than me by almost twenty years, Bobby was a fit, silvering, handsome rogue who'd treated monogamy like a disease before Ichi rolled into town. Then he fell hard, swore off all other men, and became a fiercely loyal husband. He was still a dick, though, and he often dragged me on long runs or hounded me into the gym and boxing ring so he could pound bruises into my delicate flesh, all in the name of keeping me healthy and fit.

Bobby could wipe the floor with me and often did. Still, he was a good guy to watch my back when I went out on my more dangerous jobs. And as a former LAPD detective who'd spent his years wearing a badge safely in the closet, he had a hell of a lot more connections with the boys in blue than I did. I'd spent my time on the force out and probably dealt out more than my share of attitude when clashing with the more old-school cops. Things were different now. I was different now. I'd come out of the other side of the shooting a different man, and Bobby had been sitting next to my hospital bed when I pulled out of my coma, sitting beside me because I was a brother in blue and ashamed he'd hidden in that closet instead of helping me batter down LAPD's homophobic walls.

I loved him like a brother. It just took me a bit to accept he loved my brother like... well... I didn't even want to think about what he and my baby brother got up to.

"Just try not to be a dick to Mister Brinkerhoff. He's an old man, and he just lost his wife," I reminded Bobby. "I don't even know why he called me. This should be something he leaves up to the cops."

"A lot of people don't like to involve the cops, because it means opening up their lives to some intense scrutiny," he shot back. "And if O'Byrne is doing her job right, she's got to take a hard look at him, because the spouse is always the first person you suspect."

"From what I remember of the old guy, he just didn't strike me as a murderer." I stood on the sidewalk, staring up at the two-story 1940s home set back from the street and shrouded by mature trees.

"Yeah. His wife also looked like the type of woman who baked cookies and gave you a quarter as a tip," Bobby murmured, closing the distance between us with one stride. "But you found her dead, wearing one of Emma Peel's hand-me-downs and holding on to enough ice to sink the Titanic."

We were about three or four neighborhoods away from my home, but we'd gone through several economic strata to get there. Los Angeles was a curious city. Most people were surprised at how small Downtown was. With its glittering skyscrapers and beautiful old buildings, that part of the city sat in the center of a vast, knitted-together sprawl, boundary lines blurred in places with a mingle of languages on the signs, alphabets changing in the blink of an eye from Korean to Arabic. We were diverse in pockets. Taken together as a whole, Los Angeles covered the spectrum from pale to intensely dark, with every shade in between and practically a slice of every language there is, but walking its streets was a cruise through different cultures and shifting streams of ethnicities and foods. Los Angeles's people were bound together by different threads, mostly living outside of the Industry, both feeding and shitting out movies, television shows, and literature to entertain the masses.

The neighborhood we were in sat up against the walls of a studio, its squatters' rights entrenched by a convoluted agreement between powerful men who'd long since started their own dirt naps and the money stream it continued to dump into the city's coffers. Open real estate was hard to come by in Los Angeles, and once the studio took an inch, it held on to it until the rocks turned to sand. Oil wells churned up product in different parts of the LA Basin, but none were ever set up inside of the studio compound.

The Brinkerhoffs' home was much like every other one in the area—a throwback to a time when the entertainment executives lived close by and movie stars were tethered to a single studio. The houses were old, but their bones were firm, their lines echoing structures found mostly in the South, with squared-off columns and broad porches facing short lawns kept green by armies of gardeners and lots of water. There was an understated elegance to the neighborhood, with ghosts of large-finned Cadillacs and dinner parties where the menu featured Grandma's meatloaf and a multicolored Jell-O-mold salad with canned pears and shredded carrots. The hint of money clung to the air, and as sedate as the street appeared, the homes themselves were worth several million and were passed through family lines rather than sold.

Climbing the few stone steps up to the porch, I shivered as I passed into the cool shade. Spring hadn't quite made its appearance, and I was wearing my second-best leather jacket, since the Doberman ate the other one. The jacket wasn't as warm as I'd have liked, but beggars couldn't be choosers, and since I'd been pretty much forbidden to buy my own clothes after coming home with a light-blush-and-faint-green camo jacket I'd have sworn on a pack of Bibles was actually shades of gray, I couldn't just pop out to get a new one.

Compromise—the key to a good marriage and also, apparently, defined as agreeing to certain things a spouse insists upon in order to continue sleeping in the marital bed. Jae didn't draw the line on a lot of things, but since I apparently couldn't dress myself—something Claudia and Scarlet also agreed on—it curtailed replacing my jacket.

"You know, I've got you with me," I said, suddenly coming to a stop on the porch.

"Dude, put your hazards on if you're going to brake like that," Bobby grumbled, taking a quick step to the right to avoid slamming into me as he came up the steps. "Yeah, you asked me to come with you."

"No. I mean I need a new jacket. My old one got eaten." A more thorough explanation was apparently needed, because Bobby gave me an odd look. "I just want a black leather jacket. Once we're done here, I can swing by a shop, and you can verify it's black when I buy it. That way Jae doesn't give me the hairy eyeball when I come home with it."

"You need your husband's permission to… oh, the Easter-bonnet jacket," Bobby snickered. "Yeah, I can do that for you, Princess. Though why he'd think you couldn't figure out something was black—never mind,

I wouldn't trust you either. How they ever let you be a cop, I don't know. Can you tell which one is the green light? Should you even be driving?"

I lifted my hand to knock on the front door, muttering at Bobby under my breath, "Fuck you. I drive—"

Gunshots blew the glass insert out of the door, and I lunged at Bobby, taking him down to the porch's painted wooden floor. Shards and splinters rained down on our heads, and it took me a moment before my brain processed someone was seriously trying to kill us. I shoved at Bobby to crawl away from the line of fire, and he flipped over onto his side, glaring at me.

"Where's your gun?" he shouted, trying to be heard over another round. Car alarms were going off, and somewhere, someone was screaming at the top of their lungs in full-out terror. Thankfully, I didn't seem to be the one who was screaming.

"I don't have a gun!" Of course I yelled that back during a long stretch of silence so the shooter could probably hear me quite clearly.

"Why the fuck don't you have a gun?" Bobby pushed me off of his legs and began to scramble backward.

"Because I didn't think I would need a gun to talk to an old man about his dead wife!" Another shot blew out the top of the doorframe, and I weighed the risks of putting myself in the line of fire to get to the steps leading to the yard. "Stay away from the windows. Try to get off the porch."

Bobby took a way out I hadn't even considered, launching himself up off of the floor and over the hip-high decorative stucco wall surrounding the porch. It had a wide enough sill to provide him leverage to catapult over. It seemed a lot closer and safer than the steps, and I went over the same wall a second later.

He landed in a bush.

I landed in the cluster of cacti.

"Fuck!" Swearing didn't help the prickles of pain along my thigh and arm where the oddly fuzzy-looking cactus pierced through denim and leather. Rolling off left me clear of any more thorns, but it still smarted like hell, and I'd somehow torn my second-best jacket on something sharp in the flower bed. "Bobby, you okay?"

"Yeah." He was already up in a crouch, scanning the area around us, and I reluctantly followed, feeling every burr and bruise I'd collected over the last twenty-four hours. "Sounds like the shooting stopped."

I didn't hear any sirens, but that didn't mean the LAPD wasn't on their way. Torn between staying down and not being mistaken by the cops as the shooter or going in to check on the state of my potential client, I poked my head up just in time to see denim-clad legs sprint across the porch and down the steps.

"He's doing a runner," I shouted, taking a long stride forward to give chase. But Bobby grabbed me by the back of my jeans.

"I'll go. You go check on the old man," he ordered, already on the move. "Call 9-1-1! Make sure they know you're in the house."

There was no arguing with him. There never was. I took the stairs two at a time, realizing I'd dropped my phone somewhere when I couldn't find it in my pocket, but I was betting the house phone would work. The Brinkerhoffs were of an age where being without a landline was inconceivable, or at least I was going to bank on that. The inside of the house was dark, the curtains drawn tight against any sunlight, and the plaster walls were burdened with a deep honeyed-oak wainscoting and crown molding. The lack of light dragged the walls down to the floor, shortening the high ceilings above my head.

The foyer was like the one in our house—opening into a wide archway on either side leading to a massive front room to the left and the kitchen on the right. I could see the remnants of an elegant-yet-comfortable living space, blossoms of doilies scattered about the floor, mimicking a spray of tulips lying among the ruins of a cut-glass vase. The davenports were a taupe velvet and sliced apart, the fabric cut so thin I wondered if our assailant was a sashimi master. A wooden coffee table as heavy as the darkness in the room sat up on its edge, one of its legs smashed and dangling from a single bolt.

A glance toward the kitchen told me there was as much chaos wreaked in there as the living room, heavy crocks of flour, sugar, and salt bashed to smithereens on a sea of red Spanish tile. The refrigerator doors were open, and the freezer's contents were scattered about on a small round table set into an eating niche. Our shooter had taken the time to tear open bags of frozen vegetables and dump out everything onto the floor and counter. Ice cube trays were emptied, the cubes left to melt on the cushions of the kitchen chairs. All of the drawers were upended, mingling silverware with the flotsam and jetsam people gathered in their kitchen's nooks and crannies.

I stood still and listened. Then I called out Brinkerhoff's name, the echoing stillness in the shattered house staining my panic with fear. A low moan came from down the hall, and I sprinted toward it, snagging a cordless phone from the side table as I went by. I dialed 9-1-1 mostly by feel and dropped the phone on the floor when I entered the small room at the back of the hall.

Arthur Brinkerhoff was beneath a mattress, his frail shaking body pinned down by its heavy weight. Dark purple splotches marbled the papery skin stretched over his finely boned skull, a fringe of white hair circling the back of his head and spotted with blood. His lip was swollen and split, black speckles clinging to the corner of his mouth, and his eyes were crazed when I pulled the bed off of his chest.

The man was a fighter. I had to give him that, because as I crouched over him to pull him out of the mess he'd been trapped under, he gave me a solid left hook across my nose. I saw enough stars to qualify as a planetarium, but other than a little bit of ringing in my ears, it felt like my sinuses were still intact. I grabbed at his flailing arms, securing his wrists in a loose hold, mostly because I was afraid if I gripped too tight, I would shatter his delicate bones.

He was a lot older than I remembered, dotted with age spots and worn with grief. His baggy brown pants were dark across the crotch. The stink of stale urine hit me in the face. I didn't know how long he'd been under that mass, but it couldn't have been more than a few hours. I'd only spoken to the man that morning, but he was lost somewhere, trapped in a terrified maze with no anchor to pull him free.

"Arthur," I practically shouted into his face, hoping to shake some reason back into his unseeing eyes. "It's Cole McGinnis. You called me. You're safe now."

"McGinnis." His watery eyes fixed on my face, and he grabbed at my shirt, his surprisingly strong grip stretching out the cotton fabric. He swallowed hard, and tremors shook through his thin arms, rattling his chest and legs as shock rippled through him. "You've got to save my Adele. They're trying to take everything I have left of her. You've got to stop them. *Please*."

FOUR

"I SWEAR to God, Los Angeles would be a safer city if I just threw *you* in jail," O'Byrne snapped, shoving her jacket back with a flourish and planting her feet into a firm stance. "I'm pretty fucking sure criminals would break in just to beat the shit out of you."

"Just charge admission so I can have a water bed," I grumbled back, fidgeting on the short wall enclosing the Brinkerhoffs' front lawn while an EMT cleaned out one of the cuts in my forehead. He'd already picked out a couple of chunks of glass, closing the tiny wounds with butterfly bandages, but from the clicking of his tongue against the roof of his mouth, I was going to be there for a little bit. "And I'll need conjugal visits. At least once a day. Three times on Saturday."

"Three?" The EMT's eyebrows lifted. Smirking, he shook his head. "Your girlfriend must be hot or your ego's bigger than you are."

"My husband is hot, and I need the three times to keep him happy." I hissed at the sting of antiseptic on my cut flesh. "Saturday's when we do laundry. Pretty sure those three times will be me folding clothes."

They'd taken Arthur Brinkerhoff away only moments ago, strapped down to a gurney and wrapped up in a thin blanket to fight off the shock bleaching his skin to a grayish white. Bobby was being interviewed by a stern-looking detective named Bishop, his eyes drifting off over her shoulder as he watched the crime-scene techs begin to go over the shot-up porch with a fine-toothed comb. I studied the techs for a minute but couldn't see what had Bobby so entranced. For all I knew, he was planning dinner and taking a mental inventory of what he had in his freezer.

"You about finished up there? I've got some questions for him," O'Byrne growled at the EMT. "Assuming he's got any brains left, because I wouldn't be surprised if they slithered out of that hole in the back of his head."

"You know, if I wanted to be abused like this, I'd be sitting at my desk, letting my office manager take shots at me," I grumbled back. The medical tech laid one last Band-Aid down and declared me fit to drive home. "At least there I get pie."

The wall was covered with the same stucco that was wrapped around the house's exterior, minus the bullet holes. It was wide enough to straddle, but it had to be done carefully because one of the Brinkerhoffs really liked succulents, planting more of the prickly beasts on the inside of the wall. I'd tossed my ruined jacket into the Rover's back seat, and the EMT plucked a few short thorns out of my flesh before moving on to the glass bits. I didn't know where the bullets went, but a quick inspection of my SUV reassured me it hadn't been hit. I couldn't say the same for a gleaming black sports car parked in front of the Brinkerhoffs' house. It took the brunt of the shoot-out with two shattered windows and a deep crease across its roof. It didn't look like the kind of car Arthur Brinkerhoff would drive, but California was a car-mad state, and oftentimes people drove the most unexpected things.

Since Arthur had married Adele with her odd proclivities, maybe he was really into unexpected things. Hopefully I would have the chance to ask.

"Did they give you a prognosis on Brinkerhoff?" I asked O'Byrne. "Guy was beaten up pretty badly. What kind of asshole beats up an old man?"

"You were a cop. You should know what assholes can do," she replied, standing on the lawn but avoiding the bristle of cacti starting along the wall about six inches behind my foot. I had to twist to clearly see her expression. Then, after a warning twinge from the scar tissue along my ribs, I pulled my leg over the wall and sat facing her. "And Dawson is your best friend. That's like having a ringside seat to the Asshole Circus."

If my brother Mike hadn't already married his wife, Mad Dog, I could have seen him with O'Byrne. She was the kind of woman who could haul in a hundred-pound tuna during a deep-sea fishing trip, then after a quick shower, slide into a copper sheath dress for an elegant night on the town. If I liked girls—and I wasn't scared to death of her ripping my head off like a praying mantis—I would've asked her out. I probably wouldn't have survived the experience, but I'd have given it my best shot. Because it would've been a good way to die.

We were almost friends. At the very least, colleagues who respected each other at some level. I'd been helpful to her in the past as a consultant, and she'd eased my way through a couple of cases with some pertinent information. But I was pretty sure she was tired of seeing me in the middle of her investigations, especially since I seem to show up without her asking me to be there.

"Give me the rundown on the old man," she said, her eyes resting momentarily on my face as she angled her body, moving to allow the crime-scene techs a bit more space to walk by and giving her the opportunity to watch them work. "You said he called you?"

"Yeah. I got the impression he didn't have a lot of faith in the LAPD solving his wife's murder." I shrugged at her fierce glare. "Don't look at me. I'm just telling you what happened. I told you last night I felt some kind of obligation to them. It's not like I expected to get shot at when I arrived."

"Was there any warning at all? From the shooter?"

I had to stop and think about what happened, slowing the incident down in my mind and sifting through the stuttering fragments of memory. The brain does funny things when hyped up on adrenaline and fear. It takes slices out of events, sometimes long stretches where everything slows down and you can see every grain of time. But most often you're more likely to be left with bursts of things—a bit of a loud boom, the spark of the muzzle flash, or the shocking heat of blood hitting the skin. There wasn't anything I could find in the microfilm-like spools embedded in my brain. What dominated the memory was my concern for Bobby and then me being pissed off about ruining yet another jacket. It was a stupid fixation, but sometimes that's just how the mind worked. It grabbed at the things that it could handle, sloughing away the moments too incredibly overwhelming to hold on to.

Still I searched, looking for any small clue vivid enough to stand out as a warning.

"Not really. And when the guy went by, I didn't get a good look at him. Just sneakers. Casually dressed. Maybe a hoodie." I snorted a brief laugh, glancing across the street where a studio squatted across a good stretch of the neighborhood. "I don't think he was an assassin. Don't those guys get dressed up to go out to work? Italian suits and polished loafers? And why was he tuning up Brinkerhoff? The place was tossed, but it didn't look like he was carrying anything when he went by us."

"Those are all questions I've got but no answers. I was kind of hoping you had some." O'Byrne's eyes narrowed when one of the techs began working on the sports car. "I'm wondering if that vehicle belongs to our shooter. There's a garage in the back, off of an alleyway. It's got a couple of cars in it. We're going to run the plate and registration, but something tells me that piece of flash isn't going to belong to our victims."

"I was thinking the same thing, but you never know. Jae's been lusting after vintage Mustangs lately. I blame my brother Ichi for that. For all we know, Mrs. Brinkerhoff's tastes ran to sleek and fast." I met Bobby's eyes, and he frowned at me, trying to tell me something silently, but I couldn't figure it out. "I really don't have anything to give you, O'Byrne. I didn't talk to him for very long on the phone, and he was out of it when I pulled the mattress off of him."

"There's too many odd threads in this. Something is going on, and I'm going to find out what that is. I've got a dead woman dressed in leather with a handful of diamonds lying in the backyard of an expensive mansion with nobody in the area reporting a robbery, and now I've got you and your buddy, Bobby, walking in on some guy working over the dead woman's husband. Then you're telling me he's probably not going to talk to the cops, so that's just another wall I'm going to have to climb on this case. Do me a favor. Whatever you dig up, I want you to call me. I don't care how small it is or if it looks like it's not connected to anything. You call me."

"What makes you think I'm going to dig something up?" I hadn't given much thought about what I would do after she cut me loose, but something wasn't sitting right in my guts. I just hadn't had time to dig through it and figure out what. "Technically, he's not even my client."

"I know you, McGinnis," she replied with a smile crocodiles would envy. "You're going to slink off back to wherever your kind holes up and chew on it until you decide justice needs to be done. Then you're going to fall headfirst into whatever cesspool this case crawled out of. So I want to know your every step along the way, because I don't want that husband of yours to buy his Mustang out of a life insurance payout."

I didn't like being that predictable, but she wasn't wrong. I hated the feel of how weak Brinkerhoff looked when I pulled him out of the pile he was buried under, and the angry black-purple bruises on his arms and face stuck with me. He'd been beaten pretty badly, to the point where I was worried if he would make it through the night. He was old and at an age where the body couldn't take that kind of damage. But like O'Byrne, I didn't have anything to go on.

"You're that sure I'm not going to leave things well enough alone?" I snorted. "Not like somebody's going to drop into my lap with a lead. The old man didn't even tell me what he wanted to talk about."

"Yeah, I'm *that* sure," she replied, a knowing smirk on her lips. "Here's a hint. Why don't you go look up Montoya's boyfriend. You know, the guy who hired you for the job? Also not so big on talking to the cops. Maybe you should go digging around there. You might be surprised at what you find out. Just remember you've got my number, McGinnis. Be sure to call, because I'm going to come after your ass if you don't."

THERE WERE spots of Los Angeles that rarely saw the sun, and in the densely packed maze of beautiful buildings lining Downtown's streets, it wasn't hard to see the bones of a bygone era. There were entire blocks of stone and metal whose shadows held the ghosts of noir detectives and gum-snapping dames. Downtown wasn't where tourists came to see the glitter of Hollywood or the beaches running up and down the 101. There were a few here and there, drawn to places like a bookstore with a tunnel made of sculpted novels or the Symphony Hall built out of steel and resembling a piece of origami made by a one-eyed drunk raccoon. I wasn't a fan of the building. It sat above Little Tokyo like a giant mutated metal mushroom, waiting for Alice to come by and take a bite out of it so she could grow smaller or perhaps slip back through the looking glass.

Downtown Los Angeles was the beating heart of the city, stitched together from bits and pieces of the people who'd wandered there. Some souls were looking for a dream they would never fulfill while others were simply looking for a way to escape a drab, dreary life. It was a harder city than a lot of people imagined. Nobody really knew what waited for them on the star-studded sidewalks. As beautiful as the face Los Angeles wore was, much of it was theater paint, smoke and mirrors hiding her bloodied fangs and wretched soul. Still, I did love her. She was vibrant and flamboyant, with rotted parts we all struggled to cut out, as if somehow we would be able to cure her of the cancer humanity brought to eat her alive.

I guess I wasn't much different from the people who came looking for that dream they would never fulfill, but that didn't mean I wasn't going to keep trying. The Lady of the Angels was worth it, and sometimes you find a dream you didn't dare to imagine. Like falling in love with a Korean man named Kim Jae-Min.

Who was probably going to kill me once I dragged myself home and he saw the condition of my face.

"It isn't too bad, right?" I studied the constellation of butterfly bandages across my temple, using the metal napkin dispenser I'd plucked from the middle of our table. "It looks worse than it is. Bet you once I peel these off, you'd hardly notice."

"You just keep telling yourself that, babe." Our young waitress, a long-legged redhead in a retro pink '50s uniform she'd paired with black fishnets, tapped her pencil against an order pad. "Not like I would toss you out of bed for eating crackers, but you look like I would have to spend a lot of time kissing those boo-boos before we got down to business."

"See? This is why I don't like doing jobs with you," Bobby growled at me from across the table, then plucked the napkin dispenser out of my hand.

"It's like you go out of your way to get us killed. And"—he peered at the waitress's name tag—"Laura, I'll have a catfish po'boy, a side of onion rings, and a red velvet donut. Water's fine to drink. And since we're talking, I'll let you in on the fact that he's married to another guy and possibly the biggest piece of trouble I've ever met. Not somebody you want in your life."

"Hey, if I was into hot daddies, I'd have hit on you," Laura snapped back. Patting my shoulder, she bumped me with her hip and gave me a smile. "I hope the guy you're married to isn't him, because you deserve somebody who treats you better. What'll you have?"

"No, I'm married to somebody a lot prettier and nicer. I'd show you a picture, but the asshole I brought with me would probably kill me with a spoon." I took another quick glance at the lunch menu. "I'll do the Reuben, also with onion rings, but with a piece of Oaxacan chocolate bread pudding for dessert. And to drink, an iced tea with sugar. *Please*."

She walked away with a snap to her hips, and Bobby plucked a few napkins from the dispenser he'd taken away from me. Waiting until Laura returned with my tea, he leaned over and said, "Tell me you're not going to chase after this thing with the Brinkerhoffs. Let O'Byrne handle it."

"Can't do it," I replied, plucking the lemon out of my tea and sliding it into his water. "There's too many questions that don't have easy answers, and I owe Adele more than just one 9-1-1 call to the cops to tell them I found her."

"You don't even know them," he pointed out. "It's not like you guys were friends. They're just an old case."

"I got the feeling O'Byrne was asking me to dig into it." I had to raise my voice to be heard above the din of a group of women laughing at a nearby table. The diner was popular, both for eating and filming any scenes that needed an authentic-looking retro space. It was the kind of spot where coffee cost a nickel and the donuts were bigger than my cat—a slice of old Los Angeles tucked in between more modern storefronts. "She told me to talk to Montoya's boyfriend. I don't know what that's about. She said he wasn't one for talking to the cops, but he's hooked up with one."

Detective Dante Montoya was someone I'd met through Bobby at the boxing gym where both of us spent an inordinate amount of time beating the shit out of each other. It was a good way to keep fit, and Bobby always had some kind of trick to show me, something safer to do with gloves on and guaranteed to help me end a fight. Unless of course he was the one whaling on me. Then he would pull a rabbit out of his hat and I would end up kissing the canvas.

Montoya and I had gone a few rounds ourselves. He was good for a solid workout, but we never made plans to spar, only hooking up when we ran into each other down at JoJo's. And since it was always good to change up partners, he was always up for a few hits. We were pretty evenly matched, except he didn't fight as dirty as Bobby did. But then nobody fought as dirty as Bobby did.

"You sure it was Stevens who called you about the job?" Bobby asked. "Did you meet up with the guy?"

"Yeah I met up with him. Down at his shop in Hollywood. I grabbed a windup metal Godzilla for Jae when I was there." I murmured a quick thank-you to Laura and inhaled the rich scent of hot corned beef and sauerkraut as she dropped off our plates. The onion rings were crisp, crackling hot, and steaming, with a side of jalapeno aioli. I was going to hurt. "Seemed like a nice enough guy. Kinda wound up tight but okay."

"Montoya told you what he used to do for a living?" Bobby returned the favor of lemon in his water by sliding his aioli over to my side of the table. "Before he opened up that store?"

"Stevens told me most of his business comes from dealing with high-end collectibles," I said, passing the ketchup over to Bobby before he asked for it. "Said the security thing was something he dabbled in once in a while. So I'm guessing maybe he worked for a company like Mike's. Seemed to know a lot about alarms and perimeters."

"Sometimes, Princess, you are just too fucking precious for words," he growled back at me, grinning evilly. "Rook Stevens was Montoya's white whale. He didn't work for any security firm. He was a fucking cat burglar. One of the best in the business, and never once did those silver bracelets cops put on him ever lead him to a jail term. So, still think it's a coincidence the old lady was found behind the house he asked you to check out? Somebody knew about those diamonds she had on her, but the bigger question isn't how they got there but why they didn't take them off of her after they killed her. I'm going to go out on a limb and say O'Byrne thinks Stevens has fallen back into his old way of life and Montoya's none the wiser, so she's going to use you to sniff him out. He used you to find out if Mrs. Brinkerhoff was still lying on that lawn, and O'Byrne is using you to find out if he was the one who put her there."

FIVE

"WANT ME to come with you?" Bobby asked from the relative safety of a palm tree's shade. "I mean, I can if you want."

It was a magnanimous offer, especially since Ichi's tattoo shop, Hizoku Ink, was only a few doors down from Rook Stevens's memorabilia store. I either hadn't remembered that tiny little fact or it just hadn't sunk in, because I'd been to Hizoku enough times to nearly call it a second office. I'd actually been in Potter's Field a few times before but hadn't connected it to Montoya's lover. That also could have been me lacking the particulars instead of being obtuse.

Either way, we were close enough to Ichi to make Bobby fret.

It was kind of adorable to see my once-lothario best friend wrapped up tight around a wedding ring and marriage vows. Less cute was that he was doing unspeakable things to my baby brother, but Ichi could take care of himself and probably gave as good as he got. It wasn't that I was squeamish about what they were doing. I didn't want to dwell on Mike and Maddy having sex either, despite having clear evidence they'd done it at least once in the freakishly gorgeous baby girl they had a few years ago. Lisa Rei McGinnis was going to be a heartbreaker once she realized she'd won the genetic lottery, and I was doing everything I could to keep my niece off the straight-and-narrow path. Mike didn't stand a chance. Between me buying a motorized kid-scale Ferrari for her to tool around in and Ichi applying temporary tattoos to her arms and shoulders whenever she wanted to change things up, Mad Dog Junior was going to be a kick-ass woman in a leather jacket and glittery combat boots.

Or at least that's what we were all hoping. So far her favorite things were dinosaurs, muscle cars, fairies, and books. And we were doing everything in our power to encourage her to keep pushing boundaries and take no prisoners.

Mike *really* didn't stand a chance.

Neither did Rook Stevens if he had anything to do with Adele's murder. Cop boyfriend notwithstanding, if he crossed into my life and brought death with him, there were going to be consequences. I didn't care how much Montoya loved him.

"Just tell Ichi I'll be by later to say hey. Jae might've already called him to see if you guys were coming for dinner. There was some furious fish chopping this morning when I left, so either we're going to be overfeeding the cat, or we're going to be feeding the two of you." I glanced down toward Potter's Field, where there appeared to be a small line forming outside the door. "I might be a while. Place looks like it's busy. Stevens might not be able to break away."

"If I don't hear from you in an hour, I'll send somebody to get you, Princess," Bobby drawled. "Just make sure you're in the right tower."

"Is that a gaming joke?" I cocked my head at him.

"Yes it is. You know you're getting old when you aren't up with current games and music, Cole." He shook his head, *tsk*ing at me with a few clicks of his tongue.

"Some of us aren't so desperate to avoid aging that we marry somebody twenty years younger than us," I stabbed at him with teasing, sharp words, knowing I could score a hit.

"Just remember that someone is your brother," Bobby shot back.

"Yeah, and it's something I try to bleach out of my mind every single night after I'm done brushing my teeth." I gave him a light shove toward Ichi's shop. "Get going, old man. Try to stay out of trouble while I'm gone."

"That's a shitload of funny coming out of you, dude," Bobby said, giving me a punch back on my shoulder. It hurt. And not just because I was still a little bit tender from my pinball run through the garden and then my tuck and roll off the ledge of the Brinkerhoffs' porch into the cacti patch. Bobby was a muscular, solid man who kept fit and trim by torturing me. And since torturing me was one of his favorite hobbies, he was extremely fit and trim. "One hour. Then I'm coming to get you."

"What's the worst that can happen?" I asked, walking a few steps backward and flinging my arms out in mild protest at Bobby's derisive snort. "It's pretty much a glorified toyshop. Not like anybody's going to drive by and shoot the place up."

THERE WAS an air of excitement around Potter's Field as I approached, a buzzing energy more in line with a movie premier than a place someone stopped by to grab an action figure or lunch box. This part of Hollywood had its own feel, far different from the street-hawker, carnival-like atmosphere found farther down, by the Chinese Theatre and the Roosevelt. There were still sporadic iconic funky-colored stars studding the sidewalk, but it was a grittier, more authentic Hollywood on this end of the boulevard.

We were far from the out-and-proud of West Hollywood and a good couple of miles from the packaged glitter of the Oscars and people dressed as superheroes charging for a photo. Big name-brand stores didn't drift down this way, leaving the sun-battered buildings to a hardier, more desperate crowd. There were spots of gentrification and sleek storefronts like Ichi's tattoo shop and Stevens's memorabilia store, but for the most part, it was a landscape of psychics, smoke shops, and cheap clothing. There was a Denny's a few blocks up, open twenty-four hours, and a refuge for runaways and prostitutes. I'd spent many a dollar at that Denny's, both as a cop and as a private investigator, plying witnesses with cheap coffee and stacks of fruit-covered pancakes.

The bones of old Hollywood existed, though, elegant structures studded with sleek lines and copper inlays now a blue-green from years of weathering. Potter's Field took up the first level of one of these buildings, stretching out to the height of nearly four floors. But from what I could see, it was only two stories. In any other neighborhood, the rent would've been exorbitant and outright buying the building practically unheard of, but in this part of Hollywood, it was almost within reach, and from what I understood, Rook Stevens's reach was pretty long.

Now I was questioning how he got the money and what he was doing to get more.

I jostled past the line coming out of the front door, much to the angry muttering of the people standing not so patiently in the brisk breeze. Whispering a few apologies and reassuring a woman holding a stack of books that I wasn't there to cut into the line, I made it in. A purple-haired, broadly smiling woman sat at a table a few feet past the entrance, a display of novels set up next to her. A harried-looking young man operated a cash register just inside the front door, ringing up customers after they plucked a book or two from the selection in front of them. From the sound of the woman's thick accent, she hailed from a part of Ireland where there was a bit of sea nearby and rolls of vibrantly green countryside. I couldn't understand a lot of what she was saying, but she seemed excited to see everyone, signing whatever they put in front of her and chattering up a storm.

Potter's Field was a haven for all things geek and magical. I had to give Stevens credit for the layout of the place—a combination of museum, theme park ride, and gift shop. It was hard to focus on one section of the store, mostly because the eye was drawn practically everywhere. There was an enormous, elaborate soft sculpture of a creature I think I recognized from a movie dominating the far end of the sale space, but other things caught my attention as well, including the massive spaceships hanging from the rafters. They glittered with sparkling lights and meticulous paint jobs, the spotlights above their graceful forms casting shadows down on the floor below. With the ceiling painted black, the ships stood out, occasionally bleating out a sound effect or flashing a concentrated beam of light across the far wall.

I hadn't noticed all of this before. I'd been focused more on getting in and out, or perhaps Stevens had ramped up the floor design since I'd been there. There was a whiff of paint in the air, so it was not outside of reason to think they'd remodeled. It was now a little bit of chaos and a lot more flash than it was before, but the crowd seemed to love it, wandering around through the displays and asking the black-shirted staff a million questions about everything they found.

Nobody stopped me as I wandered through the sales area and toward the employees-only section of the store. There was what looked like a pretty-well-stocked employee lounge to the right and a long hallway leading toward a fireproof steel door set into the back wall. I hazarded a guess the hallway led to storage, mostly because the closed door directly to my left had a sign that said Office on it. I knocked, then opened it when I heard a gruff voice tell me to come in.

The office was fairly large, a broad rectangular space with a seating area near the door that took up two-thirds of the room. A sturdy wooden desk that would've been at home in any governor's office was set back away from the entrance, positioned with its short end against the wall so whoever sat behind it was facing the door. Long stretches of narrow windows set near the ceiling provided a bit of illumination, but mostly the room was lit up by a constellation of recessed lighting set into a drop ceiling covered by punched-tin tiles. Decorated in a mishmash of Art Deco, retro toys, and video games, the wall separating the office from the main store was dominated by an enormous television, its dormant screen reflecting the man sitting on the couch across of it.

I'd pinged Rook Stevens as someone who preferred to stay behind the scenes, a puppet master of sorts who loved to put on a good show but didn't like anyone to see his face. He was the ringmaster and the Wizard of Oz wrapped up as a strong-featured, pretty young man with mismatched eyes and a wary gaze. I gave Montoya credit for building a relationship with this man, because he struck me as someone who didn't like entanglements… or least not romantic ones. But that also could be because I hadn't earned the right to sit in his inner circle. Jae had been this wary, opening up only after fits and starts of trust-building events.

"I was wondering when you were going to come by," Stevens said, not looking up from the comic book he was reading. "The coffee pot's fresh. Grab some if you want."

I didn't really want any coffee, but it seemed prudent to pour myself a cup as I figured out how to deal with Stevens's insouciance. If he'd planned to set me up to discover Adele, then I was going to have to come at him carefully. I only had Bobby's word on Stevens's past, but Bobby was as reliable as a sunrise. There were undercurrents in Stevens I had to negotiate, fast-moving rapid waters hiding boulders I could get hung up on, and I wondered if I'd come to a battle of wits totally unprepared and not armed to the teeth.

"Cream's in the fridge if you want it." He nodded with his chin toward the squat steel box the coffee maker sat on. "Then you can tell me about what happened the other night and why you look like somebody took a potato masher to your face. O'Byrne came by to shake me down, but I didn't have anything to tell her other than what I told you—it was just a security job and I wanted basic recon. Nothing more. Nothing less."

The coffee was strong, a bracing punch of dark roast powerful enough to make me want to check my nose to see if it was bleeding from the impact. I added a little bit of cream in the hopes of scaling back its pungent hit, but it swallowed the milky swirls as if it were a black hole eating one of those starships hanging from the store's ceiling. I reconciled myself to not being able to sleep later on that night and sat down in one of the armchairs next to the couch.

"So you didn't know Adele Brinkerhoff? Or why she died holding a handful of diamonds?" I watched Stevens carefully, but there was nary a flinch. There would be no poker games in our future, because his face betrayed nothing, to the point where I wasn't even sure he knew who I was.

"No. Who was she to you?" he asked, finally putting down the comic book and sliding it onto the low table in front of him. "To be honest, I also don't know the people who were having sex in the guesthouse either. The place was supposed to be empty."

"Her husband hired me in the past for a case," I replied, leaving out any mention of her confirmed infidelity and fondness for bondage and leather. "He also contacted me to look into her murder because he doesn't have a lot of faith in the cops. Doesn't think the LAPD can bring her killer to justice."

"*That* is the understatement of the century." Stevens chuckled, reaching for his own cup of coffee. "The LAPD misses more than it hits."

"You're hooked up with a cop," I reminded him. "A pretty good cop."

"Whose dead partner tried to plant evidence on me to frame me," he shot back. "Montoya *is* a good cop—a great one—but they're few and far between, and even he can get tunnel vision sometimes. Let's not fuck around with this. Someone told you I was on the wrong side of the law at one point, and you're here to poke at me to see if I knew about any potential heist that could explain the diamonds you saw. Right?"

"I'm also looking at whoever pulled a home invasion on her husband this morning. When I got there to meet with him, I was greeted by a bunch of gunfire, and after the shooter bolted out of the house, I found him beat up and clearly out of it." I risked another sip of the coffee, bracing myself for the moment when the stuff would make me see time slip away around me. It hadn't happened yet, but I was certain it wouldn't be too long before I started to see pink elephants dancing by. "O'Byrne said nobody reported any thefts, so either no one's missing those diamonds yet or—"

"Whoever had them shouldn't have had them," Stevens finished for me. He flowed back into the couch with a fluidity so smooth it made me wonder if he had any bones at all. "What did O'Byrne tell you I allegedly did?"

"O'Byrne told me nothing," I corrected. "Somebody else told me you used to be a thief. Now I don't think there's a coffee shop where criminals meet to chat about what they've pulled off, but if you operated at the monetary level those diamonds live on, then there's hope you would at least know who Adele could have been working with. If it *was* a burglary."

"Montoya told me you'd been a detective on the force. I can tell. You think like one," he muttered, raking a hand through his long caramel-streaked hair. "I'm not going to point you toward someone who can give you information, because that's how people end up in jail. I didn't know about the beating the old man took, but that doesn't change anything. I'm sorry about the lady you found, but I really don't know how she got there and I sure as hell don't know who she was working with."

"I'm not asking for anything other than a place to start," I replied, leaning forward. "I don't care about the diamonds. What I do care about is Adele Brinkerhoff's death. If she was caught up in something illegal, that's one thing. But someone busted a hole through her chest and left her literally holding the bag."

"If I had to come up with a theory," Stevens began, scratching at the bit of scruff along his chin. "She was set up. Probably by her partner or partners."

"She was kind of old. That's what doesn't make sense to me. You're talking about a woman who looked more like Granny from those Tweety Bird cartoons than a cat burglar."

Stevens laughed at me, to the point of a tear forming in his green eye. Wiping it away, he said, "Burglars come in all shapes and sizes. Some guy dressed in black in that neighborhood is going to get a lot of people to notice him, but put an old woman in Chanel or a sweater set, and people are going to give her directions to their silverware drawer. The best thieves look harmless. The fantastic thieves look helpless. She sounds like the perfect setup to get a gang to slip into a house with nobody inside of it."

If I hadn't seen Adele Brinkerhoff in action, I would've scoffed at Stevens's theory, but she'd been more than competent in hunting me through a topiary while wielding a shotgun. The woman who came by with her husband a few days later had been somebody totally different, still strong-willed but meeker, a staunch, law-abiding citizen who wouldn't ever be caught dead in bondage gear. I realized I still clung to the idea of Adele Brinkerhoff being the grandmotherly woman who'd perhaps once in a while walked on the wild side. Maybe I had it wrong. Maybe she was in fact a wild, lawless woman who every once in a while faked being a grandmother.

Her husband's anguish was real, though. Arthur Brinkerhoff mourned his wife. I'd heard it in his voice, felt it down in my bones. She may have led him on a merry dance through their lives, but he was devoted to her and wanted to know who killed her.

"Then why leave the diamonds?" I had my own suspicions, but I wanted Stevens to confirm them. "They were loose and in her hand. She was found on the lawn of a house that was mothballed by its owners while they trotted around Europe. O'Byrne said there were housekeepers that came in every once in a while and a son that periodically dropped in to stay in an apartment over the garage. But there wasn't any sign of a break-in there."

"I don't know the answer to that," Stevens admitted. "The bigger question is why did somebody beat up her husband? Maybe they weren't pulling off a job that night. Maybe those diamonds were part of a heist she already pulled and they were meeting there because they knew those properties were supposed to be empty."

"There's a lot of maybes floating around. It would also mean that whoever killed her knows that neighborhood." The leather jumpsuit was perplexing, but it would've given her cover, blending her into the shadows of the overgrown garden bordering the house's back lawn. "Still, why leave them?"

"Did anybody check to see if they were real?" He grinned at me, Cheshire-wicked and cunning. "Did the cops get an expert to look at them, or someone with a jeweler's loupe and a little bit of knowledge about stones glanced at them a couple of times and called them good?"

"I don't know," I admitted. "But I can ask. Why?"

"Because that's one of the most basic scams between thieves, especially ones that don't trust each other," Stevens replied. "They might have killed her because she was passing off bad merchandise, or maybe discussions just went sideways. Either way, there's probably a bigger haul out there and her former partners are looking for it. If I were you, I would start with the old man. Find out who she was working with, and if he's clueless, then buckle yourself down someplace safe, because if they were willing to kill her because she double-crossed them, they're going to be more than happy to kill you because you're getting in their way."

SIX

"Do you lead with your face into things?" Jae carefully plucked off one of the bandages, its ends soaked through after my shower. "When the shooting starts, do you say to yourself, 'I am too pretty. Let me put my face right into where it can take the most damage'?"

The Band-Aid removal wasn't painful, and I could have done it myself, but Jae liked playing nursemaid. It also gave him a chance to scold me. He'd already sighed when I informed him I lost yet another jacket to the case, and I'd given Ichi my shut-the-hell-up glare when he chimed in on Jae's argument that I should drop the whole thing. Our predinner visit was mostly spent cataloging my injuries and me refilling my glass with Hibiki, wondering when I was going to get some food instead of the shit they were piling up on me.

In the end I had no idea what I'd eaten other than I thought it was some kind of fish battered in miso, and the buzz I'd gotten from the whiskey was light enough to be burned off by a hot shower. Jae wasn't so easily shaken off.

"I went to ask a few questions, not end up in a shoot-out." My defense was weak—even I could see that. I should have expected something to happen. Something *always* happens. "I called the hospital to see how Mr. Brinkerhoff was doing, and the nurse said I can drop by during visitors' hours tomorrow morning to talk to him."

"You're probably going to have to take a number behind the police," Jae reminded me. He had a sultry purr to his voice, a velvety thrum I adored, and despite him working stuck adhesive from my skin, my body was heating up under his touch. Since all I was wearing was a towel around my hips and he was practically straddling me as I sat on the edge of our bed, he couldn't help but notice. "Tell me you're not getting turned on because this hurts. I don't think I'm ready for that kind of adventure with you. With your luck, I'd end up tied to the bed with you passed out on top of me wearing only a Batman mask because you thought it would be sexy to leap across the room and you hit your head on the dresser or something."

"It sounds like you've thought that through," I mumbled, shifting the towel so it sat more comfortably across my lap. "Batman? Really?"

"The way you're going, it's going to be Deadpool," he remarked sarcastically. "I'm surprised you didn't come home with more toys from that shop. You like those kinds of things."

"I like the shows and books, but I don't want a lot of stuff cluttering up my life." It was a habit mostly, years spent being yanked out of military housing and shuffled around to the next stop on my father's Tour of American Bases. Moving often was easier if you didn't have a lot to pack, and my stepmom, Barbara, was strict about Mike and me fitting our things into only two boxes with a suitcase for our clothes. "I got that Godzilla for you the last time I was there."

"You have five Chicago Cubs jerseys and four signed baseballs." Jae snorted, smearing something on one of the deeper cuts. It stung, but I held off any sign of pain by biting my lip.

"That's different." I winced when he smoothed the lotion into the crevices of the cut, mostly because the sting prickled and grew when he moved it around. "It's the Cubs."

"Remember that when you're throwing things at the TV." He studied my face, turning me with a firm hold on my chin. "Some of these really didn't need bandages. Was the EMT gay?"

"I don't think so." Maybe that was the wrong answer, because the butterfly bandage he put on stung nearly as much as whatever it was he'd smeared on me. "I didn't notice. Married to you, remember?"

I went for romantic, snagging his hand, and kissed the ring I'd put on his finger during a ceremony that seemed to go on longer than a double-header. All I got in return was a withering look and a disgusted snort, followed by another smear of pain gel across my forehead.

"Sit still," he ordered sternly, but there was a twinkle in his gold-flecked brown eyes. "You're moving around too much."

"There's ways of making me stay still." I wiggled my eyebrows at him, pulling a sweet smile out of his mock frown.

Laughing softly, Jae straddled my lap, pinning my thighs to the bed and sliding the V of his legs across my groin. The towel was trying very hard to contain me, but it was a lost cause. A low growl thrumming through Jae's throat cautioned me to keep my hands planted on the mattress when I tried to slide them up his hips, but it was difficult to concentrate on staying still, especially since the wet towel was bunched up against my abdomen and his heat spread across my damp skin.

"This is not helping me stay still," I cautioned, steeling myself not to groan when Jae shifted on my lap, allegedly to reach a small slice on the other side of my forehead. "Babe, a man can only be so strong."

"You've had worse," he murmured, kissing the cut briefly. "I have faith you're man enough to hold on while I finish taking care of you."

He was good at testing my limits. He should be. Jae's been testing them for years now, and I'm not too proud to admit I buckled every time.

I'd fallen for him practically from the moment I first saw him. It wasn't love then—maybe fascination with a heavy dose of lust—but he'd intrigued me. That day he'd been another grieving relative in a house full of pain and sorrow, but then something happened between us in the kitchen as he chopped up vegetables. In the middle of all of that death and a tangled weave of lies I'd been caught in, Jae teased me about spaghetti.

It'd been unexpected and pretty much laid the path of our relationship from that moment on. He was complicated in ways I couldn't begin to understand and possessed a simple philosophy on things I could only envy. I counted each day with him as a blessing and was pretty sure *he* counted each day as a mild curse. We'd come through so much together—his family pretty much declaring him dead and my father making sure I understood every insult from him was simply another handful of dirt on my grave.

There were also times when it felt like he could read my mind, so I wasn't completely surprised when Jae whispered softly, "Do you know the exact moment when I knew I couldn't live without you?"

"Pretty sure it was when you stopped me from eating the raw bitter melon," I teased with a playful boast. Considering that happened within the first half hour of us meeting, it was a very far stretch.

"No, that was the moment you were trying to figure out how you could get into my pants," he lobbed back at me. He moved again, and the towel finally gave up its battle and slid to the floor. It was getting harder to think with my dick coming up with all sorts of much more interesting things to do besides me sitting on the edge of the bed getting plasters put on my face. "It was after. When you dug Neko out of my building after it exploded and then you came to tell me she was okay. I hated you so much because I didn't want to be in love, especially not with a man. And really not with a man who knew everything about me."

"Everything I found out about you just showed me how fucking strong you are, *agi*." The endearment was *wrong*. One of the many things I'd fucked up in my pursuit of the beautiful, rangy Korean man straddling my lap, but it'd become a thing between us. A stupid, silly misspeak we'd built up into something special, although whenever I slipped up and said it in public in the middle of Koreatown, I got some pretty funky looks. "Are you about done with my face? Because I would really love to move you down my body."

We'd made love a thousand times before, and with any luck, we would have many more times together before one of us slipped away to join the stars. I treasured the feel of Jae's mouth on my skin, hissing at the painful pleasure of his teeth nipping at my nipple, then returning the favor, making him gasp. We knew each other's bodies, explored the familiar landscapes, but it felt new every time.

He had a faint brown mottling on his right hip, more like a cluster of freckles the length and width of my thumb—scarring from when he fell on a briquette fire when he was nine. I liked kissing it, making him squirm. He was ticklish in places, and where my lips made him writhe and buck beneath me, my tongue and teeth made him moan.

And the noises I drew out of him with my fingers were both heaven and hell to my ears.

I longed to bury myself into his heat, lose myself in the clench of his body around mine, but I knew better. Sex is like whiskey, always better sipped and savored, especially when it's aged, mellowed with affection, and shared with someone you love.

"Cole-ah," Jae ground out between his clenched teeth, arching in response to my touch. "*Now.*"

I gave in to my husband's demands, but on my terms. I was bruised and smarting in some areas, but the stretch of his lean form beneath mine more than made up for any aches and pains. Jae dug his fingers into my shoulders, probably adding to the welts and marks already on my abused skin. We rode each other gently at first, but then the heat we'd built up between us consumed our patience. The tug and twist of Jae's body around my shaft was exquisite, pulling the tender threads of my climax out from my very core.

There were so many small moments I wanted to hold on to, bits and pieces of sensations I needed to engrave in my memory—the chiming of our wedding rings when our fingers touched, the bite of gold into the webbing of my hand echoing Jae's tight hold on me, and the familiar sting of being stretched. I knew he was feeling every one of my thrusts.

We were slippery and salty, damp from our exertions and needing even more. His heels dug into the back of my legs, a quick reminder of how flexible he could be. I was wrapped up as tight as a gift, ready to spill apart at the seams when Jae began to shake. He bit me, definitely adding to the contusions on my skin, and the sharpness of his teeth into my flesh made me lose control. Wrapping my arms around him, I rocked into him, taking him with me over the edge.

When we both lay panting and wrung out, I realized I was half off the bed, and at some point, the dog had not only brought her wet tennis ball into the room, I'd apparently ground it into the floor with my foot. I wasn't sure what was more damp—my toes from dog spit or the rest of my body from making love to Jae.

"I stepped on your dog's swamp ball," I gasped into Jae's ear. "It feels disgusting."

"That's exactly what someone wants to hear after having sex," Jae muttered, not so gently pushing me off of his torso. "Kick the ball downstairs and we can go take a shower."

"Last time I took a shower, we ended up here on this bed getting sweaty again." I rolled over, trying to get more of my body on the bed. "How about if we just skip the shower and go right back to what happens after it? Minus the tennis ball."

He propped himself up on his elbow, studying me. I knew what I looked like. As hard as I worked to keep my body prime and in shape, I'd taken a lot of damage over the years. The keloids along my ribs stretched around like kelp tendrils over my skin, twisting down into my muscles in the most inconvenient places, often going into spasms when I moved the wrong way or firing off the wrong signals for shits and giggles. I had starbursts along the ridge of my shoulder, souvenirs from the night I lost both my best friend and my lover. Jae had a matching scar on *his* opposite side, a battle wound taken during one of my cases. It was smoother than my healed-over wounds, leaving me to wonder if bullets soaked in betrayal and hatred scarred the flesh.

"I love you, *hyung*," Jae whispered, pressing his mouth against mine and stealing away my breath in more ways than one. "I think you're right. Let's skip the shower. But get rid of the tennis ball first."

THE MORNING came in fits and starts, sunbeams breaking through the low-lying cloud layer with an enthusiasm I normally only saw in sullen teenagers dressed in all-black baggy clothes and trudging behind their parents while shopping at the Grove. With daylight expressing a fierce reluctance to participate in the sun's scheduled rise, I dressed as warmly as I could, pulling a leather-and-wool Chicago Cubs jacket from my closet. I'd gotten halfway down the stairs when Jae spotted me and made an all-too-familiar turnaround motion with his index finger.

"What?" I looked down the stairwell, then at my clothes. "Black jeans, gray shirt, and a Cubs jacket. The jacket's gray and red. This should all go together."

"That shirt isn't gray. It's closer to Pantone 559, and it belongs to Bobby. He must've left it here, and it got mixed up in your laundry." He made the motion again, emphasizing his point by stabbing at the air toward our bedroom. "It's like the universe hates me. I got rid of everything in colors you can't see, and they still show up in your dresser. Go change your shirt. You look like a washed-out Christmas tree."

I came back downstairs and got permission to leave the house after grabbing another T-shirt I was fairly certain was gray. I wasn't sure if they were all just fucking with me or if they were really greens I couldn't see, but since everyone including Claudia had opinions about my sartorial attempts, I just changed my clothes.

Opening the front door, I found Bobby standing on the stoop, about to ring the doorbell. He grunted a quick hello to Jae, who offered to give him a cup of coffee, but he held up a steel tumbler, sloshing it about.

"What are you doing here? Did you want to come with me to the hospital?" I checked the time, calculating how long it would take me to get to the medical center they'd taken Arthur Brinkerhoff to. I wouldn't be allowed into the ward for another hour, but it would take me about that just to get through the Wilshire traffic. "Isn't your car at the shop? How'd you get here? I didn't hear your bike."

"Ichi dropped me off," he rumbled, picking Honey up when she danced over to his feet. "How's my baby girl?"

I peered down the walk toward the front of the Craftsman, not seeing my brother's car or his Harley. "My brother can't come in now? He just drops you off and leaves?"

"He does when he's driving the crazy old cat lady to LAX. Not only did he agree to take her to the airport, I'm stuck with her cats for two weeks while she's out of town." Honey slobbered all over his face, not happy unless she covered every inch of his skin with spit. Her tongue made scraping noises against his unshaven chin, and she wiggled happily in his hands. "Yeah, I was planning on going with you on whatever you were doing today. Considering you've been shot at two days in a row, it probably isn't a bad idea for you to have backup. You might want to reconsider carrying while you work this case. You might need it."

I was very much aware of Jae still standing in the doorway. I felt the weight of his anxiety when his expression flickered with concern before he buried it beneath a placid mask. I was still licensed to carry a concealed weapon and routinely went down to the range with Mike and Bobby to keep my marksmanship up, but it had been a long time since I actually carried a gun with me. A darkness had consumed me when a madman hunted through my family, nearly killing Mike and injuring practically everybody else. Jae had that man's blood on his hands, and I had the burden of that guilt on my conscience. It was probably foolish *not* to take a weapon with me. It was certainly naïve for me to have faith I wouldn't be shot at because I didn't have a gun on me, but… the pain and worry in Jae's eyes kept me from opening up the gun safe in the hall closet and taking out my Glock.

"Let's see where this takes us first," I replied. Then I leaned over to kiss Jae goodbye. "*Saranghae-yo.* I'll call you later. Text me if you want me to bring food home for dinner."

"I love you," he murmured back, twisting his fingers into the fabric of my T-shirt, refusing to let me go. "Maybe Bobby is right. Maybe—"

"I'm just going to talk to an old man in the hospital," I reassured him, tucking some of his hair behind his ear, mostly to trail my fingers along the soft skin at the nape of his neck. "I've got a lot of questions for him, and he hasn't even really hired me. If things start to look dangerous, I'll consider it, but for right now, the gun can stay where it is. And you better let me go. My husband picked the shirt, and if you wrinkle it, he might get mad."

"Yeah, I hear he's a real asshole sometimes," he teased back, giving me a silly smile.

"I think you're talking about Bobby," I corrected haughtily, sniffing with mock indignance. Bobby barked a short laugh, and Honey joined in, trotting back into the living room with a few yips. "My husband is a delight. I worship the ground he walks on."

"Can we get going before I throw my stomach up like a starfish? The two of you are making me sick," Bobby groused loudly, scraping the heels of his boots against the cement stoop.

"Good thing you're going to the hospital, then," Jae snarled back playfully. "Just take care of my hyung. We've got an anniversary coming up. Anything happens to him, I'm taking Ichi with me to Catalina, and the two of you can sit here and rot."

SEVEN

"YOU GOING to be okay going in there?" Bobby asked, glancing at the shards of glass and concrete poking up into the Los Angeles sky.

"Why wouldn't I be?" I gave him a quick glance, but past anguishes were building the pressure inside of my chest. As a best friend, Bobby was both fantastic and maddening. He knew me well enough to know when to push and when to back off, but me and Bobby usually chose to do the exact opposite. Stupidly enough, that's exactly what I needed in a best friend, but in this case, I told myself I was going to be okay. "Hell, I haven't been here in so long they're starting to send me Please Get Shot postcards in the mail because they miss me."

It'd been forever and a day since I'd spent hours on my knees in this hospital's chapel, praying for my brother Mike to survive a bullet meant for me. There was so much blood on my hands, some of it so old it stained my skin and I was never going to be able to scrub it off. Sitting in the Rover, bracing myself to wander around halls I knew too well and knowing I'd never get the stink of death and antiseptic out of my nose for days afterward, I wondered if chasing after Adele Brinkerhoff's murderer wouldn't bring me right back here again.

"Am I doing the right thing?" The steering wheel had an odd bumpy pattern along its inside ridge, and it sang with a bass moan when I ran my thumb over it. "Jae says I can't help myself, that I wouldn't be able to put this aside because that's not who I am, but I'm wondering what I'm bringing to my front door if I pursue this."

There was a kernel of self-loathing in my gut twisting into existence just for thinking about walking away. It was difficult to even consider, much less do, but there I sat, debating starting the Rover and going back to a life dominated by taking pictures of cheating spouses and finding lost dogs. I didn't know if that life was enough for me, but it certainly seemed safer for everyone I loved. I'd already lost so much and risked so many. I didn't want to lose anyone else. I couldn't afford it. My heart was already taped up and stapled together. Another tap from the ball-peen hammer of Fate, and it would shatter.

Bobby turned to face me, leaning against the Rover's passenger window. He was staring at something past my shoulder, but that was just how he thought. It was a way for him to gather up his ideas, bundling them into a tight cannonball before he shot a hole through my chest. I could always depend upon him to give me the truth, unvarnished, mostly painful, but always accurate. We disagreed on a few things in life—I still hadn't quite gotten over him sneaking around with my younger brother behind my back—but I loved and respected him.

And while not diplomatic, his heart was always in the right place, and whatever he told me, it was always said with a modicum of objectivity. He'd been a good cop, balancing the law with what was the right thing to do, since sometimes they didn't go hand in hand. He would sooner buy groceries and diapers for a woman caught shoplifting because she was desperate to feed her kids. Still, there were times when he wanted to protect me from myself, and while I could understand that, right now I needed that objectivity.

"You and I have been through a lot of shit," he rumbled, rubbing at his eyes, then blinking rapidly, probably trying to clear his vision. "It's been a long time since you opened a can of worms. And that's kind of what your cases end up being sometimes—a very large can of poisonous, Cole-chomping worms."

"I think those would be called snakes," I broke in, trying for some levity. But the stern look I got told me it wasn't appreciated. "Sorry. And?"

"Jae is right. You've always got to climb up on that white horse and ride to the rescue. And when you do, we're all scared as shit that one day you're going to run into a dragon too big for you to take down." He sloshed his coffee tumbler back and forth, then popped it open to take a sip. "The question is right now, is this that dragon? How deep does this go? Because the pieces of this puzzle aren't lining up. You've got a dead geriatric dominatrix with a handful of diamonds, and her husband is lying in the hospital after getting worked over by some guy in a hoodie who took a few shots at us. On top of that, the only reason you were there was because you were doing recon for a cat burglar who says he's given up that life, but who knows for sure?"

"You think Montoya would be with him if he wasn't?" I didn't know Dante Montoya, not like Bobby did. My gut told me Montoya was not the kind of man who would be in bed with a criminal—metaphorically or physically—but sometimes love did weird things, and ethical corners get cut when the heart is involved. "I talked to Stevens. I couldn't get a good read on him."

"I think Montoya would need proof Stevens was out there pulling jobs, but no, he wouldn't be there unless Stevens was riding the straight-and-narrow line." Bobby frowned at his tumbler, then fit it back into the cup holder between us. "Let's assume you're not going to get paid for this. And I know money isn't a problem, but you're going to need some kind of legal standing to get your foot into a lot of doors, especially since you and I both know you're going to have to shove that foot in between a few cracks to get inside what's going on.

"You feel responsible for her being dead. Don't deny it. And I know it doesn't make any sense, but that's just how you think. You found her body, and now you need to find her murderer, even though O'Byrne will be working it on her end." He glanced up at the hospital, peering at it through the somewhat bug-speckled windshield. "And up there is a man whose heart is broken because somebody took away the love of his life. You know how that feels, and you know what it's like to live without answers to the questions that keep you up at night. So yeah, I don't expect you to do anything but chase this down, Cole. I'm just going to have to be right beside you in case that dragon is too big."

"I appreciate that, Bobby." I patted his shoulder, lightly squeezing it before letting go. "Thank you."

"You act like I have a choice," he grumbled at me, opening the door. "Don't forget, Princess, I married your baby brother. I come home without you and there's not going to be enough left of me to sleep in a dog bed, much less a couch."

ARTHUR BRINKERHOFF was asleep, hooked up to what looked and sounded like a DJ mixing board more than any medical device I'd ever seen, but it had been a while since I'd been lying in a hospital bed, waking up to a new litany of pains and bruises. He was frail, his nearly translucent skin draped over his bones like tissue paper dampened by ugly blotches of purpling watercolor splashes. His eyes were practically slits in his face, and his upper lip swollen to a plumpness big enough to touch the tip of his hooked nose. His chest rattled beneath the hospital gown decorated with thin yellow stripes—probably meant to be a cheerful touch of color, but it only served to highlight the sallowness of his skin. Dried blood flecks dappled his forehead—dribbles from a cut closed with a butterfly adhesive—but there were stitches along his jaw and neck, clear-cut evidence of deeper wounds.

He looked exactly as I thought he would, so I wasn't surprised when I came into the room and found him lying in the hospital bed looking like a Ramses the Second cosplayer who'd gone too far.

The drop-dead gorgeous blond sitting in the chair beside the bed definitely was a shock, though.

She was everything a detective novel needed to ratchet up the suspense—icy golden hair, long legs, and a face gorgeous enough to launch a thousand ships, be they Viking or gondola. I was used to beautiful. I spent most of my days around Jae, Scarlet, and Claudia, so while I wasn't immune to beauty, it took a lot to steal my breath away.

This woman certainly had that *a lot*.

If I were straight, I would've been in trouble. When she glanced up at me with her wide baby blues and gave me a small shy smile just a hair short of sexy and a finger breadth away from wicked, that look told me all I needed to know about her. I wouldn't be able to trust her as far as I could throw her... well, if she was carrying something heavy, because she didn't look like she weighed that much.

She was dressed to kill, a pair of red stiletto heels giving a splash of color to her black pencil skirt and dove-gray blouse. But then, for all I knew, the tucked-in, fitted boyfriend shirt was actually some shade of pink I couldn't see. I still wasn't buying the whole "there were colors I couldn't see quite right," but I was reluctantly being drawn over the line of accepting a reality outside of my control.

Much like this case.

"Cole McGinnis. I'm a private investigator hired by Mister Brinkerhoff," I said, nodding at the old man in the bed. "I came to see if he was up to answering any questions."

"McGinnis," she purred at me in a smoky voice reminiscent of speakeasies and cigarettes. She was a walking cliché, but it seemed like I was stuck with her, at least until I could figure out what she was doing there. "You're the man who rescued Poppa. One of the police officers last night told me you'd be coming by."

I took the hand she offered and shook it. Her fingers were cool to the touch, without a hint of clammy nervousness. "And you are?"

I was really beginning to regret letting Bobby go on a coffee run for us. Neither one of us liked what any hospital had to offer, and there was a Starbucks drive-through not more than three blocks away. As much as I wanted more coffee, I could've used him as a foil. She was an unknown quantity, and from the looks of things—her phone charging on the side table and the thick book she'd been reading left to rest on the old man's bed—she was a woman who was a part of the Brinkerhoffs' life. Every bone in my body screamed at me, trying to get my brain to understand. This woman was a complication in an already fucked-up case.

Like I needed even more convincing about how much trouble she could potentially be.

"I'm Marlena Brinkerhoff. Adele is… was my grandmother." Every pitch and fall of her voice was filled with the poignant sorrow of a woman in mourning, and her elegant hand clasped the unconscious Arthur's fingers in a gentle embrace. It was all so very perfect and yet felt quite theatrically practiced. "I flew down from San Francisco as soon as I could. Poppa called me when Grandma was found, so I was in the air when he was attacked. I didn't discover what happened until I showed up at the house and found the police…."

She gave a little sob, closing her eyes tightly and bringing her clenched fist up to her ripe, red-lipsticked mouth. As wary as I was, my heart went out to her, and I reached over to touch her arm, probably falling into the web that she wove.

That was the problem with being a private investigator, or at least that was my problem with being a private investigator. I could never really see the cobweb strands, and my gut had often proven to be a liar.

"I'm very sorry for your loss." She folded herself into my arms before I could stop her, and I was left to stand awkwardly as I patted her back. "I met your grandmother before all of this. A few years ago. She seemed like a strong woman."

"She was. She would push me to be my best," she murmured through a series of hiccupping sobs. I wasn't sure if my shirt was going to be able to absorb all of her tears, but I also wasn't in a position to protest. The woman had lost someone dear to her, and I needed to find out who took Adele Brinkerhoff from her family. "A lot of people thought she was too stern, too strict, but I knew she loved me."

"Did she ever bake you cookies?" I had to ask. If I took anything out of this entire experience, I wanted to be reassured that grandmothers baked cookies.

The look Marlena gave me when she pulled back from my chest was an odd one, but it was a strange question. I wasn't going to be the one to tell her Adele Brinkerhoff and I met over the business end of a shotgun after I caught her doing the spank-and-tickle with another woman, but the cookie thing was important, at least in my own twisted little brain.

"She baked cookies all the time. Usually shortbread," she said with a small smile that seemed more genuine than the one she'd given me as I walked into the room. "Poppa's favorites are shortbread and peanut butter. I like chocolate chip, but her shortbread could just melt in your mouth."

"It's good you have that," I murmured, putting a little distance between us. "I can come back later when your grandfather wakes up. I just need to ask him about what your grandmother was doing that night."

"Poppa isn't able to talk to you. The doctors are concerned he hasn't regained consciousness, and they're worried there's brain damage," Marlena whispered breathlessly. "He told me he was hiring a private investigator to look into Grandma's death. And that you were the one who'd found her. He was just so upset. I told him we could talk when I got there, but now... I'm just hoping he wakes up."

With Arthur out of reach, Adele Brinkerhoff's motives for being out that night were going to be hard to ascertain unless Marlena was cognizant of their day-to-day life. I didn't have the best of relationships with my own parents. Okay, my father would sooner see me dead than cross the street to put me out if I was on fire, but I also knew not everybody had that kind of family. For all I knew, Marlena was the apple of her grandparents' eyes and she knew everything about them.

Except maybe perhaps for the whip-cracking, adulterous-lesbian-sex-with-secret-lovers thing Adele had going. I wasn't sure if I'd want any of my grandchildren knowing that about me, much less have calendar updates on when and where I was going to go to have some fun, leaving Grandpa at home to watch *Jeopardy!* in his leather recliner.

"How well did you know your grandparents?" I asked as gently as I could. "Your grandfather and I were going to go over everything yesterday, but he was seriously injured, and getting him medical help was more important than asking any questions."

"They raised me. My mother was their only child and got pregnant pretty late in life. I'd like to tell you she was someone to be proud of, but she was wild and out of control. They didn't even know she was pregnant until she showed up on their doorstep and dumped me on them." Marlena sank back down into the chair, motioning toward the empty one next to her. "Please. Sit down. Maybe talking about it will wake Poppa up or at least comfort him in knowing you're working on the case. The detective I spoke to said they didn't have a lot of leads for either the murder or the attack."

"Was her name O'Byrne?" I dug out the small notebook I'd shoved into my back pocket, ready to take down everything she said.

"No, it was Bishop. She was nice, but there didn't seem to be a lot she could do about Poppa's attacker. She had a lot of questions about what Grandma was doing and what they found on her. There was some question about whether or not there were more gems at the house and that's what that man was after." She wrung her hands together, leaning forward as she spoke. "I don't like the cops. None of us in the family do."

"A lot of people have problems with authority," I conceded. "I sure as hell do sometimes. Were your grandparents suspicious of the police? I'd spoken to them before this. I got the feeling they came over from somewhere else. Both of them had an accent I couldn't place."

"Bavarian. Which technically is German, but Poppa was always very proud of where he'd come from." Her hand drifted again to the old man, resting on his arm. "They'd both come from a very rough neighborhood there. Life wasn't easy."

"They're at an age where World War II would leave a pretty heavy mark." The chair wasn't uncomfortable, but my ass had been in more than a few of them, and I knew from experience it would do a number on my back if I sat there for very long. "Lots of conflicted authority figures there. I could see where that would shape their opinions."

"Oh no. That's not it at all." Marlena let out a short, tinkling laugh. "It's because Grandma was a thief and Poppa used to be an art forger. They only gave it up to raise me, so I know there's no way in hell she would have gone back to doing that. If she were caught, I would have to leave my job in San Francisco to take care of Poppa."

Reeling from Marlena's words, I barely had the presence of mind to ask, "And what exactly do you do in San Francisco?"

"I'm an assistant district attorney for the city." This time her smile was as deadly as the bombshell she dropped. "Grandma and Poppa would never risk me—my career—for a handful of diamonds. Especially since they were fake."

EIGHT

"A DISTRICT attorney?" Bobby repeated for what might have been the third time. "Okay, this case is getting complicated."

"It was already complicated. It was complicated the moment I stepped on Adele Brinkerhoff's body." After throwing the Rover into Park, I scrubbed at my face, trying to make sense of the whole situation. "Let's see what O'Byrne has to say first, and we can all compare notes. *Somebody* killed her, and so far we've got no one on the board who looks like a suspect."

I'd been kicked out of the hospital room a few seconds after Marlena Brinkerhoff finished adding another layer of either bullshit or cloudy motive on top of her grandmother's death. Arthur chose that particular moment to wake up and begin shouting incoherently. His hoarse, raspy voice chased me down the hall, surprisingly strong for a man who'd been given the diagnosis of brain damage and potential continued unconsciousness. Marlena shot me a textbook puppy-dog-eyes look, beseeching me to let things go for the time being while she attended her grandfather.

Beating a hasty retreat, I nearly ran down Bobby, who'd finally returned with a couple of Trenta cold brews from what had to be the longest Starbucks trip ever.

"Did you ever notice that it's always puppy-dog eyes? Like, what other kind of puppy is it?" Seizing on the ridiculousness floating about in my thoughts, I lobbed the question over at Bobby. "It's like that whole tuna fish conversation. Just tuna fish. It's never salmon fish patty. Just like puppy dog. Although maybe it's like kitty cat?"

"Princess, there is something seriously fucked up with the way you think," Bobby grumbled at me. "*Seriously* fucked up."

O'Byrne rang me up as we were leaving the hospital. The crime-scene squad was done with the Brinkerhoff household, going over it as much as they could. But considering how thoroughly it'd been tossed, there was a good chance something had been missed. Agreeing to meet her down there, we fought traffic back across Wilshire and through the neighborhood where movie stars living on shoestring finances and tethered to major studios once resided. An unmarked police car was parked in front of the house, a sleek sedan O'Byrne probably conned the motor pool into giving her because of her rank. It sure as hell wasn't because of her social graces and pleasant personality, but she was a good cop and got the job done with little bullshit and game-playing. While I could admire that, having wrestled with the LAPD motor pool myself, they preferred to be bribed with donuts and cupcakes with a healthy dose of ass-kissing to chase down all the sugar.

Neither Ben nor I were much for that kind of thing, so it stood to reason that all of the cars we'd been given were usually missing air-conditioning, smelled of puke or piss, and sometimes—alarmingly—didn't have working brakes.

"Neighborhood's quiet," Bobby observed, scanning the empty street. "Most of these places are big enough for a family, but there's a couple of small houses here and there, just enough for someone who's retired. Did O'Byrne send people out to knock on doors?"

"The day Dell O'Byrne doesn't send a cop or two out to see what the neighbors heard or saw will be the day she turns in her badge," I replied with a heavy dose of sarcasm. "She didn't say they came up with anything, but you'd think, in this kind of neighborhood, someone would come forward. It's not like anyone's going to worry about gang retaliation or their landlord kicking them out because they talked to the cops."

"Yeah, this is the kind of place where when you move in, if you don't take around a plate of cookies to every neighbor, you're not invited to the block barbecue on the Fourth of July." Bobby ducked his head and stared up at the house through the windshield. "That granddaughter of theirs is probably going to inherit this place. If she were smart, she'd begin laying tracks down to migrate to Los Angeles. Hell of a lot cheaper than SF."

"She just seemed too good to be true," I confessed, mentally scratching at the itch Marlena Brinkerhoff left along my spine. "Something's off there, and I don't know what it is."

"Probably because she's a lawyer, and deep down inside, you're always going to be a cop. Cops and lawyers don't mix, Princess. They're like mortal enemies—Road Runner and Coyote, sheepdogs named Sam and whatever the fuck Ralph was." He took one last look at the house, then nodded toward the shot-up porch. "Get out of the damn car and let's go see what O'Byrne found in old Arthur's house."

Bobby wasn't wrong. The neighborhood was an idyllic slice of Americana sat down in a gritty urban fold in Los Angeles's diverse economic landscape. In a lot of ways, the City of Angels was an oddly constructed, sometimes badly made burrito. You could take a bite at one end and get a mouthful of rich carnitas spiced with a chipotle sauce and then a few inches over, discover the guy who made it also added cold french fries and a bit of gravel. If you knew where to bite in, Los Angeles was rich and fulfilling, but there were also bits of broken glass and shrapnel hidden in its delectable, aromatic plumpness.

And sometimes, even as careful as you are, you get a mouthful potent enough to kill you.

The front door was boarded up, sealing off the shot-through glass window, but it was still functional. Surprisingly, the gunman missed the doorknob and the deadbolt. The sash windows along the front also sported a new plywood coat, and ribbons of crime scene warnings fluttered in the light breeze, anchored with pieces of duct tape to the columns framing the stoop. Bobby walked straight through. I had to battle the yellow-and-black kraken before I was allowed entrance into the crime scene. After unwrapping my face for the third time, I tied off the end to the post while Bobby bitched at me for fucking around.

"I swear to God, you can't even walk up a flight of stairs without something happening to you," he groused. "How have you even survived this long? I'm surprised you didn't stab yourself to death the first time you used a fork. Or did they only give you spoons until you turned eighteen, and then after that they figured, fuck it, he's on his own?"

"And you're my best friend," I said, slapping him on the shoulder as I went by. It stung my hand. Probably not his shoulder, but I did my best. "O'Byrne's inside. She said I could look around if I wanted to. Mostly I want to find out what she's dug up. Maybe she's got some piece of information that will give us somewhere to start."

"You know you're not a cop, right?" Bobby walked in behind me, enveloped in the cool shadows draped through the front foyer. "It's O'Byrne's job to find the murderer. Not yours."

"He's a paid consultant," O'Byrne interjected dryly from the living room. "I've got a lean budget for payroll but a slush fund for private investigators I can use to hunt down bits and pieces of the case. Mac here does a little digging for me, maybe helps close a file or two, and I cut him a check off of LAPD's treasure chest. That's how it works, Dawson."

"I get paid?" I stopped short, mired in a stack of throw pillows and hardback novels missing their dust jackets. "Really?"

"If somebody doesn't shoot you in the next week, Princess, I'm going to," Bobby promised with a snarl. "Why don't we all catch each other up on how much we haven't found. Then we can go digging through the house to find jack shit."

"Is he always this pleasant?" O'Byrne jerked a thumb toward Bobby, who'd settled down on the thick arm of a plaid-covered couch.

"Oh, this is him happy," I informed her, ignoring the bird Bobby flipped me behind her back. "Did they find anything? I'm guessing nobody tripped over a box of priceless gems and pearls while they were taking fingerprints."

"We should be so lucky. The diamonds found on Brinkerhoff were man-made—flawless, but they do something to distinguish them from natural diamonds. The expert we brought in spotted that within seconds of looking at them." She extracted a wooden chair from a pile of papers, straddling it after setting it down on the living room floor. "Dawson's right. Let's go over what we know and see if we can make a game plan. I assume you met the granddaughter?"

"The assistant district attorney?" Bobby piped up. "Did you have somebody validate that? I mean, anybody can say they're something. This asshole over here introduces himself as a private investigator, and that's only because he hopes to get free coffee."

"Once again, my best friend," I said with a shake of my head. There was another wooden chair, but it creaked when I picked it up, so I opted for a velvet wing chair instead. "How much have you learned about the Brinkerhoffs? Marlena was pretty forthcoming up until the moment her grandfather woke up. I didn't get a lot out of her except that Grandma and Grandpa apparently were pretty hard-core criminals until she came along, and she knew those diamonds were fake. Did someone on the LAPD tell her that? Or did she already know?"

"I'll have to check with Bishop." A thunderstorm briefly rolled over O'Byrne's face, and I didn't envy Bishop when the lieutenant caught up with her. "That's not something we'd tell her."

"Rook Stevens brought that up too. Asked if the LAPD brought in an expert to look them over." I began picking at a pile of papers on the floor, arranging the sheets into neat stacks on a long table next to me. "If she's a district attorney up in SF, she might have contacts down here. Someone could be feeding her information."

"Because that's what this case needs, an out-of-town DA raised by crooks and an information pipeline O'Byrne here won't be able to throttle." My stacks of paper weren't meeting Bobby's strict organizational guidelines because he picked up the whole mess from the floor and plopped the papers on the couch next to him. "You're making me crazy. You're not even looking at them. How do you know what goes with what?"

"I was looking to see if any of it was connected to a storage unit," I informed him with a smirk. "They may not have anything in the house, but they could have stuff hidden elsewhere. Stevens told me he has a couple warehouses where he keeps his high-end merchandise. Maybe that's something they teach them in cat-burglar school."

"If Marlena Brinkerhoff has somebody talking to her, I'm going to have to put a stopper on it. And good call on the storage unit. We went over this place as best we could, but there's nothing out of the ordinary—a small safe with important papers and a few bits of jewelry but nothing worth killing over." O'Byrne pursed her lips, lost in thought. "And you said Stevens didn't know her. Think he was lying?"

"He was harder to read than a comic book written in Enochian Pig Latin." I handed over the stacks of paper I'd pulled together when Bobby held his hand out for them. "He seemed pretty blasé about the whole burglary thing. I don't know him well enough to tell you if he was lying or not. I don't even know Montoya that well, but Bobby here says he wouldn't be with someone pulling jobs."

"He wouldn't," she agreed. The room was stuffy, and O'Byrne shrugged off her jacket, her shoulder holster squeaking when she twisted about. She favored Glocks, just like me, carrying two along her rig. Sighing, she blew a strand of dark hair out of her face and looked around the room. "I'm going to guess our shooter didn't find what they were looking for. He spent some time beating up the old man, then spent even more of it tearing the house apart. Either Brinkerhoff didn't tell him anything or the guy didn't like the answers he was given."

"I'm guessing Brinkerhoff said shit," Bobby interjected. Putting another stack of papers down on the table, he began to sift through a handful. "Our shooter didn't know we were coming, but Brinkerhoff did. I think the old man kept his mouth shut because he knew he couldn't fight back and was gambling on us—or at least Cole here—to show up."

"That's a big risk," O'Byrne pointed out. "He would've been gambling on Mac here coming into the house and not assuming Brinkerhoff blew him off."

"If you didn't know in the first five minutes meeting Cole that he would scale a castle wall and fight off the dragon if he thought something was hinky inside of your house, then you would have to be the stupidest motherfucker on earth." Bobby grinned at me when I flipped him off. "Brinkerhoff knows him. Hell, he called Cole to hire him to dig into his wife's death, the same wife Cole investigated before when Brinkerhoff suspected she was skipping around in somebody else's garden. He knows this idiot. What's more important, he knew our gunman wasn't going to shoot him."

"He beat him half to death," I reminded them. "The doctors weren't even sure he was going to wake up. You can't get information out of a dead man, so maybe the guy figured he would go through the house, see what he could find, and if he came up empty, he could do Brinkerhoff in. We just got here before he could get to that point on his to-do list."

"Well, right now I've got a dead woman, useless diamonds, and an assistant district attorney who probably has political connections that are going to be chewing on my neck in a couple of days," O'Byrne said with a sigh, pushing off of her chair to stand up. "Consider yourself assigned to the case, McGinnis. Dig in as deep as you can, but try not to get yourself killed. At least I know you're not going to be talking to the lawyer. I'm going to have to see if I can find out who's leaking information, but at least Ms. Brinkerhoff gave us permission to go through the house. I figured I would have to come at her with a warrant or call the whole thing off."

"That tells me there's nothing here," I said, taking in the mess. "I mean, let's think about it. Marlena Brinkerhoff knew her grandparents were criminals. She says they stopped when they took her in, but we only have her word on it."

"So what? Marlena sat at home doing her schoolwork at the kitchen table while Grandma was out knocking over banks?" Bobby snorted. "You think she's covering for them?"

"The Brinkerhoffs were never on the LAPD's radar. Not like Rook Stevens," O'Byrne said, pacing off the floor in long strides, avoiding the piles of debris. "But Stevens hit big and usually worked with a team. Or at least that's what they think. They never caught him, and most of what they suspect he did came from other thieves looking to cut deals. If Adele Brinkerhoff did smaller jobs by herself, no one would know what she pulled."

"She could have had a team, or at least someone small and wiry to help her," Bobby threw out, stacking the last of the papers next to him. "That's what they did in Victorian London, right? They had little kids shimmy down the chimney because they'd fit? Maybe before Marlena got her sheepskin, she was out fleecing the sheep with dear old Grandma."

"That's all conjecture," O'Byrne replied. "We don't have any evidence the Brinkerhoffs were anything but upright, law-abiding citizens."

"I don't know about that," I said, leaning back in the wing chair.

The house wasn't huge, maybe eighteen hundred square feet. It looked like it had three bedrooms and two bathrooms neatly packed into its early 1900s bones. While not as luxurious as the mansions in Brentwood or Beverly Hills, its prime location and vintage classic lines more than made up for its lack of space. Technically the home was considered a Craftsman bungalow, rich with polished wood and pocket doors, lovingly tended by its older European owners. It was a gorgeous house, perfect to raise a child in, with good schools nearby and close proximity to everything Los Angeles had to offer.

Considering I'd purchased a larger, much more run-down version of the house in Brentwood, I had a pretty good idea of its market value.

"This place right now could probably go for a million and a half. Property taxes are steep here. Even if they bought it years ago, it was still a pricey neighborhood. Always has been, this close to the studio," I said, taking a good hard look at the living room. "Marlena said they gave up their old lifestyle, but how did they pay for all of this? Did either one of them have jobs? Costs a lot to raise a kid, right?"

"And put it through college," Bobby chimed in gruffly. "Especially when they take six years trying to figure out what they're going to do for the rest of their lives and then when they graduate, do something totally fucking different."

"He's bitter his son opened up a coffee shop," I said, making O'Byrne laugh. "But really, where did they get their money?"

"We just started digging into their finances, but I've got to step carefully," she replied. "I might be investigating a murder, but there's still a lot of politics I've got to wade through, especially with her job up in San Francisco. I sniff at the wrong pile of dog shit, and it's going to end up in my face."

"You worried more about your career or catching a murderer?" Bobby growled, lifting his eyebrows at her.

"I'm not only going to pretend I didn't hear you say that," O'Byrne replied with a snarl of her own, "I'm also going to not shoot you for saying it. You know how this kind of crap works, Dawson. You did a full ride with the LAPD during some of its shittiest times. Even as cleaned up as it is now, there's still a lot of the good old boys left over from those days, and they're just as filthy now as they were back then.

"I'm lucky enough I've got Book as my captain, but some cops, like Bishop, are stuck with some real assholes. This case is already screwed up, because it crosses over several departments and there's some infighting going on, but that doesn't mean I'm not going to do my job." She did another circuit of the room, stopping at odd points for reasons she didn't share. But I got the feeling she really wasn't seeing anything beyond her frustration. "If I find out Bishop didn't say anything, then I've got a damned leak. That means I would have to watch my back and my mouth around everybody in the department except for probably Captain Book. Well, and the two of you. So, someone's got to speak for the dead, and in this case, Adele Brinkerhoff seems to only have the three of us. Are you assholes in or not?"

"Do I get paid the same rate as Princess?" Bobby cocked his head, smirking at her. Since he pretty much rewrote the definition of cocky, I wouldn't blame her if she decked him, but O'Byrne was a better person than I was.

"Have McGinnis pay you," she shot back. "He apparently doesn't need it."

Their now-lighthearted bickering faded into a waterfall of white noise, because the odd feeling I got about the room finally settled in and I took a good hard look around. The place was a mess, but I got the sense of a comfortable placidness to the home, something violently disturbed by the intruder who'd beaten the hell out of Arthur Brinkerhoff. Picking up one of the books, I glanced at the spine, curious as to what Adele or Arthur would find interesting to read, but somehow a dry account of animal husbandry written by an Englishman in the early 1900s didn't seem like a titillating choice. The books were all stripped of their dust jackets, or perhaps they never had any to begin with. Scattered about like confetti after a three-year-old's birthday party, I was struck by how they were all shades of dark green, oxblood, and brown.

Their subject matters were a range of nonfiction and the occasional unheard-of novel by an unknown author, not something I would have chosen to line my shelves with, but I didn't know either Brinkerhoff, so I couldn't really say what held their interest. Leaning back, I tried to see the room as a place where I spent my evenings, sitting with my spouse and talking, because if I wasn't mistaken, the television wasn't plugged in, and it was too far away from an outlet to get any power.

"This is all window dressing. This room. Their lives," I said, standing up to join O'Byrne in her pacing. "These books are like the kind you buy by the yard to make your shelves look good. But they're worn, more homey. And look at the walls. What do you see?"

"Other than some really nice wainscoting, they're kind of drab. I think they call that paint color oyster," Bobby said. "It looks just like my grandparents' house used to. My mom's house probably looks this way now. Don't give me that look, Princess. You know things went to shit when I came out. I just haven't been over there."

"Look, we know they live here. All of the neighbors we talked to say the same thing—nice older couple, raised their grandkid right and put up Christmas lights every winter. The old man hands out full-size candy bars at Halloween," O'Byrne commented. "There's clothes and toiletries thrown about upstairs in the bedrooms, and the guy even went through the hall closet and pulled out all the towels. I think there's even a half-eaten gallon of butter brickle from Thrifty's in the freezer."

"Did you find any BDSM gear?" I asked, turning to face her. "Anything out of the ordinary? A rubber ducky in a leather mask?"

"No." If O'Byrne could have tossed me into a cell on a 5150 at that moment, she would've buckled the straitjacket on me herself. "They're, like, fucking seventy years old."

"Adele Brinkerhoff had a thing going with at least one other woman—a thing that included bondage gear and French ticklers, which I only know about because I had to look it up. And when she died, she was wearing a leather jumpsuit. Or a romper. I'm not sure what the difference is, but the old woman had a bit of a kink going, and that's got to be stored someplace. If not in this house, then somewhere else." I gestured toward the walls. "Look around you. Marlena Brinkerhoff told us Arthur used to forge art for a living. My guess is he's a painter, because I can't see that there's a lot of money in forging sculptures, not to mention trying to move the damned things, but the walls are fucking empty. There's not even a velvet painting of Jesus or those big-eyed freaky fucking children on the walls.

"I live with an artist. They can't stop arting. They can't help it." I finally had their attention, and O'Byrne began to look around her with a calculating gleam in her eye. "Even if he gave up forgery, he wouldn't give up painting, and there's not a damn thing in this house that points to either one of their lifestyles. There's no pictures on the wall either. Marlena Brinkerhoff graduated from law school, and there's not one damned photo of her in a cap and gown? Maybe I'm missing all of it and it's hidden somewhere else in this house, but it doesn't seem like this place is real. And I have no idea on where to start looking for where their lives are stashed."

"You might not," Bobby said from his perch on the couch. "But I bet you their granddaughter knows."

NINE

"O'Byrne's got you on a leash," Bobby grunted, the punching bag rocking in his hold when I connected with a couple of hits. "With that consulting thing, she's pretty much got another detective in her back pocket that dances to her beck and call."

My punches in no way moved him. Bobby had long mastered the art of planting himself firmly and using his knees and hips to absorb any impact. I still tried, though. It gave me something to do besides not gnaw on my frustration. Bobby wasn't wrong. There were things I couldn't do for Dell O'Byrne. Gathering evidence and actually arresting someone was outside of my purview, but if she tapped me to help with a case, I could run down leads and feed her any information I got. As far as I was concerned, Arthur Brinkerhoff hired me, and he was my first priority. But O'Byrne definitely had tangled me in tighter.

My problem was I was unsure about what exactly I was chasing down. Adele's murder weighed on me, and despite the possible criminal activity she was involved in, she didn't deserve to die in the middle of a wet lawn with a hole punched through her chest. I just didn't know where to start looking for who killed her and who attacked Arthur.

"I think we need to see if Arthur is up to talking." Shifting my feet, I tried a couple of uppercuts. They strained my damaged shoulder, but the burn was light, not the stinging, tearing alarm of something going terribly wrong along my joints. "Every time we dig, we just come up with more questions. I need answers."

Bobby and I did our best thinking when either eating or sparring down at JoJo's. Since he and Ichi were once again freeloading dinner off of me and Jae, our evening meal would be a large one, probably tons of barbecued meat and a million little plates of *panchan*. While I loved *kalbi*, there was something special about picking through all of the tiny white plates filled with things I still haven't figured out after all these years of being with Jae. Panchan was kind of like food-based Cracker Jack prizes— some things I recognized by shape, while others were always pure surprise. The slivers of slightly sweet fish cake with thin slices of burdock root and jalapenos were probably my favorite, but there was a dish of almost sugary cuttlefish strands made with a spicy chili sauce I'd fallen in love with. They were the kind of hot Jae and Ichi found spicy, but the two of them also mixed lava in with their breakfast smoothies.

I liked to think I'd grown a lot since meeting Jae, especially considering all of the food adventures he'd taken me on, but I still really hoped tonight's panchan wouldn't include the bright pink baby octopi he and my brother loved.

"Are you thinking about food or your husband? And don't deny it. You've got that look on your face, Princess. Why don't you try to focus?" Bobby asked, bumping me with the bag. "Less drooling and more punching. Where do you want to go with Brinkerhoff? If your little theory about them hiding their lives away holds up, the granddaughter's going to know about that, and she's going to try to block you out."

"Depends on what's more important to them," I said, shifting up my punches with different angles. "She and Brinkerhoff are going to have to decide what they want more, finding Adele's murderer or protecting their secrets."

"I don't think either one of those exists without the other," he suggested, pressing his shoulder up against the bag as I began to intensify my strikes. "Let's assume Adele was ripping somebody off with those diamonds she had. So either they came from a stash they squirreled away somewhere, or she did a job recently and that was her haul."

"O'Byrne said Stevens worked with teams, but it was probably more likely Adele either worked by herself or with her husband. They weren't anyone the cops noticed, or at least they weren't big enough to draw attention to themselves." Stepping back from the bag, I shook out my arms, sweat drenching my T-shirt. I had another ten minutes with the bag. Then we could hit the showers, worn out from spending an hour in JoJo's gritty, no-frills boxing gym. "Arthur's too old now. If she was going to do a job and needed help, she'd have to tag somebody else."

"Not like that woman was a spring chicken. There's no way she was limber enough to pull off a burglary," Bobby growled, tapping the bag to remind me I still had time on the clock to work through. "If they were hurting for money so bad she had to pull off a heist, why not sell that house? It's worth a hell of a lot, and they could buy something smaller."

"When I first ran into her a few years back, she was plenty enough limber and spry," I replied, ducking back into a fighting crouch. "She kept up with me while holding a shotgun. And I think she was wearing heeled boots. Wasn't like I was taking fashion notes. I was running for my life. She looked about the same when I found her. A little pillowy, but you and I both know that's kind of deceptive. Women hide a lot of muscles in those curves of theirs."

"True," Bobby agreed. He gave out a little grunt when I punched the bag, leaving me with a small sense of satisfaction. Also, he wouldn't be able to return the favor, because he'd already done his bout. Going second had its advantages because sometimes holding the bag left me as bruised as going a few rounds when Bobby needed to work off some of his adrenaline. "If the granddaughter is smart—"

"Marlena," I corrected as gently as I could while plowing another punch into my target. "She's an assistant district attorney. Let's assume she's got two brain cells to rub together."

"Okay, Assistant DA Brinkerhoff has a lot more to hide than where her grandmother's stash is. If she's got any political aspirations, she doesn't want any of that dirty laundry to be pulled out of the hamper."

"She's the one who told me about their criminal dealings," I reminded him, dancing back a step to shake out my arms again. The workout helped limber me up, loosening tight joints and sometimes even helping me think. "Looking at everything, it makes me wonder if she's playing a long chess game of sorts. By closing off access to Arthur, she's going to be controlling the narrative and any information we get. It won't matter if Arthur wants to find Adele's murderer. It's going to be Marlena who guides us through things if we let her."

"So we just have to get you in to talk to Arthur without her being around." He checked his watch, and I knew he was simply adding minutes to my end time for however long I stopped to gather my thoughts and talk to him. "Divide and conquer seems like the best thing to do. I'll have to keep her busy while you sneak in and talk to the old man. You've got five minutes left, Princess. Then you could hit the showers."

Having Bobby as a best friend meant going through a lot of physical activities, usually on days when running five miles in the rain was the last thing I wanted to do, but it helped me keep fit. Since I was married to a slightly younger man with a hell of a lot more stamina and flexibility than I had, keeping myself in fighting form was smart. Sad to say, being a private investigator and sometimes ending up in very sticky situations wasn't enough of an incentive lately for me to get out of bed at 5:00 a.m. for a run or a boxing bout—not when I had Jae in bed next to me.

Of course, that was probably a lie I was telling myself. I liked the burn of my muscles being worked through their paces, and the aches through my body reminded me of how far I'd come since that fateful day Ben tried to end my life. He'd taken away everything I loved—my boyfriend, my career, and with his suicide, a man I considered my brother as well as my partner. And as much as I'd gained since that day, I was also carrying around a bunch of scar tissue and healed-over wounds I needed to stretch out once in a while. Doing yoga with Jae—or at least attempting to do yoga, since I wasn't as graceful as he was and yoga seemed to be based on the positions a cat cleaned itself in—wasn't as effective at getting my blood pumping and my muscles aching as boxing was.

I also really like to hit things.

"We're close enough to the hospital to hit the start of visiting hours. Won't hurt to see if Arthur's up for a little conversation. Even if he just gives me a name, I'll have some place to start looking." I squared off, going for a round of body shots on the bag's thick form. Sweat was beginning to sting my eyes, and I was really looking forward to a lukewarm shower in the locker room. I spoke between punches, knowing Bobby could keep up. "Do you think you can keep Marlena out of the way for five minutes?"

"I think I can do that," Bobby promised, grunting again when I gave a good punch into the middle of the bag. "Let's face it, between the two of us, I've spent more of my life lying to myself about preferring women. Hopefully that will at least hold me over until the old man gives you something you can work with."

THE BEST thing about JoJo's was it had parking, a premium perk in Los Angeles's urban sprawl. Since the city and building owners were serious about guarding their lots, it was usually only somebody incredibly stupid or an idiot willing to risk his car who parked someplace they didn't belong. The worst thing about JoJo's was the parking lot was pretty much a glorified wide alleyway jammed in between two looming, run-down warehouses. You didn't go to JoJo's for a workout on treadmills while a talk show played on big-screen TVs mounted on the walls or to try your hand at the newest weight machine positioned in front of a wall of mirrors. It wasn't the kind of place you could pick up a smoothie after you were done, and there were no free water bottles waiting for you at the reception desk.

Shit, there wasn't even a reception desk.

It was an old-school, no-frills boxing gym where trainers took their up-and-coming fighters to test their skills against men and women who'd been around the block more than a few times. If you could hold your own at JoJo's, you had a good chance in a ring where money exchanged hands and your night ended with blood smeared on the mat—hopefully not your own.

So the guy walking down the parking alley toward JoJo's front door stuck out like a Persian in a whirl of Tasmanian devils. I wasn't sure if a group of Tasmanian devils was called a whirl but it seemed likely, and I'd just come from the gym, so I knew what it was like in there.

There was still a bite in the air, something Los Angeles wouldn't fully lose until July or August, but the black hoodie he had on was a bit too much. Too new. His pointed-toe Italian boots and indigo dark jeans came off much too flashy for anyone intending to go a few rounds, but more telling was the fact that he held a small duffel up against his side, his right hand tucked into its partially open zipper. His face was flat of emotion, carved out of a Slavic hard stone and nearly bloodless—a splash of white with bright blond hair cropped short against his square skull. His jaw was set with the determination I normally only saw in nutcrackers at Christmas, and he stared straight through us as he strode down the alleyway with a firm purpose.

He made no attempt to hide himself among the vehicles, and there was no indication he'd stepped out of any of them. No jingle of keys or juggling of his bag, just straight ahead and careful to keep his hand inside of his duffel.

"*Fuck.*" That was all the warning I got from Bobby, but it was enough. We both dove between the parked cars when the guy shook the bag off his hand and came up with a wicked-looking gun.

I don't know who choreographed gunfights on television and movie screens, because things never went as smoothly as depicted. Bobby and I had been walking side by side, and when we instinctively jumped to protect ourselves, we ended up on opposite sides of the alley. I landed in a scatter of gravel, barking my elbows and forearms on the broken-up asphalt. Rolling over onto my side, I spotted Bobby in a full crouch, protected by an enormous Ford truck with his hand clutching a weapon that looked a hell of a lot like the one the guy had in his duffel bag.

There were no guns on me. The duffel bag I'd been carrying held only a stainless steel water tumbler and sweat-soaked clothes. It wasn't like I could check under the minivan I was hiding against for a Glock or Colt duct-taped to its undercarriage. Something told me that the man or woman with a stick-figure family dancing across the back windshield and an I Love to Brake for Flower Sales bumper sticker plastered below a personalized license plate declaring somebody loved Gigi wasn't exactly going to be sporting firearms anywhere in their vehicle.

I could've been wrong. It *is* California, after all, and we're known for our contrary natures as well as our kick-ass tacos, but regardless, I seemed to be the only one who'd come to a gunfight with a gym bag.

A bullet shattered the minivan's side windows, showering me with bits of glass. Since I still sported a few of the deeper cuts left on me from the Brinkerhoffs' door, I pressed my face up against the car's wall, making sure my feet were hidden by the tire. Across the way, Bobby gestured at me with his gun, a questioning look on his face. I was taking that to mean he was asking where the hell was my weapon, but he also could have possibly been suggesting he was going to kill me for once more getting us into trouble simply by doing my job.

To be fair, he gave me that look a lot, for quite a few different things. One thing I knew for sure—I wasn't going to scream across the alley to tell him I didn't bring a gun with me. I hadn't planned on being Doc Holliday to his Wyatt Earp that morning, or really any morning, but I was going to have to do something quick because another shot rocked through the van, and as far as I could tell, Bobby's side of the alleyway was hot-lead-free.

I was definitely the target.

I really didn't like being the target.

"Okay, McGinnis, do something," I muttered to myself, glancing up to see Bobby returning fire with a quick one-two from his weapon. "You're a sitting duck."

There was silence in between the shots, and sadly, none of it was filled with police sirens or outraged yelling. What I did hear was the sound of leather-soled shoes scuffling across the gravel-flecked asphalt alleyway, a sure sign the gunman was getting closer. My Rover was, of course, at the far end of the parking stretch, literally the last car along the row opposite of JoJo's gym. I usually park there to avoid it getting scratched, and with any luck, it would survive this little dust-up without any bullet holes. I could only hope the cars in front of it would take the damage.

Mostly because my insurance company was beginning to believe I had somehow moved into the middle of a war zone instead of living in a Craftsman in Brentwood. My rates were through the roof, and I was pretty certain the Range Rover dealer had a second house in Cabo, considering how many times I'd had to replace my car.

"The stupidest things go through your head when you're trying not to die," I scolded myself, looking around. "*Think!*"

I hated JoJo's parking area. It wasn't maintained well, and there were potholes big enough to be home to a sarlacc, enormous craters formed by the rapidly changing cold-hot Los Angeles winters. There was only so much stretch and give that asphalt and cement can take before its integrity breaks down, leaving bits and pieces of patched-together parking lot scattered about in clumps. I was crouched next to a particularly large crevice and holding a mostly empty bag.

"Cops are going to be here anytime soon!" Bobby shouted, glaring at me across the pavement.

He made a motion toward his face, mimicking somebody talking on their phone, and I was sad to say I had to disappoint him by pointing toward where I'd parked the Rover, where my cell phone sat hidden in the console, charging itself out of the red zone on the power pack I'd brought with me. My best friend flipped me off, so I returned the phone call mimicry, then pointed at him, cocking my head to the side while shoveling as many asphalt bits into the bag as I could.

Our miming conversation was quickly interrupted by another round of bullets. After the thunderous strikes of projectiles hit the row of parked cars, setting off a chorus of screaming alarms and whooping klaxons, I spotted Bobby's gym bag lying a few feet away, sitting in what little sunlight was able to reach in between the tightly packed buildings.

No one was going to be riding to our rescue anytime soon unless someone heard the gunshots over the gym's loud music and arrhythmic grunting… and then cared enough to call the cops. We weren't exactly in a neighborhood where cops strolled by to check up on its law-abiding citizens in the middle of the afternoon. On the edge of an industrial area, it was more likely to get a private security car with a rent-a-cop to stop by long enough to get his fool head blown off because he was curious instead of calling in the authorities.

The pointy Italian shoes made their appearance on the other side of the minivan, and I took that as my cue to move.

Like I said, gunfights were never graceful in any way. They were never a ballet of bodies twirling about, coats flying up behind the participants' backs, arms windmilling about in a martial-arts pose evoking the idea of a praying mantis or slumbering tiger. They usually were made up of short bursts of activity, followed by punches of adrenaline and a mouthful of thick spit because that's what fear did to saliva.

I came in swinging. The gym bag was heavy and new enough that I had faith the straps would hold. I probably shouldn't have packed it as tight with broken asphalt and cement, but it was my life on the line. If I pulled a shoulder muscle while trying to survive, I literally could live with it.

The first crunch was satisfying, catching the guy straight across the face. The bag's weight shifted, pulling me around so it was unwieldy, making it an inelegant weapon, but I wasn't looking to score points with any fight judge. I needed to take this guy down, and fast. Up close, that wicked-looking gun wouldn't miss, and I'd promised Jae not to get shot. He really disliked me coming home with more holes in my body than I left with, so using the momentum I'd built up with my initial bag swing, I twisted around and caught the gunman again, slamming the bag into the side of his head.

Blood splashed across my hands and over my bare arm, its metallic stink nearly as hot as its splatter on my skin. The guy stumbled back but held on to his gun, its muzzle skittering through the air in an unfocused spiral aimed at the far warehouse's wall. His finger flipped across the trigger, and the gun went off, puncturing one of the paper-covered upper windows set high on the building's brick façade.

I didn't know if he reloaded or how many more bullets he had left in his gun, but it wasn't anything I was up to chatting about. I swung the bag up, connecting with his chin. Then I let it go, fixing my stance as he stumbled about. His fingers failed him, and the gun went flying, opening him up for my fist.

He was just tall enough for my uppercut to catch him across the jaw and loosen a few of his front teeth. Bits of broken white enamel were mingled in the blood bubbling out of his mouth, and I hit him again, popping him hard in between his eyes and above the bridge of his nose, then following up with a body shot, hammering his ribs. My shoulders were strained from swinging the heavy bag, but my brain and body remembered each lesson Bobby gave me on how to fight.

Boxing might be a gentlemen's sport, but I wasn't interested in being a gentleman, and Bobby taught me every single dirty trick he knew. The guy was still on his feet, and I needed to make sure he was in no way, shape, or form able to run once I was done with him.

So I grabbed his balls with my left hand, squeezed and twisted hard enough to make his eyes pop out, and hammered at his face with my right fist.

It took him four seconds to go down, but I didn't let go until his back was up against the asphalt and Bobby's foot was on the man's discarded gun. Sitting back on my haunches, I tried to catch my breath, my chest heaving while my brain sifted through all of the adrenaline coursing through it, trying to find a single sensible thought amid the oh-my-God-we're-all-going-to-die sparkles overloading my senses.

"Did it ever occur to you that I had a fucking gun?" Bobby growled at me, the welcome but too-late-to-the-party sound of police sirens finally breaking through the neighborhood's uncaring silence. "I could have shot him."

"You threw away your gym bag. The one with the phone in it," I reminded him, scrambling for an excuse. Gasping, I continued to jab wildly at him, using my words in probably ineffectual punches to ward off his quite reasonable logic. "I couldn't risk you throwing it at his head."

"You are so full of shit, Princess. You didn't even fucking think about it," he countered, effectively putting an end to my argument. "You recognize this guy?"

I studied what was left of his face, something that was practically impossible to do since he was writhing around in pain, but I got enough of a look to know I didn't recognize him. Shaking my head, I flexed the tightness out of my hands, then stood up, nearly bumping into what was once a sleek sports car whose back end now resembled swiss cheese.

"Never saw him before in my life, but I can tell you one thing about him," I said, then cocked a smirk at my best friend. "We've now got somebody to question besides Arthur Brinkerhoff."

TEN

"I DON'T see why O'Byrne couldn't let us watch them interrogate that guy," I pointed out to Bobby as I scraped at the paper on my beer bottle, "or at least get back to us about any answers he gave. How the hell does she expect me to move forward if I don't have any place to start?"

"This is where I remind you that you're not a cop," he said, clicking the tongs at me. "O'Byrne doesn't owe you anything, including answers."

The tongs' scalloped ends were coated with sesame seeds and green-onion bits from the marinade Jae soaked the short ribs in before turning everything over to us to grill. As much as I liked barbecuing, Bobby had an obsession with it, and it was simpler to let him take over the tongs. He just had a bad habit of using them to emphasize his points as he spoke, clattering them like castanets during a furious flamenco dance.

As dreary as the day grew, the addition we had added to the back of the house included a covered lanai, perfect for evening barbecues and lounging in reclining chairs with a cold beer. We had a larger outdoor kitchen built on the far side of the lawn, complete with a fire pit and enough outdoor furniture to host a birthday party attended by fifty preschoolers. I knew that last bit for a fact because our niece, Lisa—Mad Dog Junior—celebrated her latest circuit around the sun in our backyard, complete with a bouncy castle and at least three puking children who'd eaten too much cake and ice cream. I also knew from experience that the cost of cleaning a bouncy castle was about the same as getting a car detailed.

The addition not only gave us a back patio but also pantry space, a larger mud room for our washer and dryer, and after reconfiguring a few walls, a dining room we apparently desperately needed. When various members of my family—including Bobby—gave me shit about the lack of a dining room, I reminded all of them about the office at the front of the house where I actually did some business and employed my favorite person in the world, my surrogate mother, Claudia. *That* dining room had been converted over to a conference area, but now it was the employee lounge where Claudia and Scarlet spent a few afternoons during the week watching Kdramas on the large-screen TV mounted to the wall.

I couldn't remember the last time I'd actually had a meeting in the elected conference room, and when given a choice between taking the conference room back so the main part of the house had a dining room or building an addition, I'd choose the addition. There was no way in hell I was going to take away Claudia's stories, and since I'd already supplanted a few of her biological sons as her favorite, I wasn't going to give up my spot anytime soon.

I'd already given my damned tongs to Bobby. There was only so much a man could sacrifice for his family.

"Did you miss the part where I feel like I'm responsible?" I countered, debating if I should grab the tongs the next time he clicked them at me. "You don't have to help me out if you don't want to."

"You're going to get your fool head shot off if I don't help you," Bobby shot back. "Today was a good example. What the fuck were you thinking?"

"He wasn't thinking," my older brother, Mike, said as he came through the open french doors connecting the dining room to the lanai. "I don't even know what happened, and I can tell you he wasn't thinking. What happened?"

Mike was still thinner than I was used to seeing him. It'd been years since he nearly died under a hail of gunfire, a victim of a psychotic murderer intent on making me pay for Ben's suicide. But he hadn't gained back all of the muscle and stockiness he'd lost in the hospital. The pain and stress drew grooves down into his skin, lining his face with an age he shouldn't have been showing, especially considering he'd pulled heavily on our mother's Japanese genetics. Shorter than me by a few inches—despite the violent spikiness of his favorite haircut—Mike was a solid bulldog of a man who'd taken a few years to get used to me being gay. We'd been estranged when Ben tried to kill me, but after his marriage to Madeleine and the birth of his daughter, we'd fallen into a more easy relationship.

Being Mike's brother was hard. That was something Ichi and I both agreed on. He seemed to take a paternal outlook to being an older brother, pushing for his younger brothers to be more ambitious and accomplish more in our lives than what we had so far. Ichi and I had different ideas on what we counted as a success. I liked my private investigation business and being married to Jae. That took up a good portion of my time. Ichiro, despite not having my influence growing up, broke from his own traditional Japanese father's expectations and grew up to become a world-class tattoo artist. I think in a lot of ways Mike regrets not being born to Ichiro's father, because the two of them really sound like they would get along.

Mike's stuffiness was the sole reason I felt it was my obligation as an uncle to make sure Mad Dog Junior had a solid bad influence to help guide her through life and its obstacles. Mike, however, did not share that view and constantly reprimanded me for things like the drum set I bought for her when she was two.

"Cole-ah is investigating a murder, and someone tried to kill him and Bobby today. Bobby is mad because he had a gun and didn't get to use it. I am irritated because, instead of letting Bobby use his gun, Cole decided to beat the man half to death with a bag of rocks," Jae remarked, nudging Mike out of the doorway with his elbow. His hands were full with a tray of vegetables and marinated chicken thighs. "Bobby, move the kalbi to the upper rack. The chicken is going to take longer to cook, so put it next to the flame. The zucchini and corn can go wherever you have room. I can keep it warm in the oven if it's done early."

"Notice you don't snap at him when he tells you how to grill." After toasting Bobby with my beer, I took a long draw. "Grab a beer, Mike. And where's the kid?"

"The kid and Maddy are at tumbling class, then having a girls' dinner at some fondue place," Mike said, stepping out of Jae's way. "And I've got a bottle of water because I'm driving. I'll be picking up my girls after I mooch food off of you guys."

"Long story short, instead of attacking the guy with my gym bag filled with asphalt from the parking lot, I should've let Bobby shoot him. Or I should've let the guy shoot Bobby. Those were apparently my only two options," I said, sneaking one of the mushrooms off of the vegetable tray. Jae gave me a pointed look, but I wasn't sure if it was because of my sarcasm or stealing the mushroom. "I'd like to point out two things. One, I took the guy down without getting shot, and two, Bobby thinks I should carry a weapon until we close this case."

"There's a third option," Mike piped up, settling down on a bench next to the grill. "You can always stop investigating the murder."

"You obviously have not met our brother, Cole," Ichi said, joining us on the patio. I was thankful we'd built it as wide as we had, not only because it extended the restructured pantry into a dining room, but because apparently the patio was going to be where we all hung out. The conversation had gone from Bobby beating up on me to everyone else joining in to take a punch. Ichi gave Bobby a quick kiss, then joined Mike on the bench. "He's not going to stop investigating the murder. And I hate to say this, but I agree with Bobby. If Cole is going to get shot at, he should be able to shoot back."

Sitting together, it was obvious Mike and Ichi were related, despite their different styles. Mike was exactly what you would want to see as the CEO of a private security firm specializing in providing protection for celebrities and millionaires, while Ichi, our younger half brother, looked every inch of the bad-boy rebel tattoo artist who took down my best friend's bachelorhood within a year of meeting him. I was definitely the whiter sheep of the family, inheriting more of the Irish from my father, but I definitely lean toward Ichi's way of thinking.

That said, I was surprised he advocated me carrying a gun. He'd been born and raised in Japan, fully entrenched with an antipathy toward firearms, and had been very vocal about me not carrying a gun when I got into a bad place a few years ago. To hear him say I should be armed made me stop and think.

I was thankful for Jae's warmth and weight against my legs when he sat down on the recliner next to me. Moving to give him more room, I rubbed at his lower back while handing him my beer, knowing he'd want a sip. He took the bottle and began to smooth down the paper, undoing all of my hard work. My wedding ring was bright against his black T-shirt, its weight as comforting as the man who'd put it on my finger.

"I promised Jae I wouldn't carry a gun," I reminded all of them. "I also promised to love, honor, and obey him, so I think that's all covered like an umbrella insurance policy. It's not up for discussion."

"You're not in the same place that you were in, agi," Jae murmured, surprising me. "Do you want to talk about this now? Or later?"

"It doesn't matter what any of them say, you're the only one that matters in this." I stilled my fingers but kept my hand pressed against Jae's body. His heartbeat throbbed my palm with the steady rhythm I knew as well as I did my own breathing. "I don't want you to ever be scared of me."

"I don't ever want to be scared *for* you," he countered, twisting about until he nearly faced me, his leg draped over my knees. Glancing toward the grill, Jae prodded Bobby, "You've had two times when someone shot at you. Listening to you describe both times, it sounds like two different men shot at you. Yes?"

Jae wasn't wrong. I didn't get a good look at the guy at the Brinkerhoff house, but he was younger, not just because of what he was wearing but because of how he moved and how erratic his gunshots were. Although the guy in the alleyway didn't hit us, his aim was better, his groupings tight and precise. We'd been protected by tons of steel and plastic, and if Bobby and I hadn't been as paranoid as we were, he could have taken us out easily.

"The shooter at the Brinkerhoffs' could have killed both of us if he'd held off. I don't think he was looking to kill us," Bobby responded carefully. "But I got the feeling from how he took his shots that he wasn't used to handling a gun. More of a kid or somebody who was afraid of them. The guy today was a professional. And even though Cole here went all psycho on him, he wasn't going to talk. Or at least not there."

"O'Byrne is going to keep him locked up tight. One thing we've got going for us is he won't be remanded over to release, not with a couple of attempted murder charges on him." As happy as I was about California restructuring the bail system, I didn't have high hopes a lawyer couldn't weasel the guy out of custody. "At the very least, they'll be able to hold him for a few days, maybe a week, and if we can break this open before he gets out, chances are he'll just go away."

"Even if he does get out, he might just disappear," Mike added, "unless you've made the job personal, in which case, I not only suggest you carry a gun but you should probably carry two."

I wasn't going to say anything either way. Did I wish I had a gun on me while I was kissing the pavement in the alleyway? Hell yes. Was I probably going to end up in another situation where I was facing down a muzzle without anything to protect myself? It sure as hell looked likely. But I had a job to do, and I was going to do it to the best of my abilities. I wasn't going to try to persuade or cajole Jae, and unless he asked—

"What do you think, Cole?" Jae asked, bringing my thoughts to a screeching halt. "Because what I wish and want isn't reality. You have dangerous cases, and this one seems to be getting more treacherous with every day that goes by. I don't want to lose you, not after I fought so hard to keep you. Do you think you should carry a gun?"

Marriages are tricky things. Some guys complain their wives say one thing but mean another. The truth is everybody is like that. No gender has a monopoly on hiding how they feel and saying what they think the other person wants. It's not a good basis for a relationship, but a lot of people do that. I have the luxury of being loved by a handful of strong-willed people. Whenever I've stumbled, I reach out to Claudia, Scarlet, and Maddy for marriage advice. Not because they'll side with me—because that's certainly not the case—it was more that they'll always give me frank, no-holds-barred advice.

It's been years since Jae and I exchanged rings, and I've gone to them quite a few times because I've stumbled over obstacles both of us have placed in my path. I've come away from those years with a single, hard-learned truth—my marriage will only last forever if I'm honest with the man I love.

"Yes. I think I'm going to have to," I finally said, rubbing my thumb across his ribs. "You're right. It's not like before. But I also don't want any of this to bleed into my life. The last time, things got too crazy and I almost lost a lot of you. I can't risk that. Yes, I want to help O'Byrne bring down Adele's murderer, but if the price of that is too high, if it's going to cost me one of you, then I'm going to walk away."

"I have never been afraid of you," Jae reassured me with a soft kiss. "Just be careful, and remember, if someone tries to kill you, you kill them first. No one gets to take you away from me. No one."

I WAS still fat and happy and filled with food when Mike ambushed me in the kitchen. I was expecting it. My older brother didn't like me making decisions on my own, despite me having gone through over three decades of walking, talking, and eating without his immediate assistance. His controlling busybody nature was one of the main reasons his daughter received very loud musical instruments and possibly a muscle car when she turns sixteen. I loved Mike deeply, but he was like an octopus—once he got ahold of somebody, he never let them go.

Even if he was strangling them to death.

"Are you sure you're okay?" That was his opening gambit, one I recognized from many verbal chess games we'd played in the past. I nodded, and he barreled forward, intent on leading me by the nose to wherever he wanted me to be. "You know I still want you to come work for me. You could head up—"

"Mike, stop." It was hard enough to load the dishwasher exactly how Jae liked it to be arranged without fending off my brother while trying to concentrate on my own personal game of reverse Jenga. "Just stop."

I didn't know what to do with the glass baking dish, because the damned thing just didn't fit and I couldn't remember the precise arrangement it needed to go onto the rack in order to be cleaned properly. Consigning it to a hand washing, I put it in the sink, then leaned against the counter to face my brother.

"I appreciate you a lot. And I'm glad we're at a point where we can talk and scream at ball games together, but I'm not a little kid. I haven't been a little kid for a long time," I said gently, shaking my head to stop him from interrupting me, because I could see that happening. "I have you and Maddy to thank for dragging me out of that darkness Ben put me in. Out of all of that shittiness, us getting back on a path to being brothers was the best thing that happened to me.

"I'm going to be the first one to admit I was pretty fucked up and you were there when I was just pretty much a zombie. And I need you to understand that I'm not spitting in your face, because I love you. I love the hell out of you and Maddy and the screaming terror you call a daughter, but you need to see me as I am now." Clasping his shoulder, I squeezed lightly, pulling him in a little bit, just so we were closer. "I'm a lot healthier than I was five years ago. Hell, even three years ago. And I have all of you to thank for that, but I also worked hard to get in a better place, to fix some of the things that were broken inside of me, and I can't be a grown-up if I use you as a safety net. There may come a time when I want to change professions, and if you've got a place for me then, maybe I'll see if it fits, but it goes both ways now. If you need something, you know you can depend upon me. I've proven that. And I will die to protect what's yours, because it's mine as well… family, I mean. Those ugly clothes you wear while playing golf are going to be the first thing on the bonfire if your life ever crashes and burns."

"There's nothing wrong with my golf clothes." Mike sniffed indignantly, and we both ignored the tears dampening the edges of his eyes. "You really should take up the sport. It'll help you relax."

"Do you really want me to start playing a sport where they give me a weapon I could use to bludgeon people? Isn't it bad enough that Bobby's got me in a boxing ring?" I teased, drawing my brother in for a tight hug. "I'll be okay. I've got a permit to conceal carry, and if things look a little crazy, I'm going to tap out. I've learned that lesson. Deal?"

"I don't think you have," Mike argued, mumbling into my shoulder because he was that much shorter than me. "But I trust you to hear us if we tell you it's going too far. And O'Byrne will kick your ass if you get shot."

I laughed despite the emotion choking both of us. "That's only because she doesn't want to do the paperwork. Now, why don't we head back into the living room, and you and Bobby can argue about what kind of gun I should carry so I can ignore you and just take the Glocks that I like."

ELEVEN

WIPING MY bottom lip clean of whipped cream, I sighed, "I don't know which god is responsible for Mexican hot chocolate, but I would risk human sacrifice and the plague of frogs to tell them thank you."

I wasn't overexaggerating. When I first came out to California, kicked out of my family home, the front door bolted shut behind me, I didn't have a lot of experiences with food other than sausages and the occasional casserole. Although I came from Chicago—a city with fantastic food—the McGinnis clan was pretty much a mayo-on-white-bread kind of family. The only mustard I'd run into growing up was yellow and usually found in a giant squeezy bottle next to a container of watery ketchup. Our meals were rotated throughout the week with a burnt roast served on Sunday, slightly sweet spaghetti on Monday, and by the time Friday rolled around, I was very thankful for my plate of fish sticks piled high on a mound of macaroni and cheese.

My brother and I were raised to be suspicious of anything that wasn't processed within an inch of its life and, in a pinch, could be used as a salt lick for roaming deer in the winter. We played enough sports to keep us reasonably fit, but when puberty hit me, I shot up and Mike shot out. Anyone seeing us knew we were brothers because we looked alike, but there was also a lot of speculation about the McGinnis boys actually being a pair of lab mice plotting to take over the world, mostly because I was short a brain cell or two and Mike had a big head with enormous ears.

Mike fled to California first, and I followed in my brother's footsteps, unsure of what I wanted to accomplish but knowing I couldn't survive another winter in Chicago with very little money and no family to depend on. As much as I loved the Cubs, I had to seek out warmer climates, just in case I was going to have to sleep outdoors.

When I hit Los Angeles, my older brother was still suspicious of nonprocessed foods, but a chance encounter at a taco truck having a three-for-one-dollar midnight blowout to empty their steam table opened up our minds to the delectable, savory world of California Mexican food. It was also serendipity—or perhaps God was smiling down on me—because the older woman manning the grills that night threw in a couple of large Mexican hot chocolates and a bag of cinnamon-sugar *buñuelos*.

We gorged that night, getting fat and happy on *carnitas*, *carne asada*, and *adobada* tacos piled high with lettuce, crumbling white cheese, and *pico de gallo*. But as delightful as the tacos were, the hot chocolate hit something in my soul I never realized needed filling.

And it has been a favorite of mine ever since. Especially when things have gone balls-up and I needed to get my head on straight.

From the skeptical look on O'Byrne's face, I didn't believe she felt the love the rich, dark cinnamon-infused hot chocolate could bring to a dreary day, but as the saying went, you can lead a horse to water but you can't make them put on a bikini and do the breaststroke.

"He gets like this," Bobby informed her, his hands nearly swallowing the paper cup filled with bitter coffee he'd gotten from the cafeteria truck parked outside of Central. I'd had their coffee before, and my stomach still had a hole in it from the last cup I'd drunk, close to seven years ago. Bobby claimed to like it—further proof Bobby was missing a few marbles. "So this guy isn't saying anything?"

"Not a damn thing, and so far, no asshole in a suit has come forward to try to get him out. We're running fingerprints and facial identification but haven't come up with anything yet. There's a pool going that he's a pro, with some pretty good odds on one of McGinnis's ex-boyfriends hiring him to take Mac out," O'Byrne said, making a face when I looked up from my hot chocolate, the sweet richness now tasting of ash on my tongue. "Sorry. That was shitty to say and… *fuck*."

"Look, I know I'm not exactly a favorite with a lot of the old-timers, but most of them are assholes anyway," I shot back with a shrug, tasting my chocolate again and finding it just as sweet. "So if he's not talking, then we've got to go to plan B—trying to get something out of Arthur."

"I called San Francisco to see if I could get someone to give me a read on Marlena Brinkerhoff, but no one's saying a word." O'Byrne picked through her nachos, most of her attention on the people passing by the arrangement of bolted-down steel benches and rickety tables some bureaucrat thought would make a good place to eat in the shadow of LAPD's imposing glass headquarters. In a couple of months, the concrete courtyard would be broiled in an unrelenting Southern California sun, and anyone with half a brain would eat at their desks like normal people did. O'Byrne plucked one of the green-tomatillo-sauce pods I'd gotten from the truck off of the table, cracked it open, and shook it all over her nachos. "They apparently are reluctant to give out information on anyone who works up there. I can't get anyone to confirm nor deny she's with the DA office, but with the crazies these days, I can't blame them. The captain's going to go through official channels, but he thinks I'm barking up a very short tree and there's a grizzly bear sitting on top of it, waiting to bite my head off. I *hate* politics."

"And let me guess—you don't have any idea who's feeding her information," Bobby interjected. "Did Book back you in using McGinnis here on the investigation?"

"He hates politics as much as I do, but he plays the game better. His brother's a captain up with SFPD, so I'm going to guess his official channels are probably a lot more sneaky." She flicked off a piece of onion, moving it to her napkin. It looked like every other piece of onion, so I didn't know what it did to offend her, but obviously it had to go. "We all know what happens to people who sniff around other departments and offices. That kind of thing comes back and bites you in the ass, even if it's just crossing the t's and dotting the i's on a case. People don't like getting looked at, especially people with secrets. If Marlena Brinkerhoff has something to hide, I want to find out what it is and how it relates to her grandmother's death."

"Right now we're just throwing wet spaghetti against the wall," I said, inspecting the onions on my food in case they were infected with whatever fouled O'Byrne's nachos. All of the white bits were white, and all of the green bits next to them were green. Most of the red bits were red, but with tomatoes, they usually ran the range of deep crimson to light pink, so I was going to have to push the I Believe button that my tomatoes were fine. "Can you send me a picture of the asshole from the alley? Bobby and I are going to try to shake Marlena off of her grandfather, and I'll see if I can get him to give me some answers about his wife. I'd like to see if he can identify the guy who shot at us, or at least recognize him. If our John Doe isn't going to cough up any answers, maybe we can get them another way."

"Hopefully we'll get a hit off of his prints, but having Brinkerhoff look at his mug shot isn't a bad idea. Just don't wear the old guy out," O'Byrne warned. "I don't want Marlena Brinkerhoff to have a leg to stand on if she comes after the LAPD because she thinks her grandfather's too weak to answer questions. She isn't letting us in there, but you're a different story. You work for the guy. You have an in I don't. Just be careful."

"Telling Princess here to be careful is kind of like telling a giraffe to watch its head in the trees," Bobby said with a chuckle. "Asshole knows the trees are there, but he's going to hit his head anyway. Come on, kid, drink the rest of your hot cocoa so we can go to the hospital and shake down an old guy."

A SLIGHT drizzle smeared headlights through the intermittent swish of the Rover's wipers. The overcast of the morning finally gave in to its promise to fuck up Los Angeles's traffic by dumping what was probably just a half a cup of water over twenty square miles and turning everybody's day to shit. We'd gotten into the SUV without getting wet, but the sprinkles chased us up Wilshire and down to the hospital, bringing us to a standstill at nearly every light. I didn't know what it was about Southern California drivers, but as soon as there was a hint of water in the air, the gears in their heads overloaded and they began to do stupid things, like the asshole who decided to play chicken with a fire truck and not only lost in a spectacular fashion, lodging his Lexus underneath its front end somehow, but also consigning us to a level of Dante's hell where we all drove around in circles wishing we were dead.

By the time we were finally free, it was nearly afternoon and Bobby and I still didn't have a solid plan on how to get rid of Marlena if she was standing watch in Arthur's hospital room.

"Neither one of us is dressed well enough to pretend to be an FBI agent." Bobby looked down at his jeans and T-shirt, then over at mine. "And neither one of us have fake credentials to convince anyone of that bluff."

"I just want to ask the old man some questions, not douse him with holy water to see if he's the undead and I have to go find his grave to salt and burn it," I replied, shoving the Rover in between two small import cars to the left of us who were refusing to acknowledge my turn signal. I was willing to pit the three tons of steel I was driving against their plastic windup cars any day, especially since I'd been polite and had my signal on for nearly half a block. I eased in, and the traffic stilled once again. "Hospital's at the next turnoff. We better come up with something, because right now, he's our only lead unless O'Byrne can shake that guy's name out of the trees."

Parking in the hospital's structure was definitely a business expense I was going to pawn off on O'Byrne. If you asked me, I was fairly certain that's how the hospital got the organs for their transplants, because it cost a kidney and a liver to park there. As usual, I cursed the lack of covered walkways as we sprinted across a short sidewalk to get to the visitors' entrance. The drizzle was easily shaken off, but Marlena probably wouldn't be as courteous. She struck me as someone who needed to control her environment, tightening her grip on any information flowing in or out of her life.

I couldn't shake off the instinctive dread I had every time I walked through those doors. Even though it had been years since I came in, cold with shock and shaking with fear, I relived every moment of those horrible days when I walked through those automatic glass panes, speckled with the blood of somebody I loved and wondering if I would ever see them alive again. I brought so much violence and pain to everyone around me and was filled with such an intense guilt that I stumbled over my own feet before we got to the elevator.

Bobby knew me well enough to pat my back a few times and murmur, "It's okay, Princess. Everybody walked back out."

"Not Rick," I reminded him, then grimaced. "Not Ben."

"No they didn't. I'll give you that, but there's one thing you've got to remember," he said softly, ruffling my hair as if I were a little kid. "*You* walked out of here. And you've got a good life now. Your head's on straight, and I've got your back. We've also both got guns, so if we run into trouble, try not to pick up a rock and smash the guy's head like you're trying to open up a coconut. I'm surprised that guy's mug shot even looks human. You literally beat the shit out of him with a bag of bricks."

"Use what you've got at hand," I said, smiling at him when the elevator doors opened and a wave of hospital staff vomited out its long steel box. "Jae tells me that about cooking."

"Yeah, Jae's talking about making an omelet," Bobby snorted, stepping aside to let a couple of nurses out, "not about you making scrambled eggs of some guy's face."

We were squished in by a horde of ordinary people looking for joy or answers amid the hospital wards. A young man with a smile so broad his full beard couldn't hide it clutched a bundle of balloons announcing someone had a baby boy while an anxious-looking older Latinx wrung her hands around an old, worn rosary, her lips moving rapidly but her prayers silent. It was a long elevator ride of emotions running the gamut from exhilarated to resigned, and we stood in the middle of it, two stones worn down around the edges, having already been caught in that river.

We had to fight our way out past the balloons, wishing the guy luck, but I was pretty sure he heard nothing past the white noise and glee in his own head. Mike had a similar look on his face when Mad Dog Junior was born, and considering she was a pretty kick-ass kid, I tended to smile like that too once in a while.

"I wonder how Marlena's childhood was," I pondered, shoving my hands in my pockets while we waited for the nurse on duty to finish with the two women in front of us. "Like, did her grandfather explain to her the difference between Monet and Manet and how to tell when a painting was fake?"

"Have you ever considered seeing a doctor about that brain of yours? Because you wander off places that make absolutely no fucking sense," Bobby muttered at me under his breath. "She obviously did okay, because she's a goddamned district attorney. Unless she's pulling the longest con ever and set up her career just so she could get Grandma and Grandpa out of jail when they got caught. For all we know, they've got a château down in Belize they're paying off."

"Let's just see if he's in the same room and—" I stopped when a noise made me look down the hall and the double doors separating the waiting area and the nurses' station were flung open and our quarry emerged.

The clip of quick-stepping heels beat a machine-gun-fast staccato against the hospital's hard marble floor. Marlena Brinkerhoff moved like a shark cutting through the currents, her face cold and set into a stony mask. There was more than a little bit of fire in her enormous baby blue eyes, and her gaze flicked over me as if she had never seen me before in her life. She was dressed to kill in a pinup-style librarian's tweed skirt and a red liquid silk shirt so fluid it clung to her breasts, flowing over their plump curves as if woven from water. Pushing past a small gathering of people waiting by a row of uncomfortable-looking chairs, recognition finally broke through her focus when she saw my face.

She stumbled.

Nothing so graceless as to twist her ankle or miss a step, but there was a slight hesitation before she brought her foot down again. Her pause was only long enough if you were looking for it, and I was certainly looking for it. She was just as beautiful as she had been the first time I'd seen her, but something had changed. The sweet, devoted granddaughter act was gone, and in its place was something much more dangerous and probably much more real.

"There's our girl," I muttered at Bobby. Breaking off from the line, I stepped into Marlena's path, bringing her up short before she could reach the elevator doors. There was a bit of murmuring from the people around us, but we were now far enough away from the orderly line to be considered no longer another supplicant waiting to speak to the attending nurse. Smiling, I said, "Hello, Marlena. My associate and I were just coming to see you and your grandfather. I had a couple of questions I needed answering and was hoping you could spare some time."

The tightening at the corner of her eyes told me time was the last thing she wanted to give me. In fact, I got the distinct impression that if Marlena had a pair of metal chopsticks secreted somewhere on her body, she would've done her very best to shove them into my eyeballs in the hopes of punching through my skull and out the other side. That impression didn't go away, even when she gave me what should have been a charming, glittering smile and then held her hand out to Bobby to shake.

If I were Bobby, I would've checked her rings to make sure they didn't have tiny needles tipped with poison before I took her hand.

"I really don't have the time," she said with another tight smile. She shifted her body, angling it slightly, and very quickly glanced back down the hall. "I'm actually very late. I'm meeting someone downtown. One of the district attorneys from the Los Angeles office. And my grandfather is really in no shape to speak with anyone. Maybe next time call ahead and I can make more time."

"We just need—" I began, but Marlena shook her head, tucking a strand of hair behind her ear.

"I'm sorry. But I have to go." She did that little touch thing on my arm, a practice taught at seminars, one of those body cues to communicate sympathy and compassion while telling somebody to fuck off. "Perhaps tomorrow."

"Tell you what," Bobby replied with a grin as sharklike as her determination to get off the ward floor and into the elevator. "How about if I ride down with you and we can talk along the way? McGinnis here can maybe touch base with your grandfather's doctor and get a better idea about how he's doing."

She was too fidgety, and for a moment there I thought she was going to argue, but the elevator doors opened and she practically leaped through them, reaching the relative safety of the lift. Bobby was close on her heels, stabbing at the buttons before Marlena could protest, and I got a wink from him right before the doors shut.

Gambling Arthur Brinkerhoff was in the same room as before, I headed through the small crowd and down the hall. There wasn't much celebration on this floor. It was mostly filled with anxious tension when most of the conversation revolved around pleas to God or condemning Him. The air was cold enough to hurt my nose, but it was typical for a hospital. They were pretty much cryogenic chambers, possibly preparing the ward's patients for the steel drawers that awaited them in the morgue downstairs.

The machines in Arthur's room had multiplied since I'd last been there. Now everything beeped and chimed and sang, loud and cheerful enough that I should've looked for a blue hedgehog collecting gold rings, but the man lying in the hospital bed looked even more fragile than he had before. Tubes were plugged in and taped down practically all over his body, and he was motionless, his eyes still beneath his paper-thin lids. I didn't know if the machines were keeping him alive or if he was breathing on his own. Honestly, considering how many bruises and welts I could see, I was surprised he was still around.

What surprised me more was the stout Teutonic woman sitting on one of the chairs next to his bed. She was perhaps thirty, maybe more, but her age probably would never really matter. She was a block of a woman, staunch and strong, the type of person who could probably build a log cabin if ever she got stuck in a snowstorm, and milk a wandering reindeer so she could make her own cheese. Her light blond hair was cut short, framing her square face, and her skin was lightly freckled, her thin mouth unpainted and set into a stern line. She was dressed in a practical way—a nondescript blouse and black slacks, a pair of no-nonsense loafers on her broad feet. There was something so familiar about her that I could only stare at her, trying to place where we'd met before.

"Who the hell are you?" she snapped, her words a leather whip across my tender skin. I knew that voice. I'd heard it before, only raspier with age.

"Cole McGinnis," I informed her, not liking the realization digging sharp claws through my guts. "Arthur Brinkerhoff hired me to look into his wife's murder. Who are you?"

"I am Marlena Brinkerhoff," she replied, rising up from the chair, a Valkyrie ready to do battle to defend her fallen grandfather. "And I know all about you, Mister McGinnis, so get the hell out of my grandfather's room before I call security."

TWELVE

"I WAS backpacking through Mongolia when I got the call about Mama," the real Marlena said, staring at the now empty hospital bed in the room. "I was in the air when he was being attacked, I guess. It's all a blur. I can't even tell you what day it is. When I landed in LAX, I had messages from my boss in San Francisco, asking me if my grandfather was all right. Soon as I found out where he was, I headed straight over. The detective on the case left me your name on my voice mail but I already knew it. You're the man who Poppa hired to catch Mama cheating on him."

A battalion of scrub-wearing nurses and attendants had bundled the old man off for parts unknown a minute or so before, unwrapping him from his nest of tubing and transferring him to a gurney much like a pit crew servicing a racecar between laps. She'd sat down back into her chair, only the tightness around her mouth and the shadows beneath her eyes giving me any indication of how tired she was.

"You must've just gotten here, then." I knew all too well what she was going through, and there weren't any words I could say to make her feel any better. She'd been delivered a one-two punch, and I was going to have to scrape at her freshly inflicted wounds to see if she had any information about the blond bombshell posing as a Brinkerhoff. Going slow was probably my best bet, especially since she hadn't called security yet to have me removed. "They said they were going to be a couple of hours. Do you want to head down to the cafeteria and get something to eat or a cup of coffee? You're probably dead on your feet."

She stopped staring at the bed, focusing on me for the first time since they wheeled Arthur Brinkerhoff out to be lubed and x-rayed by trained professionals. There was a hardness to her face I recognized from her grandmother's expression on the night Adele chased me through a topiary garden with a shotgun. I could see the woman Arthur had probably fallen in love with mirrored in Marlena's strong features. There was a quiet beauty to her, a strength and resolve I hadn't seen in the fake Marlena. The other woman who'd tried to pass herself off as a Brinkerhoff had packaged herself as sexy and mysterious—something to tickle a man's fantasies—but the woman sitting in the unforgiving, much-too-hard-on-the-ass hospital chair promised nothing but the truth. And possibly if you were man—or woman—enough to win her over, you would be set up for life with someone who would love you and fight to the death for you.

The fake Marlena definitely wouldn't even consider getting a hangnail for someone else. I'd fallen in love with Jae when he wrapped himself in secrets and frothy familial lies, but I'd seen the man who ached to live out in the open—a snarky, intelligent soul who longed to be held in bed and loved being kissed on the neck while cooking. I'd been willing to walk away from him loving me, but I hadn't been willing to let him be smothered by his family's hatred. It'd taken years before he felt comfortable enough to hold my hand at a farmers' market. Marlena Brinkerhoff was definitely not that person. The only reason she wouldn't hold her lover's hand was because it was filled with bags of groceries and possibly an anvil she picked up on sale.

I was surrounded by strong women, and I knew I was in for a battle if Marlena intended to kick me to the curb. So I was going to have to talk fast.

"While your grandfather hired me, the LAPD has asked me to help consult on the case. If you like, you can contact Lieutenant Dell O'Byrne at the main number, and she can verify I'm here to help." Reaching down into the dregs of my logic, I pulled a rather anemic rabbit out of my hat. "Your grandparents worked through their problems, and your grandfather thought enough about me to call me about Adele. He understood I was doing my job, and despite me being the person who found your grandmother that night, called me for help. So you've got to ask yourself, Marlena, who would do this to your grandparents and whether or not you're going to share that with me?"

To say hospital coffee was shitty was being cruel to every pile of feces ever shat out. I could have added an entire cow's worth of cream and possibly all of the sugar that they'd ever grown in Hawai'i and it still probably would be the color of pitch and taste like the oil scraped off of a pig's armpit. I don't know what Marlena was drinking in Mongolia, but she sipped at the coffee as if it were the finest wine. But then, she was also dead on her feet and mourning the loss of her grandmother.

I made some mention of what food was actually edible, but she shook her head, murmuring her stomach probably couldn't take anything in it. I was mildly surprised she was willing to drink the battery acid served up to us as coffee, but it was probably more to give her something to do besides stare at the nothingness stretching out around her.

Marlena wandered outside before I could steer us to a table, and I followed, guessing she needed a bit of fresh air or a change of scenery to clear her head. As dismal as the cafeteria's offerings were, it was filled with staff members and a few families sitting tightly around small tables, stewing in various spectrums of devastation or joy. It was getting harder to tell the difference at times, especially when the hollow eyes met your glance with a smile. The glare of the lights stole the color from nearly everyone's skin, rendering them in an ashen tone, as if they were preparing for Charon's arrival and still needed to check their pockets for coins.

I had to hustle to keep up with her, thankful for my long legs because, despite her blocky stance, she moved like a linebacker, stopping for no one but weaving through any open space she could. Once outside, Marlena blinked furiously, either surprised by the sun or refusing to give in to the emotions and fatigue of the last few days.

"Let's sit over there," she finally said, her voice tight and strained. "I'll give you ten minutes of my time—fifteen at the most—and I need to head back upstairs. I don't want Poppa to come back to the room and find himself alone."

We settled down on a bench outside of the hospital, sitting silently while bits and pieces of humanity streamed past us. I briefly wondered where Bobby was and how far he'd gotten with our faux-Marlena. I reached for my phone and was about to apologize to the real Marlena when she began to speak.

"I might as well talk to you. Maybe you can help me make sense of all of this," she muttered. "Because I sure as hell don't understand what's going on."

"Do you know about the woman passing herself off as you?" I led with the softest question I had, saving any discussion about Adele's murder and the attack on Arthur for when Marlena felt more comfortable talking. There was a fine balance between leading someone toward an answer and accidentally sending them off into areas of speculation that were useless to an investigator. "I assume you saw her or someone told you about her."

"Poppa's doctor at the hospital was surprised when I showed up. I had to prove to him that I was who I said I am, but they let this woman waltz in and begin making decisions about Poppa's life without even blinking." Her hand tightened on the coffee cup, and briefly it looked like she was going to crush it. But she relaxed her fingers and continued. "I asked him to describe her to me. I thought maybe it was one of his neighbors and he'd misunderstood, but she signed paperwork for his care. So that tells me she knew exactly what she was doing."

"Did you see her today? Did she come to the room?" While I'd seen the fake Marlena in the hall, I couldn't be certain she'd actually made it inside of the room.

The sour look on Marlena's face was all I needed to know she'd definitely spotted her curvaceous, vampy alleged doppelgänger. "She stopped at the doorway, and I looked up. I recognized her immediately from Doctor Wilson's description, and I stood up to grab at her, but Poppa opened his eyes and began to make some noise. By the time I turned back around, she was gone, and honestly, he was a lot more important to me than chasing her down."

"Did you recognize her?" I made a mental note to ask O'Byrne to check the hospital's cameras and then amended that note to tell her about the fake Marlena.

"No." She shook her head. Her lashes were wet, but there were still no tears coming, and I didn't expect any. "I know most of my grandparents' friends. And the ones I don't are because they're either dead or in Europe. Of course, up until a few years ago, I wouldn't have imagined Mama had affairs with other women. So there could be things about them that I know nothing about. I did wonder if she was somebody who'd been... intimate with Mama. She had that look about her. Maybe I'm just being judgmental because she'd tried to steal my name and identity, but she looked like a using bitch, and I've known more than a few of those in my time."

"I didn't get a chance to speak to your grandfather. He'd been attacked by the time I showed up for our appointment." I was going to get into treacherous territory, mentioning the attack to lead her to explain about the house. My suspicions were still firmly on the side of "the Brinkerhoffs didn't live there," but I needed Marlena to confirm that. "We ended up surprising a gunman who shot up the front of the house, then bolted out. I actually landed in the cactus on the side of the bungalow trying to avoid getting shot."

"House?" Marlena glanced at me, confused and worried. "They live in a high-rise downtown. They haven't lived in a house in over ten years. They sold the old place by the studios. Said it was too big for them with me gone. They said—"

I'd been around so many people who'd been lied to I'd lost count. First as a police detective and then as a private investigator, I'd had a front-row seat for every single farce and betrayal someone could dream up. Having been one of the unwitting actors in my own tragic play, I knew all too well the devastating tsunami of emotions hitting Marlena at that moment. There were things about her family I didn't understand, and I was going to have to dig through what was left of her life in order to find out who killed her grandmother and what that man was looking for in a house her grandparents supposedly didn't own anymore.

"I need to ask you a few more things. And I know I'm pushing that time limit you gave me, but it's very important. I had a feeling your grandparents staged that house for some reason, and something your imposter said made me think they had a very good reason—maybe even an illegal one—for keeping that house." She wasn't looking at me and flinched when I touched her arm, but Marlena nodded, her upper teeth clenched over her lower lip. "She told me your grandparents were… criminals in the past, specifically a thief and an art forger. Is there any truth to that?"

"Yes." Her murmur was a weak mewl, and she folded into herself, rolling her shoulders in until she was nearly bent over, cuddling her coffee cup to her stomach. "They took me in after my mother died. She'd left home when she was nineteen, because… she didn't want to live like them. For seven years she kept me away from them, even though it was just the two of us and it was hard. But what they did was wrong. She hated growing up always looking over her shoulder. Then a drunk driver hit her, and they took me in.

"At first I didn't understand what my mother hated about them," Marlena confessed, letting out a bitter, short laugh. "But we kept moving. I kept changing schools, and my grades were suffering. But it was exciting because Mama taught me things like how to pick locks and pockets and our walls always had these gorgeous paintings on them. They took me to museums, and we traveled around, living out of small apartments or vans. But sometimes, late at night, they would tell me to stay in my room and people would come over. The next day some of the paintings would be gone or Mama would tell me it was time to go and pack up my things."

"When did you find out?" I prodded. "I mean, you're an assistant DA now. I'm guessing something changed."

"I walked out during one of those visits. I can't remember why. I think I wanted ice cream or something to drink, and there was a man standing in the living room, looking over something on the coffee table. He either didn't know I was there or maybe he didn't see me, because he began shouting, and the next thing I knew, I was on the floor and my arm was bleeding." She swallowed, gulping in air. "He'd shot me. Pulled out a gun and shot me. I was nine, and he didn't even pause. Thank God Poppa jumped at him and threw his aim off or I'd be dead. I don't remember much after that. I passed out. But I think Mama might have killed him. When I woke up, some of their friends were there, and I was patched up."

"Is that when they moved to the bungalow?"

"No. Not just yet. It was about a year later. They argued a lot. I was scared, and I told them I didn't want to live with them anymore. Not like I had a choice. There was nowhere for me to go. I remember that." She snorted, giving another shake of her head. "I was almost twelve when I ran away the first time, and after the police brought me back, they said they would stop. That's when we moved to Los Angeles and when I decided I was going to be a lawyer. I needed to… balance things out, I think. I don't know. They told me they were done with that life, but it looks like all they did was create a lie for me to live in. I just don't know what to think anymore."

As much as I hated sifting through the shattered remains of Marlena's life, there really wasn't much choice. Unless Bobby cornered our imposter and she confessed everything, I had nothing to go on. I needed to find out what Adele was doing out in *that* neighborhood on *that* night. From the sounds of it, it'd been decades since the Brinkerhoffs pulled a caper in front of Marlena, but I had a slim hope she paid attention to their friends. Adele went out to meet someone she knew. My gut told me that. The fake diamonds told me she was either trying to scam someone or she'd been double-crossed.

"How much were you told about your grandmother's murder?" I asked as gently as I could.

"I know that she was found in Brentwood and she'd been shot. I haven't contacted the police yet. Silly me, I thought maybe someone would contact me, but I didn't realize that woman stepped in to take my place." Marlena set her cup down on the bench, and I was partially surprised it didn't burn through the Styrofoam and into the stone, considering she drank it black. "I suppose I will have to get ahold of that detective you told me about. This is all just such a mess. There was no reason for her to be out there. But then, I guess I really didn't know them at all, did I?"

"I hate to be the one to tell you these things, but I have to." Turning on the bench, I went over as briefly as I could the events of that night, leaving out the gory details but verifying how Adele met her demise and informing Marlena of the fake gems found on her body. The only time I got a reaction was when I told her I'd been the one to find her grandmother's body. She blinked, then looked away. "Your grandfather reached out to me because he didn't have any faith in the cops. I didn't understand that at the time, but if what you say is true, I can see why he wouldn't want the police to dig into his life."

"If what *I* say is true?" Marlena snorted, her nostrils flaring in anger and her eyes narrowed, fixing on some point off in the distance. "I can give you the keys and codes to their townhouse. Maybe there's something there, but other than that, I can't help you. I'm as in the dark as you are."

"Detective O'Byrne probably will want access to the townhouse," I replied, putting my own cup down because my stomach had had enough. "I'm a consultant on this case. Any evidence gathering needs to be done by the police. Are you okay with that?"

"I'm okay with anything that leads to my grandmother's murderer," Marlena said flatly, glancing up at the hospital towering above us. "And whoever attacked Poppa. They may have been lying to me all of my life, but they're all I had. It's just knowing I worked hard to become a lawyer—I graduated at the top of my class, for God's sake—and all of it was paid for by criminal activity. It feels like my diploma, my career, hell, my entire life is dirty. Like I won't ever be clean again. I'm going to need time to deal with that."

"I just have one last thing to ask you," I told her, brushing her arm lightly to prevent her from standing when she leaned forward on the bench. "You said your grandparents had friends who helped you relocate. Are these people still around? Do you have any names or addresses of people they're close to? They may be people connected to your grandparents through that kind of activity and you just weren't aware of it."

"Do you want to know what's funny? My grandfather's best friend is an ex-cop. His name is George Watson. He and his wife, Marie, live in the townhouse kitty-corner from my grandparents' place. There's four apartments on each floor of the building, and mostly everyone who lives there is older." Marlena smirked, pushing herself off the bench with a long stretch, then turning to face me as she stood up. "They all were very friendly when Mama and Poppa moved in, like they'd known each other for a long time. So maybe that's where you should start looking. Let me know what you find. I'll be either upstairs waiting for Poppa to get back or in the shower trying to scrub this filth off of me."

THIRTEEN

"THE BITCH stabbed me!"

As glad as I was to hear Bobby at the other end of the phone, I had to wince at the invective he slung out, especially since a group of nuns passing by clearly heard him through my phone's magnificent speaker, which only seemed to have Dolby surround sound at the worst opportunities. Smiling at a particularly stern woman in formal penguin wear, I cupped my hand over the phone, hoping to mute him a bit.

"Where the fuck are you?" Then I winced because somehow, doubling down on the profanity was obviously going to win me points with the Sister Mary Margaret brigade going past me. Luckily it seemed like they were out of earshot or I'd have gotten a ruler straight across of my mouth. "And who stabbed you?"

"I'm in the ER. Just get over here." Bobby growled at someone else, muttering they'd better bring someone with a painkiller in a few minutes or he'd chew through someone's head. "They put me in the second bed after you come in, but I haven't seen anyone yet. I've got pressure on the cut, but it's going to need stitches. Whatever you do, don't call Ichi."

So of course I hung up and called Ichi.

That phone call went as I expected it to—a lot of heavy silence as my half brother sorted through the Japanese swear words probably filling his head before coming up with some English I'd understand. The call was actually pretty short and sweet. I did my best to tamp down the smugness I felt about finally being the one calling everyone else to say someone—other than me—had been hurt. I wanted to savor the moment, but Ichi seemed to be in some hurry to see his stupid husband. My asshole of a younger brother hung up on me before I could draw my smugness out to a climactic conclusion, but the damage had been done. He was headed down to the hospital in a mild fury and would soon be there to take Bobby off of my hands.

I was dialing O'Byrne when I realized I hadn't told Bobby he'd actually been stabbed by a fake Marlena while the real one had coughed up as much information as she could. He was going to have to wait until I was done with Dell.

She picked up on the first ring, barking her name at me as if I didn't know who I was dialing. But by the sounds of a siren cutting off and loud voices coming over the phone, I guessed she was a little bit busy. I identified myself and barely got my name out when she cut me off.

"Where are you, McGinnis?" O'Byrne was walking away from whatever shitstorm she'd been standing next to. The sounds of chaos were fading. Then I heard a car door slam, and things were silent except for her breathing. "Tell me you're near the hospital. Tell me Arthur Brinkerhoff is not only alive but also awake enough for me to shake down for information."

"Last time I saw him, he was alive and being wheeled out for tests. I talked to his granddaughter—"

"Well then you were probably the last one who did, because she was just found in a parking lot a couple of blocks down from the hospital. She's got a new hole in her head, right in the middle of her forehead." She sighed long enough to send a whistle in my ear. "When did you talk to her?"

"She actually just left. That woman you found? The slinky blond who could pass as Jessica Rabbit's sister? That's not Marlena Brinkerhoff."

The swearing I got this time was Mexican, but it had as much heat on it as Ichi's Japanese. I heard Dell take a deep breath, as if she were calming herself. Then she spat out, "What the fuck are you talking about, Mac. I spoke to the woman last night for a few minutes on the phone. Bishop was with her for a couple of hours. If she's not Marlena Brinkerhoff, who the hell is she? And where the hell is Marlena Brinkerhoff?"

I filled Dell in on everything I'd gotten from Arthur's real granddaughter, including their address and the name of the ex-cop Marlena pointed me toward. My stomach twisted a bit, but I had to tell her about Bobby and the altercation he'd had with the faux-Marlena.

"Where did she stab him?" she finally asked when I was done.

"I didn't ask. It couldn't have been any place vital, because he was talking and sounded kind of mad." I shrugged to myself, thinking about all the times I'd been shot and knifed. "Of course, whenever somebody tries to give you an extra hole where you didn't need one, it does tend to make you kind of pissed off."

O'Byrne took one of those shuddering breaths I recognized from Claudia and Jae. It was the kind of intake of air used to communicate a dwindling patience. After she exhaled, she said, "I don't care where she stabbed him on his body. I want to know where did she stab him? Was it at the hospital? At a coffee shop? Where were they?"

"I actually didn't ask that, but we were here at the hospital, and he followed her down on the elevator. I'm going to guess probably in the parking garage, but I don't know. I was talking to Marlena—the real Marlena—and he was supposed to keep her—the fake one—busy while I hit up Arthur with questions, because we didn't know we had the wrong Marlena when we walked in."

"I must've run over a thousand puppies and kittens with a tractor in my past life. That's the only reason I can think of why I'm stuck with you, McGinnis."

"You're no picnic yourself, O'Byrne," I reminded her, glancing up to the sky and wondering if it was going to rain. "We still have the problem of a leak somewhere in your department or maybe even higher up. Our fake Marlena got information from somewhere, and now that she's been found out, someone decided she's expendable. I'm going to go check up on Bobby. I guess I'll see you as soon as you can get here so you can question him."

"Is he carrying?" she asked softly. "Because if he is, he's got to surrender it. I need to exclude the weapon from whatever drilled a hole through Blondie. I'll see if I can get a tech over to do a GSR test on him, but until I can get him eliminated, he's a suspect."

"Got it." I could just imagine how Bobby was going to take that, but O'Byrne was a good cop, and she wouldn't cut anyone slack just because she knew them. Rationally, Bobby would agree with that, but he'd just been stabbed, so I wasn't too sure how rational he was. "I'll make sure they don't swab his hands down with alcohol."

"I'll be there soon as I can." She let out another curse, mumbling under her breath. "Oh, and McGinnis? I'm going to put a couple of cops on Brinkerhoff's hospital room. Make sure you watch your back, because if they know that Marlena—the real one—is in town and she's spilled her guts to you, you could be next on their hit list."

"No, I get it. She's got to do the job," Bobby said, surrendering his gun to the baby-faced uniform who'd come to grab it. The kid's hands were shaking, and I wasn't too sure who he was more afraid of, Dawson or

Ichiro, who stood at the side of the bed, glowering at him. "I've got a spare set of clothes in the SUV, babe. Can you or Cole grab it so I can give them what I'm wearing?"

"I'll get it." Ichi's words were clipped, sharpened with anger. He'd probably come from the shop, because he was decked out in full cool tattoo-artist gear—torn black jeans, a 415 Ink T-shirt that had seen better days, and a leather jacket so worn-in it slithered around his compact, muscled torso. "I can't believe they think you killed her. O'Byrne knows you."

"It's procedure," Bobby reassured him, kissing Ichi on the cheek. "The best way to nail someone for a murder is to eliminate all of the people who could have done it but didn't. That way there's no room for doubt. That's what the whole legal system is about—beyond a reasonable doubt, and that's what O'Byrne needs to prove. Or at least that's what she needs to be able to put in front of the DA. I promise I didn't kill her, so the evidence will show that."

"Well, I probably shouldn't tattoo her in the next few months," Ichiro growled, stalking toward the curtains. "She might end up with a kanji that says asshole instead of peace."

"You know, your family has anger-management issues, Princess," Bobby murmured to me with a smile. "It's like all of you get really pissed off when the world doesn't agree with how you see things."

"And yet you are not only my best friend, but you fuck my baby brother," I reminded him, and the baby cop winced, his cheeks flushing red.

"I married him, didn't I?" Holding up his hand, Bobby wiggled his finger, where a glistening gold band sat. "Best decision of my life. Not so sure I made a very good one when I decided to be friends with you, but if I hadn't hooked up with your sorry ass, I wouldn't have met Ichi."

"Or be suspected for murder," O'Byrne said, ducking into the cordoned-off hospital room. She gave Bobby a rueful smile, glancing around the space, probably taking in the blood-soaked shirt lying on the bed where they'd left it after cutting it off of Bobby to stitch up his wound. "I've got an evidence bag for that. How're you doing?"

"I'm okay. McGinnis here caught me up with what's going on in the Brinkerhoff case. How the hell did everyone let that woman slide into place? We all just assumed she was supposed to be there?" He hissed when reaching for the cup of ice chips the nurse left for him. "Shit, this hurts."

"What did she get you with?" O'Byrne carefully maneuvered the bloodied shirt into the bag, pushing it through the opening with a pair of tweezers. "I'd say we'll get this back to you as soon as we run some tests, but I'm not sure you'll want it."

"Yeah, probably not." He chuckled. The edges of his bandages were already speckled with blood, and pain flicked across his expression when he moved. A handful of painkillers waited for him on the rolling bed stand, but he'd refused them, wanting to wait until O'Byrne questioned him before downing anything strong enough to knock him out. "I don't know what she sliced me with, but it was a straight blade, maybe something made to a point. Not serrated. The cut's a clean one, straight into my side with a stab. My ribs kept it from going any deeper, but it was sharp. Went right through the shirt like it was water."

"You said you followed her out of the elevator." O'Byrne handed the evidence bag off to the young cop, then pulled out her notebook. The teasing note to her voice slipped away, and she'd gone serious. "What were you doing?"

"She said she had an appointment that she had to get to, but I figured I would take a crack at her. Considering we all decided that house was pretty much stage dressing, I wanted to see if she had any information about where her grandparents—or at least who I thought her grandparents were—lived." Bobby frowned, pressing his hand against the bandage. "I was trying to keep her occupied so McGinnis would have a few minutes with Arthur. I didn't know at the time she wasn't the real deal."

The gauze was a bloodied white slash against Bobby's muscled, tanned torso, wrapped around his ribs and hiding some of the bruises I'd given him during our last boxing match. Or maybe he'd picked them up when we were rolling around in the alleyway, trying not to get shot. Either way it looked like he'd taken a beating. His focus was detached, his eyes on the floor as he went over the events.

"You follow her all the way outside?" O'Byrne began filling the page with her practically illegible scrawl. I would've hated to be her partner and try to reconstruct any of it for a report.

"Yeah. My legs are pretty long, and I had to hurry to keep up with her. She knew her way around the hospital. There wasn't any hesitation about which way to turn, and this place is like a rat's nest. You could end up in the broom closet if you go looking for a bathroom," he replied, sucking in air between his clenched teeth as he held his side. "She was in a hurry. And she didn't want to talk. I didn't speak with her that long. Not like McGinnis here did. But she was all smooth and polished in front of the nurse station. Then, when we got outside, she went a little gutter. Not LA. She didn't sound like she was from here. I'd say someplace back East. Maybe even Boston. It was the way she said car."

O'Byrne nodded, jotting in the row of hieroglyphics. "So you followed her outside, and then what?"

"She went out the Urgent Care door. You have to cut through a pretty big section of the hospital to get to it. I thought it was weird, because she kept zigzagging through the corridors." Bobby looked up suddenly, cocking his head as he thought. "She didn't go out the parking structure exit. We ended up on the main walk, toward the left corner of the main building. I was right on her heels when she turned around, and I felt the blade go in. It took me a second to realize I'd been stabbed. I kept trying to walk into her. So I forced it in deeper. Then she jerked back, and the pain hit. Doctor said she probably twisted when she pulled it out because she took a good chunk of my skin with her."

"Anybody see her do this? Any witnesses? Anybody stop and help you?" O'Byrne came at Bobby with the rapid-fire questions, peppering him with choices, but they were all pretty much the same jab to his story. There'd been enough time between them leaving the upper floor and him getting into the ER for Bobby to shoot her. O'Byrne needed to shake his story, trying to see if there was anyone she could tap to verify what he was saying.

"Yeah. Actually one of the ER doctors was coming in. I think his name is Davis or Davison. I got handed off as soon as they got me in." He pursed his lips, whistling out a low tone. "I stumbled back a couple of feet and went down. It took him a bit to get there, and there was a couple—an older couple—who were trying to help me up, but he told me to stay there until he could see how bad it was. Seemed like forever before we came inside. Must've been maybe five or ten minutes."

"I requested copies of the camera footage from that side of the building, detective," the young cop interjected. "Security said it would be about an hour, but they can download the video onto a drive for you."

"Thanks. Good job on that." O'Byrne gave him a curt nod. "Can you describe for me what she was wearing? I want to verify that's what we found her in."

"Yeah… um, Princess, can you do me a favor and see what's taking Ichi so long?" Bobby gritted his teeth again, and the crow's-feet at the corners of his eyes deepened. "As soon as O'Byrne is done with me, I'd like to get out of here, and as sexy as I am, I think I want to be dressed before I parade through the hospital again. I don't think we're going to go over anything you haven't already heard or know. You mind, O'Byrne?"

"No. It's okay. I'll have to shake Mac down for his side of the story when I'm done with you, so it's probably for the best," she said, jerking her head toward the part in the curtains. "Don't leave without me talking to you, okay? I'm going to also have to head upstairs and talk to the real Marlena Brinkerhoff before I go to the captain with this piece-of-shit story on a plate."

"Don't worry. I'm sure I'll be right back here," I told O'Byrne with a shake of my head. "All I seem to be doing is going around in circles anyway."

SEARCHING FOR my younger brother in a parking structure connected to a hospital was easier said than done. Luckily for me, despite the many levels, not many of them held a brooding Japanese man leaning against a silver SUV while smoking a clove cigarette. As usual, Ichi scored a good parking spot near the elevator, so after one quick jaunt around the lower floor, I spotted him before too long.

Problem was, as I crossed the twenty yards or so separating us, I noticed he wasn't looking too happy. At first I chalked that up to the fact that his husband had just been stabbed, but his expression soured even more when I drew near.

"Hey!" I called out to him, noticing he didn't have Bobby's gym bag with him. "Did he not throw his shit in there? I've got some things in the Rover he can borrow if he can get his big head through the opening in my T-shirt. I don't buy them in extralarge ego."

Ichi took another drag of his cigarette, then exhaled a thin, fragrant stream. "He doesn't need anything more from you. Don't you think he's taken enough of your shit?"

My baby brother's words stopped me short, a few feet away from the end of their SUV. In a lot of ways, Ichiro fit in nicely with me and Mike. He was an edgier version of my philosophies with our older brother's Boy Scout morals. He was a conflict of contradictions, pushing the envelope for his art but pretty much traditional down to the marrow in his bones. His appearance in my life had been unexpected and unwelcome, but he kept after me, cracking open my resentment about our mother discarding us and leaving me with a father who hated me. Eventually he fell into place as my younger brother. I'd been angry and hurt when he and Bobby began their relationship and hid their developing love from me, but by then, I'd grown very protective of Ichi. He'd somehow become my innocent, rebellious baby brother while I wasn't looking, and Bobby's interest in him seemed a bit incestuous, taking into account my brotherly relationship with Bobby.

But with everything we'd been through, Ichi never once spat in my face, not like he was doing right now. And I sure as hell didn't know what to do about it.

"What's going on?" The parking structure's floor scraped against the soles of my shoes, a shuffle of tiny bits of sand and gravel from God knows where. "Ichi, what happened?"

"Bobby fucking got stabbed, Cole," Ichi hissed at me, pacing off the end of the SUV with a single stride. "That's what's wrong. Did you miss that part of the afternoon? When you were chasing whatever it was you're after? Did you miss my husband getting stabbed?"

"It wasn't like *I* did it." For some reason, I fell into a whisper as if I didn't want anyone to hear us arguing. I didn't know what was going on in Ichiro's head, but I knew how he felt. I'd sat by Jae's hospital bed more than a few times and Bobby's as well, not to mention the vigil we all stood when Mike was shot. "He's fine. So he may not be able to swing from a chandelier during sex for a while, but—"

"It's not a joke, Cole. This isn't something to laugh at," Ichi said, turning to face me. His kretek burned red-hot at the end when he took another hit, holding the smoke in for a moment before releasing it in a plume. "I don't want him working with you anymore. And if I tell him that, he'll push back at me because I don't have any right to tell him how to live his life, but I can't watch the two of you do this. If Jae is okay with you trying to kill yourself every day, that's between the two of you. But I won't let Bobby do that. I can't. I never thought I would find somebody I would love enough to want to marry, and I was okay with that. Then I met him, and everything changed.

"And don't get me wrong, I love you and Mike. You're my brothers," he asserted, "but he's my husband. He's my *family*. And we both know he's older than I am, so every year I have with him is an even greater gift. He takes care of himself. He works hard to stay healthy so he can be with me as long as he can. So I don't need you to try to kill him every time you take a case. I just can't. So I'm asking you—if you love me as much as you say you do—don't take him with you anymore. I love him, Cole. More than I've ever loved anyone in my entire life, and if I lose him because of you, I'm going to lose more than my husband. I'm going to lose my brother as well."

FOURTEEN

No ONE ever came to Los Angeles in the last ninety years or so to look at the stars in the sky. Despite being the birthplace of packaged entertainment sold in long or short forms, the night above the glittering City of Angels rarely bared a twinkle in the midnight-blue veil she pulled over her head after the sun quenched itself in the Pacific Ocean.

I had a cold beer and the dark skies to keep me company. It was my third beer since wandering outside and making myself comfortable on one of the outdoor recliners. I'd packed five Cosmic Cowboy bottles into a steel bucket filled with ice and intended to work on the case, going over my notes and everything else. But the folder lay where I'd put it down, on the recliner next to the one I slouched into, and instead I worked on the beer.

It was nearly eight o'clock, but the neighborhood was already winding down. I was once again thankful for the mature trees I'd kept around the property's perimeter, forking over a small fortune to an expert to keep them healthy and sound. Their full canopies hid most signs of other houses, but the occasional sparkle of light shone through. As large as the lot was—a generous wide and long stretch—we still had neighbors, and we kept our shallow relationships as pleasant as possible, with high fences and the occasional nod of hello if we happened to see one another while getting mail. I liked it that way, especially on nights like this when my mind felt as if an octopus crawled up into it and began thrashing around in its death throes.

Honey lay along my hip, a dirty-blond rag mop with a snore like a rutting bison but possessing a cheerful disposition I sure as hell wouldn't have held on to if I'd been thrown out of the only home I'd known because my owner's parents hadn't wanted his boyfriend to have her. I hadn't been sure about picking her up from the shelter when they called to say they found her years later, but in a lot of ways, she was the first step I took in forgiving myself for Rick's death. She'd been practically a puppy when she'd been taken from me while I was in a coma, yet she remembered me when she saw me. Although she pretty much loved everyone she met and would probably show a burglar where the silverware was if given half the chance.

I was still grateful for her and even more thankful Jae talked me into getting the extrawide loungers, because while Honey was a fairly small dog, she took up more than her share of the cushions.

The kitchen's back door opened, its hydraulics squeaking loud enough to remind me, once again, to spray it with lubricant. None of the outside lights were on, and the moon was a thin curve of silvery yellow hanging on the edge of a far cloud, but I knew it was Jae coming to find me.

The only other people who would've sought me out were Bobby and Ichi, one of whom was stabbed and hopefully resting while the other made himself perfectly clear that he wanted nothing to do with me as long as I endangered his husband.

I envied Jae's grace nearly as much as I admired it. He moved silently, more of a gentle wind across the grass, where I stomped and prowled loud enough to wake the dead. I watched him cross the lawn, his face hidden by flickering shadows, the glow of the streetlamp at the front of the house kissing his cheekbone, then his temple, playing hide-and-go-seek with his features. To say I was in love with him would be like trying to paint the sunset using only black and white. He'd grabbed ahold of my heart, sinking through its torn and hardened flesh to force it to beat again while he fought me every step of the way. He hadn't wanted to fall in love with me, and I hadn't wanted to change. I'd been content in my stagnation, happy to dwell in the doldrums I'd fallen into, but neither one of us had any choice in the matter. We were… destined… to fall in love, and I woke up every morning to do it all over again.

It wasn't a bad way to live.

The sex was pretty fucking fantastic.

Thing is, Jae was never one to let me marinate in misery, and the time had come for me to pay the piper for the time it took me to drink the three beers and wallow in my guilt.

"Come here," Jae said to the dog, gathering her up while she grumbled in her half slumber. Dumping Honey in my lap, he made himself comfortable on the canine-warmed side of the recliner, then reached for one of the beers. "Does this twist off, or do I need a… what are those called?"

"Church key," I said, taking the beer from him. Leaning over Jae, I retrieved the bottle opener from the edge of the bucket where I'd hooked it, popped the cap, then sat up to hand it back. "Here."

I got a kiss for a thank-you, and I deepened it, disrupting the dog enough to send her grumbling and sliding off of the cushions to seek out a different place to sleep. Jae twisted his fingers through my hair, tugging lightly. I tilted my head back, following the movement of his gentle pull. His teeth dented into my skin, scoring a light furrow across my throat. Then he let me go, bringing the bottle up to kiss his swollen lips.

He felt good against me, much better than the dog. Jae also smelled better, so I added washing the dog to my mental to-do list, hopefully above lubricating the screen door, because it had squeaked for as long as I'd owned the house. Resting his hand on my thigh, Jae sat with me, sipping his beer and letting the unseen stars churn overhead, their shimmering journeys hidden by milky clouds and the city's blanket of lights. The air turned a bit chilly, and he shifted his weight, resting on the hip closest to me, pulling his legs up to hook over my shins, seeking out my heat.

"Did you talk to Ichi?" I heard myself breaking the quiet, shattering it with a verbal hammer forged in an anger I'd thought I didn't possess. Bobby had been mine before Ichiro's, and sitting there with my throat closed up around the pain I couldn't swallow, I realized I was angry at being replaced or maybe simply angry in general. "I'm going through a lot right now in my head. With Bobby. With Ichi. And I'm not really too sure what to do about it."

"What do you want to see happen? What is your wish for how things will be once you work through everything?" Jae asked, his fingers making circuits around my knee. "Because right now, Ichi is scared, and Bobby probably doesn't realize it. So he lashed out at you, and now you are having to eat his anger. Yes?"

"Some of it, yeah. But some of it's on me too," I replied, checking the level of beer in my bottle. It was still mostly full, so any blurring of my thoughts couldn't be explained by the alcohol. "I got pissed off at Ichi for demanding Bobby stop working with me, and then it dawned on me I was kind of pissed off about both of them shuffling me down on their list of people they love. Which is fucking stupid, because I fell in love with you, and it didn't change my relationship with Bobby."

"It did." Jae sat up a little bit, angling so he could see my face. "You stopped going out with him to clubs, and a lot of your afternoons were spent with me instead of with him, going to ball games or doing things that you both like to do. It's hard because both of you were alone for a very long time and used to just having each other. Then I came along, and he had to split his time, leaving him alone again. Then when Ichi came, you spent more time with him, learning how to be his brother, slicing Bobby's time even more."

"Then they hooked up, so…." I sighed, too caught up in my own selfish needs to have everyone sit in the box I'd put them in. "I realized I felt like I was being shoved out between them. I thought it was because I knew how Bobby was with guys and I didn't want Ichi to get hurt, but it was more about me not wanting to share them, not wanting to lose what time I had with them. And that's so fucking stupid, but I thought I was doing okay. Then today happened."

"Today happened," Jae agreed. "Ichi is a contradiction, because he is rebellious in his own culture but traditional in yours. I think it's why he and I get along so well—because we both feel like we're telling our world to fuck off but not really. We're just fighting for space to exist in. Because what we were given was too small, and your spaces are so big—too big—so we cling to traditional things because they're familiar.

"Tokugawa Ichiro was raised in Japan, by a very conservative father who is the head of a very conservative family. His path was laid out before him from the moment he was born, written down in the registry, along with the thousands of names that came before him. And he fought to crawl off of that page and become more," he continued. "But Ichi was raised in a Japan that doesn't have guns or the violence you and Bobby swore to shield people from. The guns both of you are familiar with are monstrous horrors, symbols of death and loss. We tell ourselves we are sophisticated and worldly because we've been through so much. But not like the two of you, and the violence you go through so easily scares us, unmans us. Bobby is the first person not of Ichiro's blood that he's put into his own personal registry, and he's frightened to lose him."

"I get that. I'd be scared as hell to find out I'd almost lost you. Shit, a building fell on you and I thought I was going to die, and that was before we were even together." I snorted, chuckling at the memory of digging through the rubble for his damned cat. "I understand what he's feeling."

"I don't think you do," Jae argued with a sweet smile I suspected hid a verbal knife as sharp as the one that sliced Bobby open that afternoon. "You've already lost two people you loved deeply. It tore through you as much as those bullets did, the ones Ben put into you. You woke up in that hospital alone—or at least alone in your head—because your father had thrown you out and Mike wasn't a good brother to you then. And you pushed through it. I don't think Ichi feels he's strong enough inside to survive losing Bobby. Or losing you. I'm not sure I am, but I know you love me and I know you will always fight to come home to me. But no one's ever fought for Ichi. Maybe he's scared Bobby won't. I don't know, but that's something he's got to work out with Bobby, not you. They have to talk about it, and Bobby has to make those decisions. I've learned that from you. Sometimes you have to accept the nature of the man you've fallen in love with, because those are the very reasons you fell in love with him."

"I fell in love with you because you wouldn't give me a straight answer," I teased. "You were like unwrapping a very complicated, tightly wound present who tasted like heaven after I walked through hell to get there."

"You were the most frightening, addictive temptation I'd ever seen," he confessed, laughing brightly. The stars shimmered through the night sky just for a moment, or maybe it was just me seeing the joy in his eyes. "I hated you for making me want you, for making me dream about waking up next to you. I wanted you so much I used to cry sometimes at night because it hurt. I couldn't find a way out of where I'd been put in my life, and I couldn't risk losing what little love my family gave me on the maybe of you."

"Well, your sisters love you, as evidenced by their frequent flights back here whenever there's a break in classes." I kissed his temple, inhaling the scent of the vanilla shampoo we shared. "And you have me and Scarlet and Claudia and everybody else in my crazy family, including Mad Dog Junior. I just want Ichi to understand that he's got all of that too. We're not going to go away. No matter what happens."

"You, me, and Ichi were all thrown out by the people who should've loved us the most. The difference is, you and I had people who taught us how to love, like Rick and Claudia and Scarlet. I think Ichi reaching out to you and Mike was him taking that first chance, hoping to find love from brothers he never knew. Then Bobby came along," Jae whispered, returning my kiss with a brush of his lips across mine. "And now his heart is full, and he doesn't want it broken again. I told him he had to talk to Bobby. He called right as you came outside, but I told him to give you a little bit of time."

"I would've talked to him," I protested with a sniff. "I'm just a little pissed off and mostly confused about this fucking case."

"You would've done two things—one, got into a fight with him again because neither one of you can apologize, or two, tell him it's okay and then nurse your grudge like you were breastfeeding a dragon." He shook his head, probably to cut me off before I could defend myself. Because that's exactly what I was about to do. "Don't deny it. I know you. I love you, but I know you. Now, it's getting cold, and I want to go back inside where it's warm. Grab the dog, and I will grab the bucket."

"I've got a very good way to warm you up," I said, waggling my eyebrows at him. "I don't even have to grab the dog to do it. That actually sounded a lot better in my head."

"You can warm me up all you like." Jae grabbed the bucket's handle, stashing his open bottle in the half-melted ice. "You and I are getting too old to be doing those kinds of things outside on the lawn furniture where the neighbors can see us. We have a bed—one we haven't broken yet— and a shower with hot water. Let's go use those, and in the morning, you can call your brother, and the two of you can figure out a way to apologize to each other without actually saying 'I'm sorry.'"

MORNING SLID around us, pulling the sleep from our eyes and wending a lust for coffee into the base of our brains. A splash of cold water on my face was enough to drive away the cobwebs, but it took the first hit of smoky, chocolatey brew for my mind to finally stop its wandering. I had a lot to do. Claudia was out for the day, something about the girls' trip down to Disneyland, an annual gathering of the Dubois women, the wives and children of Claudia's many sons. I forked over all of the tickets as a quarterly bonus for her, and each year it hurt more and more. But she enjoyed it, and I got to live vicariously through their family antics— stories told to me over the following weeks and usually accompanied by a souvenir they all picked out together.

As a retired bus driver for the LA school system, I imagined Claudia's pension didn't go very far and that's why she'd sought out work after they rolled her out. She'd been an anchor point in my life for so long I couldn't imagine waking up in the morning without having her tear a strip off of my ego, shake off any sugarcoating, and promptly feed it to me for breakfast. I loved the hell out of her, but sometimes it was good to have a morning by myself.

Especially since I had to wait for O'Byrne to get back to me about the ex-cop who lived next to the Brinkerhoffs and whether or not she had a chance to go through their apartment. The death of the fake Marlena was confusing. Someone hadn't wanted her to talk, but really, what was she going to say? And what did she have to gain by passing herself off as Arthur's granddaughter? I still also had no idea about who sent that guy after us in the alleyway, and more importantly, who the hell killed Adele Brinkerhoff.

My phone rang as I strolled down the front walk toward my office, the two front rooms I'd closed off from the rest of the house to separate my business from my home life. It was a good theory, but in practice, I missed having the large front stoop and the broad covered porch with its grand entrance and heavy wooden door. While I'd done a lot of work in turning a former side entrance into the house's front door, the cement slab and portico marked the visual punch of the grand old lady's original façade.

"But do I want to rent the place just to have a front door I'd like?" I muttered to myself, unlocking my phone with a swipe of my thumb. "McGinnis."

"Mac, it's O'Byrne." She sounded strained, but who didn't at this point in an investigation? The sun hadn't even made a full break from the mountains to the east, and I couldn't imagine she'd taken in enough coffee to shake off the crap she'd been wading through over the last week. "Where are you?"

"I'm about to open the front door of my office," I said, rattling my keys near the phone's speaker so she could hear them chime. "Why?"

"I found out they let our guy go yesterday morning," O'Byrne growled. "Some lawyer showed up, and I don't know what judge he blew, but I come rolling in this morning to question him and they tell me he was cut loose. The bastards are still trying to run his prints for identification, and I've got no idea about where this guy is. He could be in the wind or circling back toward you."

"That is not what I need to hear this morning," I muttered back. Wedging my shoulder against the screen door to hold it open, I went to fit my key into the knob when the heavy wooden door swung open an inch.

"I'm going to send a uniform over," she informed me through a crackle on the phone. "I really don't know what the fuck is going on, but the first thing I need to do is find this guy."

"Yeah, about that…."

I pushed into the main room, not bothering to turn on the lights. There was enough sun to wash through the filmy curtains Claudia put up a few weeks ago, pouring a bit of heavy cream into the light brown shadows pouring over the walls and furniture. Sitting at my desk was the man whose face I'd beaten in, his head shaved down to a gleaming dome and his generously bruised nose sporting a wide X bandage across his bridge. Stitches ran across his right cheek, and I took a small delight in seeing another row of stitches running from his jaw up nearly to his ear. He was dressed in an expensive suit, or at least it looked expensive in the semidark, much like an old whore who plied her trade under a flickering streetlamp so her Johns didn't know she was old enough to be their grandmother.

There was no sign of his expensive Italian loafers, but I did get a very good look at the gun in his hand—a gun he was pointing straight at me.

"Hello, Mister McGinnis," the man said with a clipped preciseness I'd only heard from fabric scissors Scarlet used while constructing one of her evening gowns. "Come in and close the door."

There were a lot of things I admired about Scarlet, performing when the need struck her and living her life as a kathoey whose powerful Korean lover kept her happy and safe. At that moment, what I most admired about her was the constant presence of squat, serious-faced Korean men whose jackets often bulged with guns and whose only job was to make sure she was safe.

I really could have used one of those men at that moment, but all I'd brought with me was my phone and a little bit of anger I had at finding a killer sitting not far from where my husband worked at the back of our house.

"Seems I found your guy, O'Byrne," I said, not breaking eye contact with the asshole in my chair. "He's here with me in my office, and for some reason, he seems to think I'm not going to kick his ass like I did the last time, just because he's got a damned gun on me."

FIFTEEN

JAE WAS right. I hold grudges. I've never seen a need not to, since the times I did get pissed off at someone, it was usually for a good reason. I think a guy coming down an alleyway intending to kill me would be a pretty good reason to hold a grudge, but some people might not see it that way.

Those people would be wrong, but who am I to judge on their lack of common sense? God knows, I've made some pretty shitty decisions in my life, but getting shot in the middle of my office wasn't going to be one of them, not if I had anything to say about it.

"Close the door behind you, McGinnis," the beaten-up asshole ordered me. "I don't want any witnesses. Especially since you've been hard to kill. I've already missed you several times, and well, now game time is over. Because of you, my girlfriend is dead and my reputation has taken a bit of a hit. The girlfriend? I can get another one. Women are easily led into doing all kinds of things if you give them a little affection, but a reputation as good as mine isn't so easily brought back to life."

"Got it, so the woman passing herself off as Marlena was your girlfriend, then? Her death isn't on me, buddy. I didn't kill her. And if you want the door closed, you're going to have to do it yourself," I replied, walking toward him. He lifted the gun another inch, following my central mass as it drew nearer to him. There wasn't any mistaking his intent. There was no way I was going to get out of the room alive if he had anything to say about it. Luckily, he was only one part of the conversation. "LAPD is looking for you. It seems Detective O'Byrne has a couple of questions she'd like you to answer."

"So I heard." His smile glittered, nearly as white as the bandage across his face, and I almost asked him who his dentist was. Although I imagine assassins probably live as healthy as they can, avoiding coffee, red meat, and cameras. "I imagine the boys and girls in blue will be showing up shortly, so we're going to have to make this quick. Which makes me kind of sad, because I would like to spend a lot of time with that pretty little husband of yours. I'm not into men, but how do they say? Any port in a storm?"

The arrogant often posed themselves in ways they learned from television or perhaps from studying despots. I'd seen it on the street when carrying a badge—young children fronting with an attitude far bigger than their bodies. And as I moved through the upper reaches of society on cases, the poses changed, but the bravado remained the same. There was very little difference between a thug snarling at me with a glittering gold grill, swearing he'd collect my eyeballs as some twisted participation trophy, and a powerful graying-at-the-temples CEO with a corner office overlooking Downtown Los Angeles and a phalanx of shark-toothed lawyers standing behind him. They all affected a loose-shouldered posture, draping limbs over chairs, desks, and sometimes the occasional mailbox or car if the situation called for it.

Apparently they taught the exact same course of attempted intimidation at assassin school, because the bruised son of a bitch affected a nonchalant air, one leg flung over the arm of my executive chair, his elbow resting on his thigh to aim his gun at me while his other hand lay on my desk, a monstrously carved, elegant stretch of tiger oak I'd restored to its original glory. The openness of their limbs was meant to convey their lack of fear, almost as if goading their prey to attack them, secure in the knowledge they could respond with deadly force before the other person could get near.

I was already near enough.

Bobby might have taught me the elegant brutality and finesse of boxing, but I'd learned how to fight in Chicago. More importantly, I attended a school where my partially Asian features made me a target and my naïve, not-so-hidden speculative glances at other boys hadn't gone unnoticed. I often wondered how my father didn't know I was gay until I told him and my stepmom that horrible, never-ending day. Trips to the principal's office were a weekly thing, and sometimes I was even joined by Mike, my squat powerhouse of an older brother, who looked even more Japanese than I did. I'd been called faggot and homo nearly as soon as I picked up my first pencil in kindergarten, so either my father was a master of denial—not something I could discount—or little kids were a lot more astute than the adults around them.

I was hoping this asshole was one of those stupid adults, and it seemed like he was, because in the middle of his need to psychologically dominate me and threaten Jae, he left himself way too open.

"That's far enough," he said, his curled-up smile tightening the skin across his face, and I knew that had to hurt, having broken my own nose more than a few times. "Time to say goodbye, McGinnis."

What a fucking cliché.

I wished I had a snappy rejoinder on deck, but truth was, I really didn't have time to banter in the style of action heroes and film-noir detectives. What I did have was the massive square avocado-green rotary phone Claudia insisted on keeping at her desk. I'd tried to talk her out of it, explaining I was going to have to angle her desk against the wall in order to feed the phone line to her sickly green beast, but when I'd unearthed it from the bowels of the Craftsman's storage shed, where I'd put all of the old things I found when refurbishing the house, her eyes lit up. Tasked with cleaning out the shed, there were quite a few things I ended up tossing, but the green monstrosity was a throwback to Claudia's childhood, and she insisted on having it.

I was very thankful my office manager slash adopted mom had fallen in love with that damned phone.

Especially when the asshole shot at me. Point blank. Aimed straight for my head. A single bullet.

If I'd still been standing in front of him, he would have blown a hole the size of New Jersey through my skull. But since I had other plans, the piece of lead with my name on it screamed past my shoulder when I lunged for Claudia's desk.

Once again, the woman had my back and didn't even know it, because her damned phone was as heavy as fuck and easily broke loose from its tether after I hooked my fingers into the space below the headset rest and yanked hard. Armed with a piece of nostalgia with the heft of a refrigerator, I clobbered him across the face.

I'd like to say I felt no pleasure in smashing apart the guy's forehead, but I'd be lying.

The first hit was hard. It had to be. There was no going back from this. I had to take the guy down as fast and hard as I could, because if he gained any advantage, I was going to die. As healthy as I tried to keep myself, there were things I'd never been able to overcome—scar tissue from the bullets Ben put in me and the chasm opening up in my chest where fear rushed in to fill. My muscles were seizing up. I hadn't stretched out that morning, and now the burn was reminding me I was getting too old for this kind of shit.

The gun went flying, but I wasn't going to chase it. I was done dealing with this asshole, and there was no way in hell I was going to leave him in any shape where he could get to Jae. His hands were how he made a living. They needed to go first. I wasn't going to leave him in any condition to ever get his fingers around anything ever again. If I didn't, he was going back to killing, and he would probably succeed if he came for me and mine one more time.

That was never going to happen. I was never ever going to walk in and find this asshole waiting for me in the dark. And I didn't care what I had to do to make that a reality.

There wasn't any blood splatter until the third strike of the phone down on his gun hand. I'd tackled him to the floor, pinning him in the chair and using my weight to hold him down, my free hand at his throat while I concentrated on pulverizing his fingers. The rotary chimed and rang as I smashed it down, its bell clapper striking the metal dome hidden in its guts from the wild flailing of my arm rising and falling. It was a curious infinity of noise, a jangle of bells punctuated by the snapping of crushed bones and his high-pitched screaming.

There might've been begging. I didn't know. I didn't care, and I wasn't listening. I'd stopped listening to whatever was coming out of his mouth right after Jae's name dropped off his tongue. I'd already lost everything once, including myself, and I sure as hell wasn't going to go through that all over again. I wasn't going to hold Jae's lifeless body as he bled out, his eyes filming over and the too-painful stillness of his heart beating one last time. Not if I could help it.

Never again.

When I was done with one hand, I started on the other, working to make sure neither one of them would ever fit around a knife's hilt or through a trigger guard. I didn't stop until I heard Jae's voice break through the rush of blood coursing through my brain, yelling at me to put the phone down, his hands desperately yanking at my shoulders.

I sat back then, actually resting against the man's twitching legs because I'd ended up in his lap, nearly as trapped in the chair as he was. I couldn't catch my breath for the fear and anger racing through me, but Jae being there helped.

"Let it go, hyung. The cops should be here soon," Jae murmured, helping me up.

My legs were numb, too rubbery to stand on, but I did my best. My fingers were cramped around the phone, and Jae had to pry them up, the rotary falling to the floor with a loud clatter. I didn't hear any sirens, but the heavy tread of running boots and shoes beat up the sidewalk and onto the stoop. My hands were wet, and I looked down at them, not surprised to see them coated in blood and sweat.

"I want to know who sent him. I want to know who brought him to my front door and put Jae in his crosshairs," I growled at O'Byrne as she came through the front door, her gun up and sweeping the room while a uniformed cop followed close behind her, covering her blind side. "And I want to be there when you start asking him those questions, because I'll be damned if some asshole like him sits a couple hundred feet away from my husband and threatens him. I don't care who started this. I'm going to fucking finish it, and they're going to wish they got off as lightly as he did. I'm done playing, O'Byrne. It's time we got some answers."

THE CITY of Los Angeles didn't put a lot of money into their interview rooms. The paint scheme ran to baby-puke green, and the metal tables and chairs looked like they'd gone through a few wars in a middle school before finally ending up providing a seat for the asses of cops and criminals alike. They were hard and mean, digging into the back of my screwed-up knee and angled so straight it was a guarantee I wouldn't be able to walk right once I left.

Assuming they would let me leave.

O'Byrne herself deposited me into the room, telling me to sit down and wait without much more than a backward glance as she closed the door. It was either a courtesy to me because I was an ex-cop or it was a subtle form of torture because there was no way I could ask somebody to use the bathroom. A fresh-faced young kid in blue wearing a badge so new it blinded me when the lights hit it came by to give me a bottle of water.

That was nearly two hours ago.

People paid a lot of money for time in a sensory deprivation tank, yet they could save themselves the expense by being dragged into questioning and thrown into an LAPD interview room. Providing they could get past the subtle stink of burnt coffee and unwashed skin—a perfume unique to police stations everywhere—the outside world stayed firmly that… *outside*.

There was not even a murmur of sound, and the frosted, chicken-wire-embedded window set into the door gave no glimpse of anyone passing by. Even the one-way mirror set into the long wall across of where I sat seemed strangely empty of life. During interrogation there were usually one or two cops sitting behind that glass, either taking notes or waiting for things to go south, ready to provide backup for the cops in the room.

The silence didn't even hold an echo. I screeched my chair back, and the high-pitched whining of the rubber feet against the thick industrial tile was swallowed up nearly as soon as it broke loose. Tapping at the table helped a little bit, but soon my fingertips began to throb.

Of course the residual stinging along my extremities could possibly have been from gripping Claudia's phone too tight as I used it to hammer the gunman's hands into mincemeat.

I was about to check the door for the fifth time to see if it was still locked when O'Byrne came in with Detective Dante Montoya shadowing her. It was odd seeing him dressed in clothes other than shorts and a tank top, because I'd spent more than a few hours trying to beat his face in at JoJo's, but the Hispanic cop gave no indication we knew each other when he leaned against the one-way mirror, his arms crossed over his chest. O'Byrne had the haunted, tired look of a cop who was reaching the end of her patience with a case. Her jacket was gone, her shoulder holster exposed and fit tight across her lean torso. There was a bit of dirt on her jeans, and either she had been rooting around in my front yard or I was going to have to have a serious talk with the cleaning crew who took care of my office. Montoya was as calm and collected as could be, his brown eyes flat and steady, fixed on my face without a hint of emotion in his authoritative expression.

O'Byrne sat down, putting the folder she'd had tucked under her arm on the table between us. She flipped it open, but I didn't look down at the papers as she rifled through them. I figured I was brought in because I'd beaten a man with the intent to cripple him—not something the LAPD was fond of—but I wasn't going to apologize for it. If they stopped using me as a consultant, I was fine with that.

My first priority was always going to be Jae, and as much as I liked O'Byrne, my husband came first.

"I don't know which way Captain Book is going to fall on this," O'Byrne said with a tired sigh, shifting back on her uncomfortable chair. "I pleaded self-defense at him, considering the guy got a shot or two off, but you used excessive force, Mac. The DA might have another opinion."

"The DA can go fuck himself," I replied as clearly as I could, stating my position in a way that no one could misunderstand. I guessed we'd had some company join us behind the mirror, especially when Montoya shifted away from the glass partition, but I wasn't there to make friends. "That guy came after me twice now. You guys had him in custody and someone with black robes and maybe an agenda let him walk, so you have to excuse me if I don't have a lot of faith in what the LAPD or the DA's office thinks."

"Doctors don't even know if they'll be able to reconstruct his hands," Montoya said, a hint of Texas-Mexican flowing through his voice. It was a different tone than the Spanish I normally heard in Los Angeles, more of a roundness to it than the staccato, rapid-fire Mexican overheard on the street. "Did you have to go so far? He may not even be able to use them again."

"If he told you he was going to go have fun with Stevens once he was done killing you, would you have just sat there and taken it?" I shot back, digging my shoulders into the metal bar set high on the back of the chair. "Because nobody comes into my place and threatens the people I love, least of all Jae. You guys are damned lucky I didn't take that phone to his face. At least he can still talk. This way I know he won't be able to come back and shoot me. Or at least he'll think twice about it. Now, have you asked him about why he came after me? And what does this have to do with Adele Brinkerhoff's murder?"

Montoya looked away, and I knew I'd scored at least one point, gouging deep into his disgust at my actions. Pacing off at the end of the table, he shook his head, then glanced at O'Byrne. "Are you going to tell him or am I?"

"The feds have swooped in. It seems like, in the DA's haste to free this guy, they didn't cross all of their t's and dot their i's. They didn't check to see if he was wanted at the federal level," she said, glancing down at the papers in her hand. "His name is Ivan Brinkerhoff, Arthur's nephew from the Ukraine. Apparently Ivan makes his living by eliminating other people's problems, and I guess, as you started digging into what was going on with Adele, you became someone's problem. I haven't been able to get close to Arthur to ask him any questions. His doctors keep blocking our access, and the granddaughter—the real one—says she doesn't know anything."

"She's an assistant DA in San Francisco," I reminded the detectives. "Could she have any pull down here? Could she maybe have yanked on a few strings and gotten Cousin Ivan released?"

"So you suspect she has something to do with this?" O'Byrne leaned forward, resting her weight on her elbows. "Because I've got two dead women, a handful of lab-grown diamonds, an old man in a fugue state, and an international killer the feds yanked from us before we could even get a peep out of him."

"I think the first thing we need to ask is, why was Adele killed?" My attention drifted momentarily over to Montoya, who'd taken up residence at the end of the table. He stood as stiff as a sentinel, unwavering and not blinking but definitely keyed in on the conversation. "I was only there that night because of Stevens. Could he have tapped me to be there, Montoya? Did he ask for me by name, or did it just come up?"

"It just came up. I told him you or Dawson could probably do the surveillance for him," Montoya said with a shrug. "He was going to have his cousin Alex do it, but he and his husband were going to be out of town, so that wasn't an option. I can verify Alex and James were gone, and Rook wanted to get the security shakedown done as quick as possible because the property's owner was coming into LA soon to start work on the place. It was just supposed to be an easy job, and Rook figured a lot of it was pretty much install cameras here and maybe take a flamethrower to the garden."

"And instead I find a couple of adulterers with attack dogs," I replied, grimacing when I remembered the Doberman who'd tackled me was more interested in licking my face than chewing my nose off. "I think me finding Adele was a coincidence, but everything after that wasn't. The attack on Arthur was somebody looking for something. It could've even been the fake Marlena, because we didn't get a very good look at the shooter, but from what I remember, they were a lot smaller than Ivan."

"We haven't got a positive ID on her body yet. Even though lover boy told you they were lovers, he ain't talking," O'Byrne said. "They're running fingerprints on her now, and facial recognition is probably going to be screwy because the coroner tells me she had some work done on her face and body. Those hips were a lie, and that pretty face didn't start off as pretty as it was when you saw it. If her prints don't come back with something, we're going to have a Jane Doe to chase down. Dawson said she sounded like she was from back East, so we might do a few reach-outs toward that coast."

"If she was working with Ivan and the feds yanked him, maybe they also have an idea about who she is," Montoya pointed out. "Providing they're willing to share information."

"Let me talk to the agent who tagged me," O'Byrne murmured, shuffling through her stack of papers before coming up with what she'd been looking for. "You were right about one thing, Mac, the Brinkerhoffs' place looks like a damned museum. If I didn't know any better, I'd say they had close to thirty million dollars of artwork on their walls."

"So maybe that's why they killed Adele," I said, turning the theory over in my head. "I looked into lab-grown diamonds, and it's becoming a pretty huge industry. Even diamond companies are beginning to develop their own lines, marketing them as pristine works of art, polished by artisans with years of knowledge so you can't even tell the difference between one grown in a lab or one dug up from the dirt. If Arthur and Adele switched up their forgery from art—something easily traceable—to fake diamonds being passed off as authentic or maybe from one of those exclusive labs, you've got a motive to kill as well as a desire to find out what else they have in their inventory."

"Because the handful that we got from the body were good but not spectacular," she commented, tapping her pen against the table. "But why have Ivan go after you? Why was his girlfriend passing herself off as Marlena? What's the reason behind either one of those people to be in the picture?"

"I don't know, but we could start by asking Arthur and maybe put a couple of questions to that ex-cop neighbor of theirs," I suggested. "He could tell you whether or not he'd seen Ivan around, or the woman."

"What we really need to do is talk to Arthur Brinkerhoff himself," Montoya growled. "He can tell you what his wife was doing that night and probably why she was murdered."

"Maybe," O'Byrne said, pulling her mouth into a tight line. "Our problem is Arthur Brinkerhoff slipped into a coma about two hours ago and the doctors aren't sure if he's ever going to come out of it. So right now our problem is whether or not the LAPD is going to charge

McGinnis here with anything, and if they don't, I have to decide if he's going to stay on the case."

"That's not for you to decide, really." I stretched my legs out, trying to ease the ache in my knee. "Arthur Brinkerhoff wanted to find out who killed his wife, and his granddaughter gave me a buck as a retainer. I'm on the case whether you want me here or not. So see if you can cut me loose, O'Byrne, so I can get back to doing the job and hopefully not get my head shot off while doing it."

SIXTEEN

"YOU SURE you're up to this?" I asked Bobby as the elevator trundled its way up, dinging loudly as we passed each floor. "I mean, you were stabbed, dude. And my brother's not too fond of me right now."

"It's a flesh wound, Princess," he said, wiggling his arms loosely. "Look! All limbs are still attached, and even if they weren't, I'd Black Knight hop after you 'cause I can't trust you to stay out of trouble if I'm not around. Look what happened at your office. And as for Ichi, he and I had a long talk about this. The two of you need to talk that out. And I get it, he doesn't like violence, but I hate people getting away with shit even more. I've been your backup for years. Not going to stop now."

"Probably should make you a partner," I muttered, pressing the top floor's button once more just to give me something to do. "For all the shit you go through, you should at least get paid for it."

"Yeah, McGinnis and Dawson Investigations doesn't have a good ring to it," he rumbled back, a slight flush washing over his cheeks before disappearing as quickly as it came up. "Tell you what—you buy all the food and we'll call it even."

"I've seen you eat. I'd rather give you a paycheck. At least that way, I won't go broke," I muttered as the doors slid open. "Since O'Byrne can't get me into the room with Ivan, she said I could try for something out of their neighbor, that Watson guy. She's already made a pass at getting him to talk, but he ducked and dodged her."

"Watson's an old-school cop," Bobby grunted, following me out of the elevator. "Might not like seeing a woman with a badge."

"That was how she saw it," I agreed. "You know how those guys are. She's hoping we'll have better luck with him. I just don't know what he can give us. Hell, I'm not even sure what we're doing now. For all we know, it starts and ends with Ivan killing Adele to begin with, and we're just chasing our tails."

"That how you see it?" Bobby stopped short, lifting his eyebrow. "Because my gut says Ivan's just a tool and someone else is cranking the wrench."

"I'd agree. We just don't know why or who." Taking a quick skim down the hall, I spotted Watson's apartment, and farther down, the Brinkerhoffs' place at the end of the expanse. "Let's see what he's got to say. Then we can do a quick look at their place. If we see anything that jumps out at us, we can tell O'Byrne."

The hallway was carpeted in standard industrial-grade gray, but there were little touches of personality along the walls, most notably niches with flowers on shelves and bright splashes of color accenting the cut-ins where ornate mirrors hung above the arrangements, bouncing light about. Despite being windowless, the hall was wide enough not to feel claustrophobic. If the doorman who'd shaken us down for our IDs after we came into the glass-wrapped lobby wasn't a sign of an upper-class clientele, the wide-enough-to-ballroom-dance hallway was a clear indicator the people who lived in the building had money.

"How does an ex-cop afford this kind of place?" Bobby glanced up and down the hall. "Prime neighborhood. Underground parking."

"You made some big bucks investing in real estate when you were a baby cop, and I almost got my head blown off by my partner, who'd been tagged by his police-assigned therapist as a danger to society, and they hushed it up," I reminded him, nudging Bobby in the shoulder to keep moving. "Neither one of us is hurting for money here, Dawson. For all we know, he invented a new type of air in his garage during his off time. Maybe managed a boy band or two."

"Yeah, there's that. How do you want to play this?" Bobby fell into step next to me, bumping me aside after we reached the door. "What are we hoping to get out of this guy?"

"Should have had this conversation out in the car," I grumbled. "Okay, here's the thing. Watson's their friend, so he probably socialized with them, maybe even met a few of their other friends. Adele was out there to meet someone that night. She was probably killed where I found her, and O'Byrne hasn't found a connection to put Adele there. No one around the area she knew, but maybe it's just someone we haven't found yet. Watson might have some answers. He might not know it, though."

"Our boy Ivan isn't talking, but he seems to be more killer than criminal mastermind. So we're looking for someone the old man and his wife hooked up with recently. Maybe even someone who made them uncomfortable," he mulled, nudging me again. "Knock on the door, Princess. We can play this by ear and see where it goes."

"Do you know him?" I searched for a doorbell, but it seemed like the building was more old-school, depending on a brass knocker hanging from the middle of the door. "Watson, I mean. Did you ever run into him?"

"Do you know how many tens of thousands of cops have worn the uniform?" Bobby scoffed. "It isn't like retired LAPD cops all get together at the beach and sing 'The Lion Sleeps Tonight' around the bonfire. And if we did, don't you think you would've gotten an invitation?"

"Wouldn't do you any good to invite me," I snarked back. "I don't even know the words to that damn song."

The man who opened the door couldn't have been more of a stereotype if he tried.

I guess I was too used to Bobby. When I thought of retired cops, I thought of him working to keep himself fit and on top of his game. Truth be told, there's tons of cops who push the limits of their waistbands while on the job, and they were a dime a dozen after desk-sitting for years. George Watson was definitely one of those cops.

He was old-school LAPD, dragged up through the days of bloodied batons and race riots quelled with gunfire and sharp elbows to young kids' faces. His face was square, held up by a thick neck and embellished by a thinning silvery crew cut, the sides shorn down nearly to his skull, leaving a glittery fur wrap around the base of his head. His eyes were sharp, steely, and mean, and they flicked back and forth between us. It was easy to see the wheels turning behind them, shuffling through scenarios where Watson would gain control of any situation that might erupt.

Dressed in navy chinos and a tucked-in dark blue polo shirt, Watson gave us a pretty good idea of how he looked in the final years of his career. His chest was broad, jutted out over a spreading belly, but his hips were lean and his legs bordered on skinny. The only way I knew he had pencils for limbs was because a small white dog poked out from between the yards of fabric swaddling his legs, pulling them tight against his knees. The chinos were worn big to accommodate his belly, their pearly button straining against the heft pushing behind it. The dog barked once, then slipped back away, leaving its master to deal with the two men standing in the hallway.

He was not the kind of cop I would ever want to pull me over. Maybe I was prejudiced based on the tightening feeling in my gut when

I looked at him, but he seemed like the kind of guy who would break a taillight just to say he had a reason to search the trunk.

"Well if it isn't the faggot Dawson." Watsons's high-pitched voice didn't match his barrel-chested body. He sounded like he'd sucked on a helium balloon before he opened the door, but the menace in his eyes didn't subside, despite the light, teasing tone he affected. Glancing over at me, he nodded and asked, "Who's the gook?"

Wow. It'd been a long time since I'd heard *that* name.

I forget I'm half Japanese. It sounds stupid, but I was raised by a fairly stereotypical military man and the corn-fed, blond-haired woman he married after my mother left. While I pulled more of my father's Irish features, the shape of my eyes was definitely my mother's. I knew I looked a little Asian—definitely not as much as my older brother, Mike—but for the most part, I was pretty ethnically ambiguous. My eyes are greenish—or at least I was assuming they were, because that's what people told me, and apparently I was iffy on that color—and my hair was dark brown, lightening if I spent time in the sun.

But I'd grown up in the Midwest, and there were places we'd gone to live where how Mike looked got him into trouble. Or rather, trouble found him. He and I made frequent trips down to principals' offices, our knuckles bloodied and our faces bruised because somebody called Mike a name.

I'd learned to deflect a lot of that, and moving out to California definitely pushed much of that back into the far distant past because we were no longer different.

Watson brought that all back.

There were a lot of things I could say to him, a lot of things my mind actively reached for, sharpening the words so I could fling them into his face and maybe cut him down to the bone. At another time I might have even wanted to punch his face. Okay, I still wanted to punch his face, but the need wasn't as strong as it would've been when I was in my twenties.

Instead I said to Bobby, with a sarcastic grin plastered across my face, "So I guess he does know you."

"Shit, I *do* know him," Bobby muttered under his breath, ducking his head to give me a hard look, then glancing back up at the man chuckling at us. "You were out of Rampart, right, Watson?"

Bobby was in the same headspace I was, caught between wanting to turn Watson's nose into a squished meatball and us needing to get any information we could out of him. People tended to not want to answer questions after getting their faces punched in, so both of us silently agreed to swallow our pride and outraged decency to push forward.

I stepped back, mostly to take Watson out of punching range and also to let Bobby lead. It didn't take a rocket scientist to know Watson wasn't going to appreciate me asking him any questions, and his resistance to O'Byrne made a hell of a lot more sense now that we added racist bigot to the equation on top of old-school cop. I stood there pondering if racist bigot was actually redundant when I heard Watson offering us a couple of beers.

That's when I also noticed I'd been left standing outside in the hall while the two of them had gone into the condo. The tiny furry scarf masquerading as a dog stared up at me from its place at my feet, its face comically screwed up with a mixture of concern and apprehension, probably wondering why the door was open and I hadn't sought the safety of its home. Dogs get like that. Or at least some do. Honey didn't like to go outside unless one of us was within line of sight. It could have been because she'd been on the street for several years and wanted to make sure she always had access to a place with food and air-conditioning, but I liked to think she just wanted to make sure she could always see the people who loved her.

Mind you, she had an unrequited love affair with Neko, so Jae and I were quite aware where we stood in the rankings of her affections—right below bacon and the cat.

"Close the door behind you," Watson called out. "Muncie doesn't like the people next door on the other side. If he catches one whiff of that shit they call food when their door opens, he'll be inside of their house before you could even blink."

"Got it," I replied, stepping over the dog I assumed was Muncie. I thought to myself perhaps Muncie didn't hate them as much as Watson thought he did and was possibly looking for a new place to live. This assumption was partially validated when I closed the door and Muncie sighed with a resignation only previously heard by Chicago Cubs fans for decades before their epic win; then the dog toddled off toward the living room.

I followed the dog.

The beer Bobby handed me was cold and in a can, its sides announcing it'd been made by the pure waters of the Rocky Mountains. I'd been to Denver. I hadn't noticed its tap water as being something especially drinkable, but perhaps the beer factory faucet they used had a filter on. Knowing Watson would notice if I didn't at least drink half of it, I popped the tab and took a sip.

Whoever was in charge of cleaning the water filter on that faucet hadn't done his job in about seven years, and I forced myself to swallow the mouthful of septic tank overflow I'd forced past my lips.

Watson was playing catch-up with Bobby, going over stories about how things were in the late '80s and early '90s down at Central and Rampart. Mostly Watson did the talking, with Bobby nodding and grunting every so often. Those decades were a dark time for Los Angeles, especially if a man or woman wore a blue uniform and a badge. A lot of good cops retired out early, fatigued by fighting the good fight and most of the time battling their fellow officers, who were as corrupt and demoralizing as the chief of police during that time. Law enforcement back then was geared toward oppression and suppression, with different response times and courtesy given to a person mostly based on their race and ZIP code. There were still a lot of cops out there who would've been very much at home during that time in LAPD's history, and from the sounds of it, Watson seemed to really miss his late-night excursions through the dark streets, armed with his baton and shielded by a badge he never should've worn.

Not wanting to join in on their trip down a memory lane Bobby and I both never wanted to visit, I began to wander around the room, Muncie trotting behind me with his tongue sticking out and never coming closer than a yard.

The condo itself was a nice one, elegantly furnished in a style that had gone out of vogue about a decade ago. The view was spectacular, overlooking Downtown Los Angeles and the mountains beyond. Whoever designed the building knew what they were about, making the most of the main space by keeping it open, leaving a clear line of sight from the kitchen to the left of the front door over to the living room on the right. A hallway leading off the kitchen probably led to a bedroom or two, guessing by the spacing between the doors in the main hall.

But what really defined the space was that view. The condo's outside wall was pure glass, broken up only by the black lines of heavy-duty girders and framing, with the rest of the walls being a standard gypsum board painted Navajo white—the cheapest and most common color used by developers. Its faint tobacco-yellow tint actually went well with the brown leather sectional and recliners in the living room, their arrangement centered on the nearly movie-screen-sized television mounted on the wall the condo shared with the outer hallway.

Judging by the pictures scattered about a set of thinly populated bookshelves, I gathered someone actually not only married Watson but also bred with him. There was evidence of a second wife, a small Filipina woman with a broad face and a thin smile, squished up against Watson's massive frame in a variety of vacation shots, including what looked like a hunting trip where he brought down a small wild boar. Since the progression of children going from babies to adulthood were tall, freckled, blond-haired, and blue-eyed, I was guessing at the second wife, but I could be totally wrong about the whole thing and Watson's genetics simply stomped hers down into a whimpering pile of thready DNA.

A niche in the wall possibly held the most interesting thing in Watson's place—a painting I'd never seen before. It wasn't like I was up on classical paintings. Sure, I knew how to recognize a Warhol, mostly by the presence of the tomato soup can, and while my exposure to the arts had increased over the years of being with Jae, to the consternation of my beloved husband, I was one of those people who didn't really know art but knew what he liked when he saw it.

The painting didn't seem to fit my perception of Watson. For all I knew, the man had depths of character I know nothing about, but since he was currently regaling Bobby with a story about how he and his partner jumped a bunch of Mexican teens coming out of a convenience store, mistakenly thinking they had robbed the place instead of just having finished doing inventory for their father, who owned the market, I was going to stick by my judgment of the man.

One thing about being with Jae and having Ichi around was that I knew more about art and how various media looked. I'd learned that lesson while following the two of them through Santee Alley and flea markets. There'd been a few times when I stopped to look at a painting that drew my eye, only to have one of them yank me away from the booth once the artist started talking to me about buying it.

Jae often chided me about how an artist would never display their paintings out in the sun, and more importantly, purchasing an original piece of art was sometimes extremely pricey. I'd been to his gallery shows, and the price tags on his photos—placed there by the gallery owner—made me blink so much my eyes were dried out by the time I finished walking the floor. I was as proud as hell of his work, but it boggled my mind that somebody would pay thousands of dollars for a black-and-white picture of my torso he'd taken while I was standing in the shower.

But one of the most important things Jae and Ichi taught me was that I shouldn't be able to see the uninterrupted pattern of canvas in an oil painting. Thankfully, Ichi was there to catch me before I spent eight hundred dollars on a reproduction printed on a piece of canvas. There should have been paint, swoops of brushstrokes and passes of a palette knife, the surface uneven and marked by the artist's efforts. It was something I wouldn't have looked for, and I was thankful for the education.

As well as not spending that eight hundred dollars.

So that's how I knew—or at least based on what little I knew—that the woman with one breast out, swaddled in red cloth and holding what looked like a dead bird while surrounded by oddly happy people wasn't a reproduction. To one side of her was a trio of men, one particularly demonic-looking one in the forefront holding a basket of produce, with another two slightly behind him, seemingly caressing his arm with loving touches.

"Bet he got distracted by the booby and didn't notice the two gay guys on the side," I muttered to myself, and Muncie grunted, agreeing with me as he plopped his butt down to begin a rigorous investigation of his privates.

The painting looked old, aged in a way I'd seen in museums and not with the bright splashes of colors I'd seen in Ichi's and Jae's pieces once I began paying attention to what they were doing. It could've just been the different style of art, especially since I was pretty ignorant about historical pieces, but it still wasn't something I'd have thought Watson would hang in his living room. I could've been wrong, and his wife—the smiling woman in the photos—insisted on having it up to compete with the television taking up most of her living room, but still, it was at odds with practically everything in the room, including the man sitting in a recliner, gesturing with his beer can as he talked.

"You like that?" Watson's voice boomed through the living room, startling both me and Muncie. The dog yelped and scrambled off, his toenails doing a frenetic salsa on the wood floor. "Arty gave it to me after I fixed his dishwasher. If I didn't know better, I'd think he was one of you guys, but he's okay. Fruity as hell what with painting all the time, but from what he said, most of the classical painters back then were men, so it is what it is. Told me to pick one out, so I grabbed that one. Had a naked woman on black velvet when I married Marie, but she made me take it down, so I figured I could at least get one tit out with this one, and she couldn't say a thing because it's all foo-foo and shit."

Bobby rolled his eyes, and I silently congratulated myself for correctly guessing why Watson liked the painting.

Taking another look at the painting, I spotted Brinkerhoff's signature, a bold yellow scrawl over a black rectangle on the lower corner. Despite his small stature and unassuming personality, it seemed like he was proud of his work, at least based on the size of his autograph. Something bugged me about it, but I couldn't figure out why.

"Did he tell you anything about it?" I looked over my shoulder at Watson, who'd gone back to his conversation with Bobby. There was little hope of steering the man toward any other topic besides himself, but I really needed Bobby to pump him for as much information as he could get about the Brinkerhoffs' social circle. "Like who he was copying?"

"Copying?" Watson laughed, sending a spray of spittle over the coffee table in front of him. "He wasn't copying anything. Arthur just sits down and begins painting. Not like my little girl, who would try to draw stuff out of one of those Japanese comic books she likes. There'd be some pencil marks on the canvas, but he would just go to town. I used to tease him about doing paint by numbers, because he'd be finished with the thing in about a week and someone would come by and pick up the painting after it was dry enough. I guess that's how they pay the rent, because they never talked about working. He had a bunch of them he said weren't good enough to sell, so I picked out that one. Painted down the black line so he had a good place to sign, and I took it down to the framing shop. You finished with that beer? Want another one?"

"Nah, I'm good." I held up my can of fermented Denver tap water, sloshing it about so Watson could hear it was still mostly full. "But why don't you tell us about the guy who'd come pick up the paintings? He's probably wondering what the hell happened to Arthur and Adele, especially since no one's been around to tell him anything. Maybe we can reach out and let him know what's going on so he doesn't get too worried."

SEVENTEEN

THE SIZZLE of cheese hitting the hot pan was loud enough to bring Honey in from the living room. She lived in the eternal hope of getting food directly from the skillet, but Jae's hard-and-fast rule of no dogs in the cooking area meant she was bound by the invisible wall keeping her from getting too close to the stove. So she set up shop as a floppy blond beggar by the dining room table. If there was one thing the dog enjoyed about the walls we'd taken down between the bundle of small rooms at the back of the house, it was that she could have a clear line of sight whenever the possibility of food popped up.

"You're not getting any of this, dog," I said, fully aware I was going to take the end piece of the bread loaf, tuck a piece of American cheese into it, fold it in half, then microwave it for the dog.

There hadn't been a plan for that when I started my dinner, but the dog knew me. She'd played on my sense of guilt from the day she came into the house. Thank God for Jae or I would pretty much have to roll her around like one of those balls people sit on in front of their desks to build up their core strength. I was an easy mark, and Jae was the only thing keeping her from looking like an oversized tribble. I would've tossed her a piece of cheese from the kitchen, but I'd learned the hard way about breaking Jae's rules for the dog. The first thing I learned was that the dog could not keep a secret and was more than willing to take the tidbit I'd given her to snack on and eat it at Jae's feet. The second thing I learned was that the universe hated me, because the last time I gave her something when Jae wasn't around, she saved it until he came home, then promptly ate it at Jae's feet.

She never did that if I gave her something outside of the kitchen. So Honey's version of a grilled cheese was going to have to wait until I was done with mine.

There was something about eating a stack of slightly burned grilled bread stuffed with plastic-wrap American cheese that brought me comfort. It wasn't something I could actually eat with my husband around, mostly because Jae questioned the preservatives I was gulping down in big bites and didn't understand that a properly made grilled cheese sandwich required a good char. The bread had to be fluffy and white, then slathered with butter—or mayonnaise, a variation I'd recently learned—and placed into a medium-hot pan to be cooked to a darkness even Satan would approve of. The cheese had to be cheap and made by the same people who brought us Americans our neon-orange macaroni and cheese in a box.

And by stack, I mean four. With Jae going out for the evening with Ichi, I'd been left on my own, and I was looking forward to getting myself sick on processed foods, drinking a few beers, and then falling asleep on the couch until he came home.

"He's going to give me shit about not eating vegetables," I muttered to myself, looking into the drink fridge for something to go with my sandwiches. "Does pumpkin ale count as a vegetable? Screw it, I'd rather have a Harp."

I'd just finished pulling Honey's snack out of the microwave when someone knocked on the door. Catching myself before I tossed the dog her sandwich from the kitchen, I called her over to heel so she would follow me into the foyer, where I could give her cheese and bread without her thinking she was getting away with something. Another knock on the door sounded before I could open it, and a quick check through the peephole showed me a very haggard-looking O'Byrne standing on my front stoop.

"You okay?" I stepped aside, and after I opened the door, I was chagrined I hadn't answered it immediately, considering how tired she looked. It was still early, about eight in the evening, but I knew the hours an LAPD detective worked. It wasn't a nine-to-five job by any means, and the truly dedicated usually work themselves into the ground every day, only to wake up the next morning to do it all over again. O'Byrne was definitely one of those cops. As she went by me, something Jae-like crawled up out of me from wherever it'd been hiding and came out of my mouth. "Have you eaten? Let me get you some food."

"Food would be good if you got some, but I've got to ask you a few things officially first." She sniffed at the air. "Something burning?"

"I made grilled cheese." She nodded, and once again I reassured myself that O'Byrne was good people. Only the true connoisseur of trash food understood a delicate touch of burn was needed on the bread to make it a true grilled cheese sandwich. "Want to come into the kitchen and talk first? I could make you a couple. Dog will probably be happy. Means she'll get another end piece if I can dig it out."

"This is actually kind of serious, McGinnis," Dell replied, pulling out her notebook from her jacket. "When I say officially, I mean I actually have to question you about your whereabouts this afternoon and early this evening. Is Jae around? It might be best if we have privacy while I take care of this."

"He's out with Ichi. They're probably not going to be back until around midnight. It's just me, Honey here, and Neko, but that's it." The hunger I'd stoked up in anticipation of my sandwiches quickly faded away. O'Byrne was deadly serious, wearing a cop face without any hint of friendship in it. "What's this about? Do I need to sit down for this?"

"We can take this into the living room and get it over with," O'Byrne suggested. "And I hate to ask you this, but is there anything on you that I need to be worried about? Gun? Knife?"

I stopped midstep on my journey toward the living room and turned back to face her. Something definitely had gone wrong, and I was now suddenly in O'Byrne's crosshairs. It was hard not to be resentful of it, especially after everything we'd gone through, but I also understood she had a job to do, even if it meant I was in the hateful position of being under suspicion for something I didn't even know what it was yet.

After taking a deep breath, I answered her calmly, "I've got a couple of Glocks in a gun safe over there in the hall closet and another one upstairs with a trigger lock in the dresser. The only knife I've touched recently was the butter knife I used on the bread for my sandwiches."

"Would you have a problem turning over your weapons if I asked for them?" She studied me carefully, her dark eyes unreadable and hard.

"What exactly do you think I've done?" There was every possibility O'Byrne was there to take me in for something. I just didn't know what. "And no. You want my weapons? You can take them. Just give me a receipt so I get them back. Now you going to tell me what's going on? Or am I going to have to sit in the back of a cop car and be taken down to Central instead of eating the sandwiches I've made?"

"The living room is fine. I hate this as much as you do, Mac," O'Byrne said, probably using my old nickname to soften any hard edges the conversation formed over our relationship. "It's just that someone got to Ivan Brinkerhoff in the hospital earlier this evening, and I just need to make sure it wasn't you. Because you've got to admit, finding out he died from a bullet hole straight through his forehead is going to lead a lot of people to you first, and if I don't ask these questions, they're going to come after you, and there's nothing I would be able to do to protect you."

GRILLED CHEESE sandwiches don't taste as good unless they are hot enough for the cheese to burn the roof of your mouth. Mine were just going to have to wait until O'Byrne was done with me, and if I were a cruel man, I would make her eat two of the cold ones just to get back at her. But I'm not that kind of guy.

Still, I was mourning the death of my crispy dinner as she made herself comfortable on the couch across of me.

"Can you tell me where you were this afternoon?" O'Byrne began, scribbling something down. I imagined it would be the time and place of our interview, because that's what I would've written down. Reconstructing a conversation into a report was only as good as the details laid down, and if there was one thing I knew about O'Byrne, she liked to keep her details straight. "Any approximate times would be helpful. As well as anyone you were with."

"Well, I started off the afternoon with Bobby—Robert Dawson— interviewing Arthur Brinkerhoff's neighbor, George Watson. We gained access to the building around two thirty in the afternoon, signing in at the security counter, then going upstairs using the elevator. We were with Watson for about an hour and a half. I got some information about paintings Brinkerhoff did—Arthur, not Ivan or any other Brinkerhoff— and discovered there was a courier who would pick up canvases Arthur finished every so often." I'd told her this on the phone earlier but it was good to catch up. "I didn't have a picture of Ivan, but I think it would be good to put one in front of Watson to see if that's who was moving Arthur's paintings."

"What did you do after you finished up with Watson?" O'Byrne nodded, reaching for the bottle of water I'd left her on the apothecary chest we used as a coffee table.

"Well, since we weren't able to gain access to Arthur's apartment to look at any of the paintings he had in there, I took Bobby home. Since Dawson lives next to Little Tokyo and we were all the way on the east side of Downtown, it took me about forty-five minutes—maybe fifty—to get him over there." I thought back to what we'd done along the way.

"Actually maybe a little bit more. I stopped for gas off of Olympic because we were avoiding the freeways, so I've got a receipt for that. I had to go inside because we wanted something cold to drink, so I grabbed a couple of iced teas. After I dropped him off, I drove home up Wilshire. I didn't get home until about six."

"Was anybody here when you got home?"

"Ichi had just gotten here. His bike should be in the carport. Jae gave me a kiss, and they hung around for about an hour before leaving. I took a shower and watched a little bit of a ballgame, then went into the kitchen to make something to eat. That's when you knocked on the door." I did some mental calculations, and while my timeline was fairly tight, it left me open in certain spots. "I guess it all depends upon when they found Ivan, because I didn't have anybody with me on the ride from Dawson's place to home and didn't stop anywhere along the way. I also have about an hour between Jae leaving and you arriving where the only alibi I've got is Honey, and she's easily bribed with food."

She was still writing long after I stopped talking. I began to regret leaving my unopened Harp in the drink fridge, and I really mourned my now totally soggy grilled cheese sandwiches. She finally looked up when I'd gotten to trying to figure out how I could hide the ones I'd made in the freezer for some later date and make new ones. Jae would find them, and he would question my sanity. They would be easy enough to eat later when heated up in a microwave, but tonight I really wanted them hot and charred.

Also my face still kind of hurt from where the blown-out glass cut me, and it was hard to believe it was just a few days ago that I'd stood on Arthur Brinkerhoff's front porch, about to knock on his front door and offer up my services to find out who murdered his wife.

"So would you say you were in the Downtown Los Angeles area at about four thirty?" O'Byrne's handwriting was precise, but she didn't lift her pen up when she wrote, so everything was connected. It looked more like the lettering on the sign of our favorite Indian food place—swirls and dips connected with lines in between. It didn't matter really, except it made it impossible to read upside down. "Where does Dawson live again?"

I gave her Dawson's address, pointing out that my brother Ichi lived with him since they were married, so technically it was the Dawson-Tokugawa residence, but that just got me a withering look. I once again reevaluated my determination to offer up hot grilled cheese sandwiches to her instead of the soggy cold ones waiting in the kitchen. It was all going to depend upon how much I liked her at the end of this interview and whether or not we ended the interview with me in handcuffs going down to Central. Because in that case, the cat would probably get the grilled cheese sandwiches, and I would have to make yet another phone call to Jae to come bail me out of jail.

Except California no longer had a bail system, and my release would be dependent upon a judge deciding whether or not I was a flight risk.

With my luck, the judge would not only decide I was a flight risk but find me a cellmate I'd arrested when I'd been a cop.

"Did they take Ivan to the same hospital Arthur is in?" Not knowing the protocols about taking care of detainees who needed severe medical attention, there was a good chance he ended up in Cedars-Sinai, right alongside his uncle. "What time did they find him? Should I get a lawyer? Am I going to get my Miranda rights read to me? Are you Miranda?"

"What the fuck does that mean? You know my name is not Miranda." So not only did O'Byrne deserve a cold grilled cheese sandwich, she also did not recognize a line from one of my favorite movies. Now I was going to have to reevaluate our friendship, but still, no sign of handcuffs or a Miranda card. "I'm going to ask for your guns just to totally exclude you, but the timeline for you to have gotten to him, gotten off a shot, and knocked out the policeman outside of his door is too tight. Especially with LA traffic. I'm not saying you're free and clear, Mac, but it looks unlikely. I've got to have all of my t's crossed on this because Marlena Brinkerhoff is kicking up a stink. Ivan was two stories below Arthur, and now she's convinced someone is going to come and kill her grandfather."

"She's not wrong," I pointed out. "Even assuming our fake Marlena was the shooter at the house and we're pointing at Ivan as the guy who killed her out on the street, we now have a third person who popped him in a guarded hospital room. And we still don't know why they came after Arthur and killed Adele. Although I do have a theory."

"Why don't you make me that sandwich you promised me while I go lock up your guns in the trunk of my car?" Dell stood up, stretching out her lean body until I heard her back and hips crack. "Then you can tell me all about the crazy theory you've got. Because right now, I'll take anything to get the captain off my ass and to close this case."

"I can do that," I murmured, moving Honey off of my right foot. "It might take a bit to make those sandwiches. Takes a while to burn the bread just right, and I still like you, so do you want two or are you hungry enough to choke down three?"

"Two, but I'll take mine with a beer," she replied, closing her notebook. "I am officially off duty as of right now, and unless you've got a smoking gun or bloodied knife you found in the alleyway by Watson's, I'm going to spend an hour with you trying to figure this shit out, then I'm going to go home so I can do this shit all over again tomorrow."

SIX NEARLY black grilled cheese sandwiches later and most of two bottles of beer put O'Byrne and me in a much better space. Honey scored part of a cold sandwich, getting it offered up to her piece by piece by a well-fed O'Byrne. I didn't mind her taking my guns. Or at least at the moment I didn't. I would have to reevaluate that conviction if I found I would need one of them over the next couple of weeks, but it wasn't like I didn't have an older brother who owned a security firm with a weapons arsenal that included a helicopter with machine guns on it. And if Mike didn't own a helicopter with machine guns on it, I was going to be sadly disappointed. What's the use of having a security firm if you couldn't have a helicopter armed to the teeth?

Neko deigned to drag herself out of wherever she'd been in the house, sitting on the arm of the couch at my elbow, selflessly willing to choke down a bite of gooey cheese and bread so I wouldn't have to do it myself. There was a bit more white around her face than there had been before, and there were times she could barely stir up enough energy to open her eyes to swat at the dog, but she seemed to do okay hitting Honey in the face just by pure instinct. Of course she was a tiny thing who'd survived a building falling on her, so I suspect the only way death was ever going to come for her was if she was asleep.

And as anyone who has a cat in their life knows, they never sleep.

"Should you be feeding her that?" O'Byrne gestured at the black furball purring up a storm at my side. "I mean, is cheese good for cats?"

"She's five days older than God, and if she wants grilled cheese, she can have it," I explained, holding another tidbit up for Neko to chew on. "If she wants a salmon, I will fly up to Alaska, learn how to fly fish, either catch one or fight a bear for one, and bring it home so she can turn her nose up at it."

"You must love Jae a lot," she snorted, taking a sip from her bottle.

"I love this cat a lot," I corrected, scratching at Neko's ears. "Do you have space in your brain to talk about what I think is going on, or do you want to do this tomorrow morning?"

"Hit me up," O'Byrne muttered, stealthily trying to hide a burp. But despite the lack of noise, I recognized the face she made behind her hand. "Tell me what you think is going on and then tell me who's behind it, because right now, I don't give a shit about the why as much as I do about who."

"I haven't figured out who, but I've got a couple of guesses. It all depends upon who they were working with, and by *they*, I mean Adele and Arthur." I gave Honey the last bit of crust on my plate and leaned forward. "Let me show you something. This is a picture of the painting Dawson and I saw hanging in Watson's apartment. It's a little blurry because I had to take it on the sly, but there's something weird about the signature. I couldn't figure out what was bothering me about it until I came home and showed it to Jae. See, that's the best thing about being married to an artist, you wind up watching some crazy shit streamed from YouTube on your TV instead of actually watching television shows. Some of the stuff is pretty interesting, but it's not something that sticks in my head. Stupidly enough, *this* did."

The iPad Jae used to sketch on was still open to the photo I'd taken at Watson's. O'Byrne made murmuring sounds of appreciation for the painting, correctly identifying it as a Rubens. The only reason I knew that was because Jae told me. So she was one up on me there. I didn't get a weird look until after I zoomed in on Arthur's signature in the corner.

"Watson said he picked this painting out of a bunch of them lying against a wall. He told us Arthur took the canvas, made a black rectangle with some paint, and then signed it." I pointed out the black rectangle with Arthur's name scrawled in bright yellow. "Do you see the difference between the black part and the rest of the painting?"

"The painting looks shiny," O'Byrne said, scooting over to get a better look at what I was pointing out. "So what?"

"One of the things Jae likes to watch is painting restoration. And I'm not talking about a couple of dings and scratches. There's this guy that fills in big chunks of missing old paint and repairs torn canvases.

He narrates as he goes, but the cool thing about it is he explains that everything he does to the painting is reversible. He uses special paints that can be removed a lot easier than standard oils or acrylics." I zoomed in even tighter until we could see the even line of black covering a good portion of the canvas's corner. The ebony cover was unforgiving, as deeply pitch and light-sucking as a monolith coming down to the ground and scaring a bunch of monkeys. "The one thing that stuck with me was something he always says. He does this thing to the original painting that glosses it up so he can see what the final colors are when he varnishes it at the end."

"This all sounds very cool, but I don't see what this has to do with anything," O'Byrne said, nodding toward my beer. "How many of those have you had?"

"Just the one. Hear me out. The reason he has to do that is because the paint he uses doesn't have any oils in it. So it doesn't have the same sheen as regular oil paint, and he needs to be able to color match with what's already there. Once he's done, he varnishes the whole thing, and you can't tell where the restoration is. Well, unless he does that crosshatch painting technique, but I only saw that once, and it looked weird. But most of the time, it's flawless. But the paint is matte until he finishes it up." With a flick of my finger, I restored the painting to the full screen. "That black part is what the paint looks like before the restorer finishes his work. The rest of Watson's painting has already been varnished. If Arthur was doing these to give away or to sell, his signature would be under that layer of varnish. And why would he put that big black rectangle there?"

"So what are you thinking?" O'Byrne took the iPad from me, studying the painting closer.

"I think if we removed that black rectangle, we'd find Rubens's signature underneath it. Maybe there's something about this painting that he didn't think was good enough to pass off as an original or maybe even one made by a student, but I'm thinking Arthur Brinkerhoff never stopped passing off forgeries." Neko demanded another pet, and I picked her up to cuddle her in my lap. "I think someone figured out he was still working his magic and tried to blackmail them. That's why Adele was out there. I think she was paying somebody off, and that somebody knew those diamonds she had on her were lab grown. That's why they killed her."

"And if Arthur was still doing forgeries, chances are Adele still had either a stash in their old house or was still pulling enough jobs," she said, narrowing her eyes. "She was an older woman. Getting into somebody's house would be kind of hard for her. They'd notice somebody's grandmother trying to break in."

"Not if she was their lover," I said with a smile. "Remember how I told you I met her? Wrapped up in a leather corset, doing a BDSM scene with a younger woman? I checked something when I came home today. That house I found her at was burglarized three months later. The only thing taken was the woman's jewelry. So yeah, I think the Brinkerhoffs never gave up their life of crime. Just like they never gave up that house. Now we've just got to find where they've hidden their loot and who the hell is ballsy enough to try to blackmail a couple of old criminals."

EIGHTEEN

O'BYRNE AND I kicked around a few options, eventually even eating the cold grilled cheese sandwiches after giving them a quick trip into a hot skillet to warm them up. She wasn't convinced that the forgeries were the reason Adele was murdered, but the attack on Arthur tied both of the Brinkerhoffs to what was going on. It was the only thing I could think of. No one had found anything in either Brinkerhoff residence to lead us to believe Adele was still operating as a thief, but my quick look at the burglary stats for the neighborhood I'd tracked her to on my first case was telling. Not only had the house I'd found her at been hit. So had the surrounding homes.

"I'm going to need evidence of the wife stealing and fencing jewelry," O'Byrne said after swallowing a mouthful of water. We'd switched away from beer nearly an hour ago, needing to keep an open mind and clear head about the case, but I was longing for a sip of whiskey, mostly because my body creaked after all of the abuse I'd done to it over the past week or so. "We can't ask Arthur. Doctors have him under heavy sedation. And since Marlena wasn't aware of her grandparents still owning that house by the studios, I don't think we can count on her to give us a lot of information."

"You guys went over the condo, right?" I asked, grunting when O'Byrne gave me a nod. "And there was nothing at the house but someone still looking for something after Adele was murdered. Since Ivan and the fake Marlena are taken out of the equation, we're still left with one person unaccounted for, and we don't know where Arthur's paintings were going."

"The granddaughter might have documentation about a storage space." O'Byrne eased back into the sofa, groaning when the cushions cradled her lean body. "You're right about someone trying to find something. And judging from the bodies falling everywhere, Arthur didn't tell his attacker where to look. Wherever this third person is, they're pretty ruthless. We can speculate Ivan knew about what his aunt and uncle were up to, based on his own criminal activity, but Marlena seems pretty sharp. It's odd she wouldn't have suspected anything."

"You like her for this?" I turned that option over in my mind, poking at it gently. "Seems kind of weird she would work hard to get to the point of being an assistant district attorney only to throw it all out for a bit of sparkle and fake paintings. Especially since the diamonds Adele had were fake."

"Apparently even fake diamonds are worth a shit-ton, Mac. It all depends on how they're branded and where they come from. I'm going to see if I can get the financials hurried up through the system. I want to know how much money the Brinkerhoffs have and how steady their income is. If we find out they're getting some pennies-on-the-dollar pension from somewhere, we'll know we're on the right track of something, because there is no way in hell they can afford that condo, especially if they didn't sell that house." She stifled a yawn, but it was still enough to trigger a teeth-bearing gape from Neko. She was the only cat I knew who reacted to a human yawning, or it could be she took it as a sign of aggression and was returning the favor. "Town houses and condos like that usually come with some kind of storage area in the garage. I don't think Marlena is all too keen about us poking around in her grandparents' life anymore, so it's probably going to have to cost me a favor with the judge to get a warrant. I don't want to burn that favor unless I know I'm going to find something."

A murmur of Korean followed by a burst of masculine laughter drifting through the open jalousies told me Ichi and Jae were back at the house. I didn't understand what they were saying. My Korean pretty much began and ended at food, smut talking, "I love you," and calling Jae the wrong word for babe. He found it hilarious. I used to find it embarrassing, but a silly thing we shared, and I was okay with it. That didn't mean I wished I could be better at languages, because hardly any of it stuck, but I could order a Korean dinner like nobody's business.

Honey was off the couch as soon as she heard the key in the door, dancing her way across the living room with a peculiar slide shuffle she only did when Jae came home. He liked to say she was happy when she heard me come up the walk, but considering I'd spotted her through the window, crashed out on the couch more than a few times when I got through the front door, I politely and respectfully called my husband a liar.

Two seconds later even the cat abandoned us, mewling her way in a gentle trot toward the man she loved the most.

"If she's telling you she hasn't been fed, she's lying," I called out to Jae. "She got a whole can of seafood pâté and then ate some of the dog's food too."

"Why did you give the dog a grilled cheese sandwich?" Jae asked, hidden from my view by the wall separating the foyer and the living room. "She's got a whole sandwich here. And don't tell me you made her an end piece in the microwave, because this is a full sandwich. And it looks like you cooked it with a black crayon, so I know it's yours."

"Didn't we eat all of them?" I muttered at O'Byrne.

"I might have given her half of mine when we were in the kitchen, but I figured she was a dog, she would just eat it," O'Byrne hissed back. "Why does your dog have a food Nazi? And why is your husband a food Nazi?"

"Because if I let him feed her human food, she's going to look like one of those giant rocks on Costa Rica," Jae said, padding into the living room while cradling Neko to his shoulder. He leaned over, taking a kiss from my mouth, then frowned at the collection of beer bottles, water glasses, and plates on the apothecary chest. "Tell me you had something besides bread and cheese and beer tonight for dinner."

"O'Byrne and I both had a package of Raspberry Zingers." I snatched one of the wrappers nearly hidden by one of the plates, then wrinkled it at him. "So a little bit of coconut and maybe some raspberry jam. Does that count?"

"Would it kill you to eat a salad once in a while?" Jae shook his head, smiling at O'Byrne. "Hi, Dell. Tell me he talked to you about something besides shop."

"Well, since it's my policy never to lie to people I like, I think it's time for me to go home." O'Byrne stood up, making a grab for the dishes, but Jae fended her off. "I can at least help clean up."

"I'll do it. The food at the showing was horrible, so I'm going to throw together something for Ichi and me to eat." Jae gave me an assessing look. "Should I just make enough for the two of us? Or are you going to pick through my dinner and eat half of it, so I should make more?"

I returned his look, taking in the pleasant view of his muscular body encased in black jeans and a tight T-shirt. "I don't know. What are you going to make?"

"Probably some bulgogi from the freezer and rice." Shaking his head, Jae put Neko down on the couch. "Never mind. I already know the answer. I'll make enough for the three of us. Dell, I'll walk you out, because it looks like my husband is way too comfortable to move."

"I can move." I sat up but didn't go farther than scooting forward on the couch cushion. O'Byrne waved me off, chuckling.

"I'll let you know about the warrant if we need it. I'll see about a storage space. We've still got the house on lockdown. Maybe want to swing by there again and just take another look. I don't think we missed anything, but you never know. There could be a piece of paper somewhere in there that didn't seem important at the time." Dell nodded a hello to Ichi, passing my baby brother by with a quick pat on his shoulder. "Good to see you, Tokugawa. I still need to stop by your place to get that ink we talked about. I just need a good four to five hours of time at one stretch to get that first sitting in."

"My table will always be empty for you, Dell," Ichi reassured her, Honey hot on his heels as he headed toward the other couch. "Just let me know when."

He stepped over my legs, not making eye contact with me as he went by. I waited for him to get settled, then followed Dell out, ignoring Jae shooing me back into the living room. My husband was playing peacekeeper, and while I appreciated it, it would be pretty shitty of me to not see Dell to the door. I would offer to walk her to her car, but she had a gun, and between the two of us, a mugger would be better off attacking me. That way, they could probably survive the experience. I knew Dell. She fought dirty and with an intent to kill.

In a lot of ways, she reminded me of Neko.

"Call me after you get over there tomorrow," she said from the front stoop. The porch light wasn't doing her any favors, but I also knew offering her a bed would get me a middle finger and a snort. "I'm going to see if we can get into the Brinkerhoff apartment through Marlena first. If your theory is right, then maybe there's a record of who's picking up the paintings and where they're going. Maybe even a big red sign that says here's the murderer."

"Let me know whenever that happens." I laughed at her flipped-up hand.

"Thanks for understanding about the guns," O'Byrne murmured, slanting a glance toward the kitchen, where Jae was rattling about. "I hated asking you for them. I just didn't have a choice."

"No. I get it. It's okay." I poked at the edges of my emotions, looking for any anger or discomfort about O'Byrne's requests and the stupidly necessary need to eliminate me as Ivan's killer. While the timeline of my afternoon pretty much excluded me, it was always better to make sure I was above reproach. At least she had enough faith in me not to take me off of the case. "Not like I was carrying them around anyway. I tried for a day after Ivan came after us in the alleyway, but the weight felt wrong. I'm probably being naïve, because we talked it all out and Jae was fine with me carrying, but I don't think *I* am yet. This way I've got an excuse to just take a pocket knife and my sharp wit with me."

"Well, at least the pocketknife will be useful," she shot back with a wink. "I'll talk to you tomorrow, Mac. And thanks for the grilled cheese and the beer."

I closed the door and stood in the foyer, debating which conversation I was willing to take on. To the right of me was the kitchen and Jae. I could go in there and talk to him about O'Byrne removing the guns from our house to exclude me for murder or I could go to the left and sit down with my younger brother, maybe even smooth over the crinkles between us. What wasn't an option was to head straight up the stairs and hide until everything went away. I did enough of that in my life before Jae, and I wasn't going to go back to that as my default reaction.

Even if I *really* wanted to.

Honey made up my mind for me, because she tottered over to the threshold of the living room, cocked her head, and gave me a silly goofy grin, barking once as if to scold me. Her tail was going a mile a minute, furiously wagging in a circular motion with nearly enough torque to lift her ass off the ground. If I didn't go into the living room, the dog was going to helicopter her way up to the ceiling, and I probably was never going to hear the end of it from Jae.

Or at least that's what I told myself as I scooped up the canine rag mop and went to beard the lion in my den.

"Do you want something to drink?" I jerked my head back toward the kitchen. "There's beer, bottles of water, and some iced tea. Both green and black. I think the green is actually popcorn, but it's pretty good."

"Tea would be good. Any kind." My brother's words were heavy with his Tokyo-Japanese accent, clipped and formal. I could nearly hear the gears in his throat grind as he finally spat out, "Thank you."

"He's as bad as Mike," I muttered at my husband, retrieving a couple of bottles of popcorn green tea from the drink fridge. Jae barely looked up from the massive amounts of vegetables he was chopping, but he spared me a small smile. "Did he tell you anything? He's still pissed off at me. He and Mike hold grudges. I don't know why I bother trying to talk to either one of them."

"You turned a man's hands into scrapple using an old phone. So I would have to say that you're not one to talk about holding grudges," Jae said quietly, fiercely mincing a bunch of green onions. "Go talk to your brother and work this out. I'm making us something to eat."

I looked at what he'd assembled on the counter, giving him a skeptical look. "You look like you're about to open a salad buffet. Are you actually cooking all of this or are you trying to give us time to get into a fight?"

"I've got some bulgogi thawing out in the microwave, and I'm going to make *soon dubu chigae*. The rice is going to take thirty minutes. That's how long you and Ichi have." His knife began moving again, expertly gutting a hapless jalapeno minding its own business on the chopping board. If ever he murdered me, I took great comfort in knowing he could probably fillet my corpse like he did the California yellowtail Bobby and I caught when we went deep-sea fishing. His blade stopped moving, but his gaze was as sharp. "Go fix things with your brother. He hates this is between you."

"Then why doesn't he start the conversation?" I muttered, pinching a bit of bean sprouts from a bowl and popping them into my mouth.

"He won't have a chance to if you stand here and talk to me in the kitchen," Jae sniped back. "Go away. I'm trying to cook. You're worse than the dog."

And with that, I fled, taking a bowl of kimchee and a pair of wooden chopsticks with me as I went.

"Here." I held out one of the bottles to Ichi, setting the kimchee down on the apothecary chest, making sure it was between us. He took the chopsticks, going through the ritual of removing them from the paper sleeve they'd come in and checking them for splinters. I wasn't offended. I was going to do the same thing in a few seconds. "Do they really give you shit in Japan if you rub those really cheap ones together to get the splinters off?"

"If you're eating someplace where the chopsticks are so poor quality that you risk getting a piece of wood in your mouth, they're going to expect you to rub them together. So no one like that would take offense," Ichi replied, picking a green leaf sliver of kimchee from the bowl. "It's considered rude if you're doing it at a restaurant or a ramen house, but they also wouldn't serve you those kinds of chopsticks. These are okay. I like the kind you don't have to pop apart."

"Me too," I agreed. "Mostly because I can never pop them apart evenly. And don't talk to me about the trick of separating them with equal force near where they're joined because it's just easier if I hand them over to Jae and give him puppy-dog eyes so he does it for me."

We picked through the kimchee slowly, ignoring the conversation we were meant to have. About three pieces in, the fire finally hit my throat, and I once again regretted marrying somebody who had a cast-iron mouth and made his own kimchee. Just as I was wondering if I was going to have to say something, Ichi cleared his throat.

"When I was growing up, everything I learned about America was through television and movies." He furrowed his brow, lost in the contemplation of his kimchee bowl. "When she was dying, our mother used to talk about the two of you once in a while. She would wonder how you looked. How you turned out. I promised myself I would at least meet you and Mikio one day. It wasn't until my father married that I realized I was no longer welcome in his family, so I came looking for the two of you."

"And you definitely found us," I said, cracking my iced tea open. "I know I was kind of an asshole to you in the beginning. Lot of anger I had to work through."

"It was understandable. Your father told you she died, and for us—as a traditional Japanese family—she didn't have a right to you anymore. I know that's hard to understand from an American perspective. It was hard for me to understand how you felt until my father began his second family and my name was no longer important to him." Ichi set his chopsticks down, resting their pepper-sauce-stained ends against the rim of the bowl. "I hated growing up as a Tokugawa. Everything in my life was laid out for me. My clothes. My schools. My behavior. Even my friends. There were expectations—no, *requirements*—to being Tokugawa Masahiro's son. And I hated every minute of it because it felt like I was dying before I even had a chance to live."

Swallowing the sip of tea I'd taken, I nodded, then said, "My father was the same way. And we all know how well that turned out."

Despite his somber expression, Ichi barked a short laugh. "You and I aren't so different there. Mike likes being traditional, and in a lot of ways, so do I, but I also want to live on my own terms. I love being an artist. I love tattooing. I love telling stories with ink, and nothing makes me happier than the look of joy on someone's face when I wipe their skin clean and reveal the piece of themselves I've pulled up from inside of them.

"Or at least nothing made me happier until I found you and Mike," he murmured. "Then I fell in love with Bobby. And suddenly I was the richest man in the world, with everything I've ever dreamed of. So, I am asking you as your younger brother and the name beneath yours in this family registry, to please understand how scared I am about maybe losing any of you."

I didn't need to see the tears in Ichi's eyes or hear the thickening of emotion in his voice to know my brother was overwhelmed. He trembled when I pulled him into a hug, his fists knotting into my T-shirt as he refused to cry. I swallowed, trying to choke down the pain in my own throat, tiny razor blades left over from words I'd held back in arguments with my own father. If anyone understood Ichi's fear, it was me. I'd reached a point of my own life where I was happy, and I knew the depths of loss more than anyone.

"Fucking Bobby doesn't take this seriously," he growled against my shoulder. "He was stabbed. Both of you were shot at. And I'm more scared than angry, then more angry than scared because he shrugs it off. That time when you and I were being shot at—do you remember that?"

"I haven't been in so many gunfights that they become a blur," I replied softly. "Yeah. You were mad at me for running in."

"I tell myself I'm used to you being like that, running towards danger to help people," Ichi said, pulling away slightly, but his hands were still in my shirt. Shaking me lightly, he laughed. "I somehow reconciled myself to having a very American action-hero-type brother who had more heart than sense. But it didn't occur to me Bobby was the same way."

Ichi really was a combination of me and Mike—Mike's features combined with my lankier body type. Our hands were the same, and all three of us were as stubborn as fuck, but Ichi was born a dreamer, an artist who could see beyond the hard lines of our world and into some mystical cosmos he and Jae could talk about. I took a good hard look at my younger brother, trying to save as much of this moment in my memory as I could. We'd only had a few years together as a family, but I loved him as much as I did Mike, and I couldn't imagine my life without him. And as much as I groused about him and Bobby, I was delighted they'd found each other. They were some of the best people I knew and deserved every bit of happiness they could get.

I just couldn't say that, because that was the code of being a brother… or at least it had been.

"In a lot of ways, Bobby Dawson is a much better man than I am. He was a cop—a good, upstanding cop—in a time when the LAPD was as crooked as shit and about as corrupt as you could get." I pushed the shock of blue-streaked black hair out of my brother's eyes. "He left the force because he needed to live his life out in the open. Kind of like you did. Yeah, he's always going to try to do the right thing, because he's that kind of guy. I learned that from him. There have been too many times when people looked away when I needed someone to step in, especially when I was a kid and Dad got too free with his fists. No one spoke up for me. Even Mike had problems with me being gay, and that made things hard. We worked through them, but it took a long time. Bobby stepped up for me when I was alone. So I kind of promised to always step up for other people, even if it meant things might go to shit for me."

"He says you're the one who made him realize he needed to be out," Ichi confessed in a whisper. "That he'd been living a lie until he got word your partner almost killed you. He'd heard you were gay and out on the force but thought you were an idiot. It wasn't until another cop tried to murder you and then he had to watch the force cover it up that he needed to step away from his badge."

"I think he was just tired of filling out reports," I said with a smile. "It's the main reason why he won't be my partner in this investigation business I've got. He doesn't want to do any of the paperwork. Bobby's a good guy. And he loves you. He doesn't take unnecessary risks, which is more than I can say about myself, because there's been more than a few times when I'm in the middle of the shitstorm wondering how I got there. He's always going to run towards the firefight. That's just who he is. That's who I've become. But I can promise you that I'm going to do my best to make sure he always comes home to you. I said that before, and I still mean it."

"I know you do. Just… make sure you come home too, older brother," Ichi said, lightly pushing at my chest. "Be careful. And whatever you do, remember to duck when someone is shooting at you. You don't need another hole in that head of yours."

NINETEEN

ONE OF the things I loved about Jae was he woke up very Korean.

It sounded weird, but it was true.

There was a span of a few minutes right after he opened his gorgeous, long-lashed eyes, blinking at the sun fighting its way into our room, when he still lay in his dreams, immersed in all of the colors and fantastical ideas simmering in his brain. His murmurs were in his native tongue—a waterfall of sounds I couldn't understand, but I felt them pour over me, golden and hot with a spark of electricity to them, even though he wasn't quite conscious. His black hair lay in a feathery cascade down his cheeks, obscuring his jaw. But his lush mouth was usually bare, plump, and slightly parted, ready for a morning kiss.

English wouldn't settle back into his thoughts for at least five minutes after those initial blinks. It took him a while to finally seize upon the fourth language he learned. I could barely say my own name in Japanese, so I was envious of the lingual rings he could dance around me.

Okay, I was envious and usually aroused by the literal rings he could dance around me, but I was man enough to admit it.

We were aging together, moving into a rhythm spiced by happiness and the adventurous leanings Jae discovered inside of himself. He blossomed, I settled down, and we found a pace we both enjoyed. It went without saying that he was the love of my heart and soul, but I said it anyway, mangling the Korean I *did* know. But he'd understand me.

Jae always understood me, even when I didn't understand myself.

"Saranghae-yo," I whispered against his parted lips. It was a more formal pronouncement of love, but it'd been the one I learned first. Those were also the words he'd murmured to me a long time before I'd told him how I felt about him. I just hadn't understood when he'd said them first. "Morning, honey."

"Honey is the dog, Cole-ah," he mumbled, his native tongue wrapped around his English with a liquid blur. "Come closer."

"I get any closer and we're going to have to kick the dog out. She's too young to watch her dads do those kinds of things." His fingers were slightly cold, and I shivered when they found me under the blankets. Stroking at my length, Jae chuckled against my neck when I responded to his touch. "Okay, see, this is why I'm always late in the morning."

"Claudia should be used to that by now." Jae's fingers moved, lightly skimming over intimate places on my body.

"How about if we don't bring up Claudia right now?" I turned him over, covering Jae's body with my weight. "I'd rather it was just you and me in this bed."

In the years between our first kiss and now, Jae and I had fought our way through cultural differences and internalized fears. It was good between us, had been good for a long time. Still, each kiss I'd given him since the first one was like a new gift. Every. Single. Time. I loved taking my time exploring his body, tasting the different textures and flavors of his skin on my tongue. I knew where each mark was on his body and the places I could make him shiver beneath me when I lightly bit there.

I could make love to him a million and one times and still want to come back for more, just for the sounds he made in his throat when my mouth closed over him and I drew him down as deep as I could. It was definitely time for him to cut his fingernails, because they made sharp aching starbursts on my shoulders and back. The sting lasted for only a few seconds, and I found I didn't mind. Making love to Jae was a visceral, primal connection we forged time and time again. I never grew tired of his touch or his kisses, and when he finally tugged on my hair, driven to the edge of his control by my mouth and fingers, I chuckled at his insistent demands.

Jae made love like he lived life. We'd once started out desperate and needy, a violent explosion of want. Then we pushed away, separated by a brittle wall of control. We'd taken that wall down brick by brick, shattering them on the solid foundation of our relationship as we built it up. Jae's passions were unfettered, sometimes even wild, and I was happy to be along for the ride. He stretched my imagination so many ways, pushing me to reach for the stars and to hold on to him as tight as I could.

I did exactly that as I slid into his tight warmth.

We rode each other slowly, stroking at ribs and shoulders, kissing what we could reach. And since Jae was a lot more flexible than I was, he could reach a hell of a lot. The stress of the past week sloughed off of me. I needed to leave all of it behind—my conflicts with my family about how I live my life, my worry I would reach for a gun to solve my problems, and most of all my paralyzing fear someone would take Jae from me.

I'd already been visited by Death way too often. I didn't need him knocking on my front door anymore. Spending a lazy warm morning with Jae in our bed was the best panacea for my troubled soul.

"Stay with me, Cole-ah," Jae murmured, raking his fingers through my hair. "Only us now."

Being a good husband, I did what I was told and fell back into the starry heat he'd laid out around me.

The friction we built up between our bodies eventually spilled over, and his tightness became too much to bear on my sensitive flesh. He left his marks on me, his fingers bruising my shoulders while his legs trapped my hips, holding me firm. We found a pace, setting to a roiling pound, and I crested first, taking Jae with me.

He dug in harder, holding me in, keeping me lodged against his body until our contact grew to that bright brittleness where my skin couldn't stand the burn anymore and I had to close my eyes, drifting away on the curls of pleasure and too-satisfied pain that sex always left behind. I kept my arms wrapped around him, fingers skimming his sweat-dappled shoulders and arms. Then Jae arched up against me, releasing the final bit of coiled tension from his body. We were sticky, damp, and probably musky as hell, but I didn't care. I nuzzled my face into the curve of his neck and sighed, echoing the tiny husky breath he let go.

"I can't move." My mumbling was lost in Jae's hair, but he understood me enough to grunt. "You've broken me. Next time, I'm on the bottom."

"That would be nice," he grunted again, this time with more force, and he shifted violently beneath me. "Because you weigh too much. Aish, you're heavy. Why is muscle so heavy? Ouch, that's my—"

"Sorry. *Sorry*." Moving was apparently dangerous, and I'd come too close to unmanning Jae for life with my knee. Half rolling, half sliding off of Jae, I landed awkwardly on the bed, somehow tangling my elbow in the sheets. "Shit, I'm stuck."

It took us nearly three minutes to get me free, but then again, I wasn't really trying very hard. After Jae caught me wrapping him back up in the linens, he did something bendy with his body and left me where I lay, a sage-cotton burrito filled with smug satisfaction and more than a little bit of arousal from Jae rubbing up against me to get me loose.

"I'm taking a shower." My beloved husband hit me with a pillow on his way to the bathroom, scoring a direct smack against my head because I was too entangled to defend myself. "If you join me, hyung, we're not having any more of this. I'm late already."

"I wasn't the one who started it," I called out, and he actually flipped me off. Not a very Jae thing to do, but sometimes he did the unexpected.

Even as tangled up as I was, I appreciated the view of him walking away. His ass was firm and taut, much like the rest of his toned, golden body, and there were a few pink bite marks on his shoulder. Not on the shoulder where he bore a slick scar from being shot—another thing he could lay at my feet—because no matter how often we got rough in bed, I couldn't—wouldn't—do anything more than kiss that spot. That spot wasn't for playing, at least not in my mind. That scar was my fault. Even though I hadn't been the one to pull the trigger, it was still mine.

"Shit, I forgot to tell you about the guns." I hadn't moved from the bed, but I didn't need to. Rolled over onto my stomach, with my head at the far end of the mattress, I could see straight into the bathroom. Jae was brushing his teeth with a distracted fury that made me worry for his enamel. His mind was probably on the things he had to do today rather than what I said, because he glanced over at me, his eyebrows creased down toward the bridge of his nose. "Ivan—the guy that broke into the office—was shot to death yesterday in his hospital room. O'Byrne came by and asked me to turn over my weapons. She took them with her for ballistics tests."

That got Jae's attention. He turned to face me—a beautiful, freckle-dusted, porcelain-skinned man wearing my bite marks and a tattoo of my Asian birth year on his body. He no longer hid anything from me. We'd started our relationship off behind a web of lies and half-truths, but while those days were definitely gone, sometimes Jae was hard to read. I usually waited for him to tell me exactly what was on his mind, but this time I didn't need any Post-it notes or carefully worded and lovingly meant remarks. The gold in his honey-brown eyes was molten, and he spat out a mouthful of toothpaste into the sink so quickly I thought he missed the bowl.

"She comes in here and accuses you of shooting the man, so you feed her?" Jae gestured wildly with his foamy toothbrush, splattering the mirror above the sinks. I had a vague hope of him not getting any of it on the art-nouveau-styled dresser I'd refurbished and repurposed as our bathroom vanity. It was a brief wish, one secured away by Jae's anger. "The two of you acted like nothing was wrong between you. I invited her to the barbecue this weekend."

I slid off of the bed and approached my husband carefully. After plucking the toothbrush from his clenched fingers, I gathered him up in my arms, then tossed the brush into the sink from behind his back. I told my cock not to get excited about being pressed up against Jae's naked body, but it had its own mind, and I could only hope Jae ignored me. I pulled him in closer, until there wasn't any space between us, and I kissed his gorgeous full mouth, tasting his ire and the mint on his tongue.

"There is nothing wrong between us. She had to ask for them. I'm a likely suspect, but I pretty much have an alibi for the time he was killed. She still needs to exclude me from the possibilities, and the only way to really do that is to check the bullet against all of my guns. She might even tap Bobby for his. It's a part of the job, Jae. Just a necessary evil," I reassured him, locking my fingers at the small of his back. "She doesn't think I killed him. She came here as a cop and did her job. If she hadn't and they bring in the real killer, the defense could poke holes in the case by asking if she excluded everyone she believed could have done it."

"She's supposed to be your friend." He wasn't willing to let go of his irritation yet. Jae prized loyalty and friendship above practically everything else. His entire life was filled with family he'd chosen, and he would do anything for someone he loved. Especially me.

"She still *is* my friend. This doesn't change anything between us. It's the job, babe." I shrugged as best I could with my arms full of a simmering man I'd given my heart to. "Look what I did to Ivan. If I was in her shoes, I would come knocking on my door too. We worked it out. It's okay. I just wanted you to know what happened and how things stand."

"He came into our house. With a gun. You could have killed him then. Why would you wait?" Jae muttered, following with a bit of Korean, which of course I didn't understand. "You can't even wait to get home before you open a box of cookies we just bought at the store. Her reasoning makes no sense."

"Is that a rousing endorsement of my unwillingness to murder someone in cold blood? Because I eat cookies in the car on the way home?" I shot him a cocky grin, hoping to tease the gold anger from his eyes. "And it's not O'Byrne's reasoning. It's just standard detective work. Eliminate all of the possibilities and what you have left or who you have left is your suspect."

"Aish, you know what I mean." He actually tugged at my armpit hair, making me yelp and pull away a few inches, but I maintained my embrace. Sometimes holding Jae was like dealing with a cat. He wanted to be held, but it would cost me a bit of my dignity. "We both need showers, and I'm going to be late if I don't hurry. Are you sure you're okay with O'Byrne? And with her taking the guns?"

"I would trust her if she told me to jump over a fiery pit," I said, making small circles across Jae's spine with my thumb. "I'm still kind of trying to decide how I feel about carrying a weapon. It's not like I'm doing anything dangerous today, and I think now that Ivan is dead, there isn't anybody to come after us. He was probably killed to silence him."

"And what about the person who killed him? You don't think they'll come after you?" Jae bit his lip and stirred against me. "I know we've gone back and forth about you taking a gun with you, but I just want you to be safe. Don't do anything stupid."

"I think I'll be fine. O'Byrne will be with me—eventually—and she's got a gun in case we get attacked by a rabid llama," I murmured, leaning down to kiss his neck. "Now, how about that shower, and exactly how late can you be?"

I CALLED O'Byrne and got her voicemail. After leaving a message on her phone, I told Claudia where I was headed and got another reminder about replacing her rotary phone. We made a quick deal on the spot. I would let her find one on the internet and buy it with the company card, and she would get a new phone out of it. Like most of my deals with Claudia, I took a hit to my wallet, but she was going to be happier for it, and when it was all said and done, that's all that mattered. I was just grateful she hadn't been there when Ivan broke into the office, because she was usually there an hour before I was and… what he would've done to her would have broken me. I would pay for a hundred ugly avocado old-school phones just for a single smile from her and to hear her call me son.

Not that I was going to tell her that, because those phones were freaking expensive and there would be no place to put them all.

I also snagged a praline turnover from the plastic container she'd brought in from her car to put into the office fridge. The treats were for her afternoon church group, a gathering of strong-minded women who spent a couple of hours every so often lamenting about their children. I'd dropped her off at the church once on my way to Bobby's and spent half an hour being told by these women about how much Claudia adored me and why her advice was so important. For all her schooling, Claudia loved me unconditionally. It was an odd feeling after so many years of my dad and stepmother. Her own sons were grateful for my presence in her life because it took a lot of pressure off of them. It seemed like, in a family of capable men raised by a powerful woman, my de facto adoption into their clan meant my fuckups were front and center and a source of great amusement among the Dubois boys.

"Are you going to remember to eat lunch while you're out?" Claudia called to me, stopping me in midstride out the front door. "Or do you need me to call you about it?"

"Why? Do you want me to bring you something back?" I felt at my back pocket, making sure I had my wallet.

"No. I brought leftovers from home, but you need to eat. Have O'Byrne take you out for some damn tacos. The least that girl can do is feed you after dragging you all over the place." She stabbed me with a steely glare sharpened with years of raising eight sons. Ancient sword masters would never be able to rival the sharpness of Claudia's maternal judgment. I felt thoroughly stabbed through, even checking my belly button to see if my intestines were on the right side of my skin. "Just take care of yourself, okay? I appreciate you bringing in a cleaner for the office. Those hazmat people did a good job. Better than our normal people. Might want to hire them full-time."

"Honey, I love you, but I'm not paying for a crime-scene cleaner to come take care of the office every other week. You're just going to have to be happy with the service we have now," I told her, saluting her with the turnover. "And I promise I'll get something to eat. Give me a call if you need anything. And if O'Byrne can't make it, I'll come right back. We're just going to take a look around. Nothing to worry about at all."

"That's what you always say," she yelled at me as I closed the screen door behind me.

And that's what mothers do. Get in the last word right before you do something incredibly stupid.

It was late enough in the morning for traffic not to be like circling a Hellmouth black hole, the suck and push of lines of cars to get to anywhere else in LA but where you were. I thanked my lucky stars I didn't have to go anywhere near the 405. Then I was forced onto the 10 by some idiot in a sports car who decided to play chicken with a fire truck.

"Glad we didn't decide on a time. I would be late as hell," I muttered to my phone as I texted O'Byrne about my estimated arrival time at the Brinkerhoffs' building. Traffic was at a standstill, and while California frowned on anyone looking at their phones while behind the steering wheel, I literally could have busted out an oven and baked a cake while waiting to move forward an inch. Still, I kept my eyes out for any CHiP roaming through the lines. "Shit, at this rate, I'll get there at about the time it would be for me to turn around and go back home."

Something unfucked itself ahead of me, and the congestion began to break up just as O'Byrne answered. She was stuck on the other side of the fuckery, and after a quick reassurance that she'd meet me there, the car in front of me began to lurch forward. I followed, glad to be finally moving and not breathing in any more gas fumes.

One of the things Marlena Brinkerhoff gave O'Byrne was the key code for the underground garage. Well, as underground as Los Angeles got. In many parts of the city, digging down was not recommended for a variety of reasons. A lot of people who didn't live in California tended to fear earthquakes. While there have been a few large ones, for the most part, we pretty much don't get out of bed unless it's a five or more on the Richter scale. I cannot count how many teeth-rattling quakes I've slept through, and since being married, I've been woken up for every single one because Jae still hasn't become acclimated to them.

And he'd been born in California.

I'm not too sure what he expected me to do in the middle of a small quake, but I was now awake for them. Thankfully, we usually found something to do after the few seconds of shaking died down. So maybe Jae wasn't so much unsettled by earthquakes as much as they made him frisky.

I didn't mind the lack of sleep.

Digging down into the Los Angeles dirt usually led to a multitude of complications nobody wanted to deal with. There were old gas lines and sewage tunnels left over from generations of haphazard, slapdash building, but going deeper presented a whole different kind of problem. Depending on where you were in the LA Basin, old infrastructure was the best thing you could find. The worst-case scenario was—believe it or not—fossils.

Sure, you could hit a pocket of crude oil in parts of LA County, but you're more likely to find a scramble of stone-encased bones that would bring your construction dreams to a screaming halt. It takes forever to extract the fossil, and where there's one, there's usually another two or three hundred. So, to avoid all of that, most high-rises either have a separate structure, or in the case of the Brinkerhoff place, are dug down just a little bit and use the first one and a half floors as parking.

In her text during the standstill traffic, O'Byrne told me to use one of the visitor spots, having cleared it with the building long before I ever woke up. The code was unnecessarily complex, a long string of numbers followed by two pound signs, then another number and an asterisk. There was a call box next to the keypunch, and from the significant lack of paint on the Help button, I imagined the security desk got a lot of calls from the senior citizens living in the building. Thankfully the light turned green and I didn't have to go through summoning Beelzebub on the punch pad again.

I don't know what I was expecting. No, I knew exactly what I was expecting. It was difficult getting older sometimes, because at some point, there'd been a generational shift, and old people—especially Los Angeles's seniors—didn't follow the elderly person template we'd all been raised up on. Sure, there were still stereotypical grandmothers with a collection of crucifixes on their living room wall and a crystal dish of strawberry candies sitting on the coffee table someone made in their shop class fifty years before, but nobody apparently told the residents in this particular building, because as I drove through the long lines of cars, there wasn't a land shark among them. Instead of aging Cadillacs and hard-finned Buicks, I counted at least seven exotic sports cars, five high-end Teslas connected to their charging units by thick umbilical cords, and six chrome-heavy Harleys. The rest of the offerings were slightly more practical—a lot of SUVs and a couple of Smart cars that should've been painted yellow and red like those pedal-powered plastic vehicles kids rode around in. I was happy to say Lisa never saw the inside of one of those, because as soon as she showed any interest in moving forward, I bought her a miniature red Ferrari to tear around in.

It was good being an uncle. I got to be cool and never the bad guy. Mike hated it, and for the most part, Maddy just shook her head and spent a lot of time in negotiations with her mini-me. I personally think Mike was just jealous because he's too short to see over the dashboard of a real Ferrari.

I found the visitors' parking easily enough, sliding the Rover into a spot next to a Mini Cooper. The parking levels were dead quiet, and only the hum of the elevators moving up and down pierced through the echoing silence. Whoever maintained the property was diligent about keeping the grounds pristine, because the floor was clean enough to eat off of and I made no noise as I walked toward the lit-up entrance door.

I had my fingers on the handle when I realized the parking levels were much more than just a place for the residents to leave their vehicles. I hadn't seen the doors as I was driving, but they were clearly visible from my spot by the entrance. Set into the wall in front of two parking spaces marked for a single apartment, the rolling metal doors were painted the same color as the wall, obviously blending them back from notice. The doors were marked with black letters painted above the upper frame, corresponding to the parking spaces and apartment they belonged to.

"Shit, all this time we've been thinking they had a storage unit someplace, and it's right here in this damn building," I muttered to myself, walking away from the entrance and searching for the Brinkerhoffs' spots. "Marlena should've known about this. Why the hell didn't she tell O'Byrne?"

Based on how the first floor was laid out, I guessed I would find what I was looking for in the far corner of the parking structure's lower level. My cell phone reception was spotty, and I had to go back to the ramp to get a strong enough signal to text O'Byrne about my suspicions. I got back a few words that she'd been tangled up on a call while driving but would be at the building in about half an hour. Depending on traffic, of course.

"Well, I'm just going to take a look," I muttered as I texted back. "If she meets me down on the second level, we can start there first."

I estimated the location of the Brinkerhoffs' parking spaces pretty well. Set as far back into the corner as possible, it was a lot darker than the upper level, the overhead lighting flickering on and off in some bad rendition of a horror-movie setting. The lower level had a loading zone and a freight elevator, its wide doors shut and empty of a lift car. It obviously was for residents to use, because there was no way a moving truck would be able to negotiate through the parking area, and someone was obviously doing something because they'd left a white van across the marked-off space, its doors firmly shut.

It wasn't until I came around the side that I noticed the business name on the van and the open rolling door of the storage area for the apartment next to the Brinkerhoffs'. Watson Gallery was discreetly lettered across the side of the van, but it was the storage unit that had my attention.

Even in the dim lighting, I could make out the masterful, beautiful paintings inside of the long space. Drawing closer, I was surprised to discover the air flowing out of the storage unit was cold, nearly crackling icy, and appeared to be coming out of a vent punched through the drywall between it and the Brinkerhoff unit. The canvases were up on their ends, sitting in something that looked more like a dish rack than any place to store a painting, but my expertise on the subject was thin at best. An ugly, twisted male face caught my eye, and I slowly pulled a canvas out using the edge of my shirt so as not to get my fingerprints on it. I recognized the painting I'd seen on Watson's wall. On this one, however, there was no black rectangle with Arthur's distinct signature. Instead there was a scrawl I couldn't make out, and it was as tempered with age as the rest of the painting… or at least made to look that way.

"Well, *shit*." I reached for my phone to take a picture of the canvas in case O'Byrne needed it for proof. "It was Watson all along."

"Don't be stupid. He isn't smart enough to pull this off," a woman said behind me. I glanced over my shoulder and recognized the petite, smiling wife Watson proudly slung his arm around in every family photo. She wasn't smiling this time, and more importantly, she had a very large gun pointed directly at me. "You have been a hard man to kill, Mister McGinnis. So I am so happy to be the one who finally gets to do it."

TWENTY

"MARIE WATSON, I presume." It was a hideous paraphrase, but when faced with the business end of a gun, my brain tended to glitch. She didn't look amused, but I wasn't exactly in a chuckling mood myself. "Let me guess. You're the one who's been moving Arthur's forgeries."

She was even smaller in person than she was on camera, which was a mean feat because I was pretty sure she'd only come up to Watson's elbow at best. I hadn't been stealthy coming down the ramp and around the cars, but I honestly hadn't expected to discover a storage unit full of forgeries and a tiny Asian woman with a big gun. I don't know why I wasn't expecting that. With the way my life pretty much had gone every single step of the way since birth, I should've naturally assumed there was either going to be someone with a gun or perhaps an interdimensional portal filled with water and a kraken pissed off at me because I'd eaten his cousin squid in a bowl of soon dubu chigae.

"Well, thanks to you, all of that is over now," she spat out with the fury of an enraged hamster. "You just had to be the one to find Adele. Of all the people in Los Angeles, that had to be the one asshole who couldn't leave things alone."

"You seem to forget the Los Angeles Police Department wasn't planning on just letting it go." I studied her, trying to gauge how comfortable she was holding a weapon.

"You should have walked away. It was bad enough I had to bring their stupid nephew into this and he wouldn't kill her, but now their damned granddaughter is down here. She'll probably take him back to San Francisco and this whole deal I've been trying to save is blown out of the water. The only reason Arthur wanted to stop painting was because Adele wanted him to." She gripped the gun tighter, her knuckles blanching down to the bone. "We could have kept this going for ten more years. Then she tries to pay me off with fake diamonds? Who does that? We had a deal. She should have kept to it."

There was something disconcerting about being held hostage by a tiny woman dressed like nearly every middle-aged Korean woman going to church in her Sunday best. There was an odd discordance to her outfit, like her closet was a time portal that she'd jumped through that morning and come out wearing a pair of polyester pants from the '80s, matched up with a '90s frilly satin blouse embellished with slightly off-brand logos. Her hair was feathered back away from her round face, lacquered black ebony water spouts that should have moved in time with a pounding soundtrack, much like the fountains at Caesar's Palace. At first glance— and possibly even a second one—she was hard to take seriously.

Except for the very mean-looking piece of steel in her hand.

The gun looked like it'd probably come from Watson, unless her taste ran to Desert Eagles. It was a lot of firepower for a small woman, and I had doubts she'd be able to control it if she did pull the trigger. But all she needed to do was punch a hole in me. One lucky shot and it would be McGinnis brain stew all over the parking structure's floor.

"What I can't figure out is why you killed Adele. Just because she wanted Arthur to stop? Seems kind of flimsy there." I was baiting her, hoping to draw her off guard, possibly giving me a chance to get the jump on her. Her dark eyes were glittering and furious, so I was either going to piss her off into talking or she was just going to say fuck it all and shoot me. It was a chance I had to take. "I thought you guys were all friends, or was she tired of the scam and wanted to quit? Or maybe he just was losing his touch and she wanted to spare his pride."

Marie flinched.

"That was it, wasn't it? Arthur's getting old, and maybe his game isn't as good as it used to be." I gestured behind me to the painting I'd pulled out, keeping my eyes on Marie and her gun. "How many times did he have to do a painting over until he got it right? That's why he gave your husband the other one. There was something wrong with it that somebody could spot right away."

A car on the level above us started up, its engine grumbling through the silence. The air was dry, scented with the untreated wood used to build storage units and the smoky pitch of the tar someone used to waterproof the walls. I shifted to my left, debating if I could make it to the van and maybe use it for cover, but Marie's aim tracked my movement.

"Adele was a mistake. Ivan went to the pickup with a ski mask on," Marie spat with a heat as deadly as the bullets her gun held. "She knew it was Ivan, because he didn't keep his mouth shut like I told him to. I told her to hand over the goods, and he said something stupid. It was supposed to be a handoff, a lot of diamonds from her past jobs, but he knew they were fake as soon as he saw them. He recognized the bag they were in."

"So what? He called her a liar and just shot her?" I shook my head at the stupidity of the whole thing, inching closer, but Marie wasn't buying it. "Those fake diamonds? They're still worth a hell of a lot of money. Apparently even when diamonds are fake, if they've got a big name attached to them, people will still pay through the nose for them."

"Stop right there, asshole," she growled at me in her high-pitched voice. One thing was certain—Marie couldn't swear for shit, because she sounded more like a voiceover from a kid's show than a hard-nosed criminal. But by my count, she had at least one killing under her belt, maybe even more if it wasn't Ivan who'd gunned down the fake Marlena that day. "She tried to cheat me and paid for it. After I get rid of you, Arthur's next. Then I'm going to work on their granddaughter and help clean out all of their shit. Ivan said Adele had a big nest egg, and I'm going to find it. No more living with that asshole upstairs, listening to him talk about how good he is. I might even kill him after I kill you, fucker."

She squeaked on the last syllable, and I would've laughed, but once again, *gun*.

The elevator rumbled, and to give the woman credit, she didn't even glance behind her when the doors slid open. That told me a lot of things—she was very confident about her ability with the gun, and she'd been expecting backup. It looked like I was right on at least the second guess, because as soon as the main doors opened, a mountain of flesh ambled out.

At some point, a bit of sperm and an egg kissed and began life. The developing cells lodged into a woman's soft flesh, cradling the growing bits of bone and tissue until it developed a brainstem and then enough solid mass to be on its way to sentience. From that microscopic spark, this man emerged as a tiny baby, and then, from what I could see, he absorbed everything around him until he was the size of a small elephant.

His thinning blond hair was cut into a pageboy I'd only seen on a film character named Rocky who preferred to grunt and run around in a gold lamé Speedo. There was muscle underneath the flab. There had to be in order to move his enormous body, because if he wasn't nearly seven feet tall and four hundred pounds, I was a rubber ducky. Wearing a blue Watson Gallery T-shirt stretched over his broad chest and ample belly, he shuffled forward toward the van, working at the string of his gray sweatpants as he walked. The look of surprise he gave me when he spotted me standing in front of Marie's gun was nearly as comical as her swearing, but that expression quickly fell away to an intense irritation, focused directly at me.

"You hired someone else?" the shambling flesh grumbled at Marie. "I'm doing it."

"No, this is McGinnis. The asshole Ivan was trying to kill." Marie still hadn't gotten the accent right on the word asshole. "Grab him so I can shoot him in the head and we can get him into the van to dump him someplace. We can move the rest of the paintings later, dumbass."

My sneaker squeaked as I moved my right foot back, digging my toe down to pivot on. Marie was still a problem, but the overgrown Dutch Boy paint kid was a much bigger one. I don't know what he was pissed off about, but the red flushing through his cheeks wasn't because he was shy and I'd tossed him a seductive come-on. He was angry—bull-in-a-china-shop angry—and something I'd done got him to that volcanic level as soon as he heard my name.

"I liked Ivan." He cracked his knuckles, sending the sound of rolling dice through the tension between us. "You shouldn't have killed him."

I didn't get a chance to tell him I didn't kill Ivan, because he was on me like Honey went after a swampy tennis ball. He moved quickly for a large man, which honestly wasn't all that surprising, because there was a lot of muscle beneath that flesh, and it was used to shoving around that weight. He huffed as he came near, a locomotive engine churning through anything in its way. I had one spare thought hit me before Dutch was within arm's reach.

Marie wasn't comfortable with the gun. She didn't trust herself using it. Not if she wanted him to grapple me before shooting me in the head.

Then my worldview filled with a rippling beige flow of skin and flab stuffed into a navy-blue shirt and sweatpants, and I put Marie to the side.

Sparring with Bobby taught me how to deal with an opponent with a lot of skill and a body tight with toned muscle. But the best thing about learning from Bobby was he often roped in various guys working out at JoJo's so I didn't get too comfortable when facing someone in a fight. Every guy came at a situation differently. Sometimes they were driven by ego and other times by the need to dominate. And every once in a while, I was paired up with somebody who was a lot larger than me and pissed off at the world in general.

I'd taken a lot of beatings from those kinds of guys over the years because they were unpredictable and no amount of strategy seemed to work... or at least not at first. Those were the types of guys that taught me the best way to win a fight was to keep moving and shoot out every hit I could.

I lost sight of Marie, but I knew I couldn't risk her getting a clear shot at me, even if she was unsteady using such a big gun. She didn't seem like the type who would be sentimental about shooting her lackey, more like a woman who would gladly put a bullet through both of us, wipe the gun down to put it into someone's hands, and pull the trigger again so there was gunshot residue everywhere.

Marie was a planner, and she was going to have to be the one who I strategized around much more than Dutch.

I just had to make sure I kept Dutch between me and that now-wavering muzzle.

The Brinkerhoffs' choice of cars ran to an old Volvo and a pair of bicycles chained together to prevent theft, so I was thankful for Watson's testosterone-driven brain because he felt it necessary to park a midget Hummer in his space. The empty spot between them was probably where Marie normally left her car, and it was wide enough to give me enough fighting room but not so big Marie could get around Dutch's heft.

Dutch's breath was ripe with onions and pickles, and he drooled like a Newfoundland puppy as he attacked, long lines of spittle trailing back across his jowls. It was going to be a risk but one I had to take because there was no way I was going to be able to fight off not only his weight but also his momentum, so I slid out of the way.

And he crashed into the wall, coming up as dazed and confused as a sunlight-blinded rhino.

I'd folded myself up against Watson's Hummer, sliding around the front end to give myself cover, and I followed through with a quick punch to the side of Dutch's head. I rocked his skull enough to jerk his face around, his chin grazing his shoulder, and he groaned, keening in pain. The howl had only reverberated for maybe a second when Marie let loose a round from her monstrous gun, deafening all of us with its thunderous boom.

The wood next to Dutch's temple exploded in a tornado of splinters, and he flinched, probably startled at the heat of the blast and then at the trickle of blood running down his face and neck. She'd shot at the space between us, obviously no longer caring if she damaged anything inside of the open locker. If I hadn't punched Dutch, I would be tasting his brains in my open mouth, and judging by the look of confusion on his face when he turned to look at me, he was still working through that possibility as he lurched to his feet.

"I didn't kill Ivan. Cops already cleared me for it." I shuffled back, keeping the Hummer's solid mass between me and Marie. "They even took my guns to check."

Dutch wasn't willing to listen to me, or maybe he hadn't quite figured out his boss was willing to kill him just to see me dead, because as soon as he was on his feet, he came after me. Trapped between the Hummer and the wall, I did my best to get away from him. I needed enough room to land a punch but not enough space to give him room to maneuver.

Glass jaws are a real thing. There's a bundle of nerves along the chin that, when hit right, sends a guy into a spiraling blackout. It was too much to hope to get the shot in right the first time, but I'd had enough practice, and I'd already rattled his brains.

"Going to kill you," he grunted at me, snarling with his chin straight where I needed it. "You cut my face."

Jesus, the guy was too stupid to even realize he'd been shot at and the bullet had done a number across his cheek. His side dug into the car's grill, and I took my shot, plowing into his chin. I felt one of my knuckles blow, popping the joint out of place with a sharp sting. Dutch's head rocked back, jerking in response to the solid hit, and I shuffled farther back, careful not to leave myself open. My left hand ached, and my ring finger swelled, throbbing with a hot pain. Grabbing at the first joint, I jerked hard, popping it back into place when Marie took her next shot.

She was really shitty with a gun, but it didn't take a lot of aim to kill a man, not when you were armed with something big enough to kill an elephant. The Hummer's back windshield blew out, and then the front followed, the bullet piercing both of them before finally burying into the air-conditioning duct running above the storage lockers' doors. She was too short to get a straight shot through the area, and the Hummer was too tall, providing us with enough cover to hide behind. But despite Dutch's eyes rolling back into his head, he remained upright, lodged between the grill and the wall.

"Stop shooting at me," Dutch groaned, but I couldn't tell who he was talking to. He didn't seem conscious enough to really understand what was going on, and I briefly wondered if I'd hit him too hard. But then I remembered he'd promised to tear my head off of my neck, so that pretty much gave me free rein. "Stop moving."

Since I hadn't taken a step away from the Hummer for fear Marie would get a clear shot, I figured Dutch was quickly losing all sense of reality. It didn't seem to stop his determination, because he pushed forward, ripping his shirt on the Hummer's chrome, and shoved through the tight space. His hands were almost on my neck before I realized he'd moved as far as he did. I heard shuffling behind me and, sure it was Marie, I took a chance and dove across the empty parking space next to the Hummer, rolling as I went.

That move always looked cool in the movies, but the truth was it only scraped up my elbows and knees and, with the slightly tacky surface of the structure's floor, brought me up short of the Lexus I was trying to hide behind. Dutch followed close on my heels, his grunting more wheezy than a bad '70s porn shoot.

He was having a hard time breathing, and a sheen of sweat plastered what hair he had across his temples and down over his broad skull. There was already a purple mark forming along his jaw, a sure sign I'd at least gotten a solid hit but not good enough to take him down. I wouldn't win a fair fight. He had too much mass, and I didn't have enough room to dance back. Not with Marie hunting me down like I should've taken that left at Albuquerque and it was now rabbit season.

Dutch was in my face before I could blink, and either it was muscle memory or just simply fear, but I jabbed him in the throat with my left, swallowing a grunt of pain when my blown-out knuckle connected with his Adam's apple. Not waiting to see if the choking strike would work, I followed up with my right, aiming just a little bit to the side of that bruise I'd already given him. Still, I wasn't fast enough, because Dutch's fingers were in my hair, knotting into the strands with a fierce grip, clubbing me in the chest with his other hand.

The shock wave of his punch made my heart skip, and not in a good way. It knocked the wind out of me, and I stumbled, unable to break free of his grasp as he went down, choking on his own tongue or spit. The clatter of his breath coming out of his open mouth wasn't good, but much like Marie, I really didn't give a shit. One of the still unhealed cuts on my forehead split open, and hot blood ran down into my left eye. I fought to regain the function of my lungs, pulling away from Dutch's thrashing body just to roll over onto my back as I tried to remember how to breathe.

That's when Marie walked down between the parking spaces, her big-ass gun lifted up as steadily as she could and aimed directly at my head.

I couldn't sit up. Hell, I felt like Dutch had just used a defibrillator on my chest, and it was all I could do to keep my stomach from crawling up my throat and emptying out onto the ground. Both the Lexus and Hummer had rims, so grabbing a hubcap and flinging it in an act of desperation was out. Marie was too far away to kick at, and judging by the smug expression on her face, she knew I was trapped. Behind me, Dutch's heels were beating at the floor, his arms flailing about as if he were fully committed to his role as a dying replicant who'd fallen into Decker's crosshairs.

"You've cost me a lot of money, asshole," she squeaked, and I wouldn't have been surprised if she wiggled her nose and somehow sprouted whiskers. I was amazed at the stupid things my brain bubbled up with, especially when it looked like I was about to die. "Now I've got to figure out where to dump your body and how to get you into the van, because Stanley isn't going to be able to do it."

"Really? His name is Stanley?" I shifted on the ground, pulling up onto my side. Something crinkled in my back pocket, and I winced, knowing it was my broken phone. I wasn't ready to die. Not when I had Jae at home and a lot of Christmases ahead of me with a niece I needed to spoil. Marie wasn't going to be the end of me, not if I had anything to say about it. "Are you going to kill him next? That's what you do, right? Pick off the people working for you so you cover your own ass? Ivan didn't kill Adele. You did. Just like you killed the girl and him."

"Wow, smart and pretty," Marie mocked me with a whining drawl. "I should feel sorry about killing you, but I don't. Say bye-bye now."

Private investigators always seem to have some smartass rejoinder before they pull their final ass-saving move, but in real life, there's really not a lot of time. Marie's finger gently squeezed down on the trigger with the perfect pressure someone obviously taught her how to do, even though they didn't school her on picking a gun inside of her weight class.

Growing up with Mike pretty much as my only playmate, we spent a lot of our time trying to figure out how to keep ourselves occupied. Back when we were kids, he couldn't throw or catch a ball for shit, so we occupied our time playing politically incorrect games of gun-toting oppressors as well as Frisbee. Now, while a phone is a lot heavier than a plastic disk, Marie was a lot nearer to me than the standard distance people stood while tossing around the disk, so I was thankful for the up-close-and-personal approach she wanted to take to murdering me. I'd already taken my phone out of my back pocket, and as she squeezed down, I flung it straight at her wrist.

She got off the shot a split second after the phone hit her fingers.

That split second was all I needed.

She lost her steady grip on the stock, her hand loosening enough to put a dangerous flexibility into her wrist. The gun boomed with the third loud and deadly report in such a short time. I was hoping to God somebody heard this one, somebody with balls enough to send for the cops or a security guard or a fucking Girl Scout if there was one outside selling Thin Mints.

My ribs still felt like they were stabbing my lungs, and I fought to roll away, hoping to avoid getting plowed through by a hot piece of metal. I didn't need to go far, because not only did Marie's shot go wide, slamming into the Lexus's front quarter panel and probably through its engine, but her loose grip had tragic consequences.

The Desert Eagle is probably one of the heaviest guns I'd ever held in my hand, and it required a firm grip and a steady aim. Shooting one usually left my shoulders in a slight twinge from the jerk of the weapon after it's fired. I'd been shooting guns for decades, where Marie definitely hadn't, because as soon as the phone struck and she loosened her hold, she lost her grip on the gun, and it recoiled straight up.

The casing popped back, and I lost its trajectory after it bounced off her forehead, but I caught the full crunch of steel meeting bone when the Eagle, powered by the momentum of its blast, slammed back into her face.

I was on the move before she hit the floor screaming, every joint and tendon in my body aching still from Dutch's punch. But I needed to get to the gun. It was my only chance of survival, because if either one of them got to it before I did, there would be no second chance.

Or at least that's what I thought, because as soon as I dropped to the ground, reaching for the Eagle with my fingers ghosting over its hard stock, I heard O'Byrne shout that she was LAPD.

"Get out of the way, Mac," she yelled in that delightful hard-cop voice everyone who prayed to be rescued wanted to hear in a gunpowder-scented parking structure. "You two on the floor, hands behind your necks where I can see them. And if you make one move towards any weapon, I'll be glad to add another hole into your head. So go ahead and flinch, if you want to know what it's like to see out of the back of your skull."

EPILOGUE

"WHY IS the kid walking like that?" Bobby jerked his chin toward Lisa, who was leaping about as if she was wearing a giant's seven-league boots. Stretching out her leg in front of her, she hurtled forward, landing on the one foot, then stretching out her other leg to take another lunge. "She looks like she's training for the Ministry of Silly Walks."

It was finally Sunday, and the Brinkerhoff case had been put to bed, or at least my part of it had been. I'd inflated the three-foot-high above-ground pool before the sun had come up, filling it up with water and locking down the steel-girder deck that came with it. It was something I was getting pretty tired of doing, and I made some noise to Jae about maybe us just putting in a permanent pool, to which he rolled his eyes and reminded me all I had to do with this one was empty it out and give it a good scrubbing. Since I had spent a few summers cleaning pools for spare change as a teenager, my memories quickly threw up every disgusting thing I had found in the filters.

Those flashbacks were dramatic enough that I stood shivering in the early hours of the morning, holding the hose in place while the pool filled high enough for me to fix it into the ladder and go back into the house.

People began arriving at about one, despite us telling them two was really the earliest everybody should get there. As a result of that, Jae and I had to scramble out of bed, where we had fallen back after a leisurely breakfast and a very erotic shower. I could have killed my brother when I opened the door, but he grinned knowingly at me, glanced down at my bare wet chest and the old pair of jeans I'd barely gotten up over my ass in time, then handed me my niece.

I'm not saying Jae could be usurped by a hazel-eyed little girl with sun-streaked brown hair, but I would die for her. Hands down. Simply die.

And she knew it.

Which was why I was forbidden to take her shopping by myself, because the threat of a pony was a real one, and I knew from experience, Mike and Maddy had enough room in their backyard to host one.

I studied Lisa for a little bit, trying to remember where I'd seen that motion before. Then I chuckled. "That's how Maddy runs when she's got her running blades on. A hell of a lot faster, but I think that's what she's doing. She's mimicking her mom."

"Okay, first I'm sorry I said the thing about the silly walks, because that's probably offensive," Bobby muttered under his breath, reaching for his beer, sitting on the ground next to the chaise longue he'd claimed as his own. "I need some help here, Princess. Is that okay for her to do? I'm not up on the whole political correctness thing. I mean, Maddy's missing her lower legs and her daughter's trying to run like her? Is that cool? And shit, even talking about it makes me nervous as hell. Your sister-in-law's got some bite to her."

"I don't think Maddy would be offended if she heard you. You guys go back a long way, and she tries to take things as learning experiences." Thinking about it for a second, I shrugged and sat up, straddling my own lounger. "Lisa's probably trying to figure out how it feels or what the world looks like when Maddy does it. She's learning how to experience what other people see or feel. I don't think it's a bad thing. She's not making fun of her mom, and Maddy's good about explaining stuff like that. I think Lisa's trying to understand her, understand how she moves. You've raised a kid. Shit, you've got a grandkid now. You know kids are curious and they're going to ask about stuff. Maddy's right there. She's got this. If it was a problem, she'll say something. They probably talk stuff out all the time."

The backyard was pretty packed, but there was a late straggler who slipped in through the gates and got a round of jeering for showing up with store-bought potato salad. O'Byrne blushed as she handed the container to Scarlet, then turned even redder when Claudia embraced her in a bone-crunching hug. I knew those hugs. In anticipation of an assault, my ribs creaked every time Claudia came near me.

Jae met my eyes from where he was poking at the chicken on the grill, giving me a broad smile and holding up a bottle of beer, lightly rocking it back and forth to ask me if I needed a new one. I never thought I would see the day when I would have a secret, silent language with a husband, but there it was—an unspoken question I clearly understood like he fully comprehended what I wanted from him later when I bit my lower lip and grinned. If anything, he turned even more crimson than O'Byrne did. Ichi said something to him, and he jerked his attention back to the conversation he'd been having with my two brothers, but I could still see the blush on his cheeks even as he turned away.

O'Byrne grabbed a diet soda from one of the ice chests on the broad, circular outdoor kitchen we'd built away from the house. I'd strung the screens up to block out a lot of the sun, taking care with the wisteria climbing up the posts and across the perimeter. It left the area cool, with the mature trees along the fence providing enough shade to keep the heat from getting too much. She dragged over one of the chairs and plopped down, cracking open the soda once she got settled.

"No beer?" Bobby questioned. "Driving or still on the job?"

"I don't trust myself not to fall asleep," she said, saluting him with her drink. The circles under her eyes were still there, but she'd gotten some sleep since I'd seen her last. "Just came back from the station. Stanley Voelker just cut a deal for a reduced sentence. He might not be the smartest guy on the block, but he apparently remembers everything he hears. He could tell the DA about everything Marie Watson was up to. They're still trying to pin Ivan Brinkerhoff's murder on her, but I don't know if they need to. She's already confessed to killing Adele and her other accomplice. I should be used to this kind of shit, but I'm always surprised what people do for money."

"What about Arthur?" I pushed back in my seat, stretching out my legs. The loungers were fairly high off the ground, something I was thankful for because both Jae and I were pretty tall and there was nothing graceful about trying to get back up from a piece of furniture that was nearly lying on the ground. "What's going to happen to him? Last time Marlena picked up one of my calls, she told me he's pretty shaken. Like the wind's been kicked out of him."

"The district attorney's office is on the fence about charging him. He was clearly forging art, and then there's the embarrassment of his granddaughter being assistant DA up in SF while he goes through an indictment and everything else that follows. It looks like they're going to offer him probation, because there's no way in hell he'll survive a trial. He's an old man that's lost pretty much everything," O'Byrne murmured, shaking her head. "I don't know. Guess we'll find out in the next couple of weeks. One thing's for sure—Marie Watson is off the streets, and I don't have to worry about someone trying to kill you when you go to get a cup of coffee."

"Like he even gets his own beer," Bobby snorted, giving Jae a broad smile as he approached with two newly opened bottles. "One of those for me?"

"You would complain like a baby if I didn't have one for you," Jae replied, passing one of the beers over to Bobby, then resting one of his knees by my hips, balancing himself against me. He put the other bottle between my legs, smiling as he said, "That's just going to have to keep you company for a while. Maybe it will help you cool off."

The icy chill went a long way in pulling back any arousal my body had stoked up, and my belly shivered in response. He smelled good— like vanilla and a bit of salt. His fingers were on my shoulder, their tips tracing over my collarbone, and I hooked my arm behind his thighs, pulling him in.

"Actually, I wanted to talk to you about something, Mac," O'Byrne said, giving Jae an apologetic grimace. "And now that I think about it, it's probably something you should hear too, Jae. Captain Book dug out a couple of uniforms who were feeding info to individuals outside of the force. Internal Affairs is dealing with it, but we don't know how long they've been leaking things out or to whom. He wants to use police consultants more until he and the rest of the brass know how bad it is. So, I guess I'm asking you if you're willing to get dragged around on a couple more cases."

"I don't know. I guess it depends on if Dawson here is finally coming to work for me," I replied, slanting Bobby a sly look. "Asshole won't be my partner, so I guess I'm just going to have to pay him a salary or something. Think we can talk the LAPD into another one of those shiny cards with *his* name on it this time?"

"I think something like that needs to be talked over with Ichi," Bobby growled at me. "What makes you think I want to work for you, Princess?"

"If you're going to get stabbed or shot at, don't you think you should at least get paid for it?" I shot back, giving Jae a quick hug. "What do you think, agi? Would you mind if I helped out O'Byrne more often?"

"Of course not. Because I love you and I want you to be happy, which means you digging into other people's lives." Jae's response was light but sauced with sarcasm. "Just tell me one thing, Dell. Are you going to be giving him his guns back, or is he just going to have to throw his phone at everyone who shoots at him? Because if he is, I'll just put a duffel bag full of rocks on his back seat. Just in case."

"I love you too, babe. And none of that was O'Byrne's fault." I chuckled at Bobby's disgusted huff. "Besides, I don't see what all the fuss is about. Sure, this one was kind of crazy, but really, after all of this, what's the worst that can happen?"

RHYS FORD is an award-winning author with several long-running LGBT+ mystery, thriller, paranormal, and urban fantasy series and is a two-time LAMBDA finalist with her *Murder and Mayhem* novels. She is also a 2017 Gold and Silver Medal winner in the Florida Authors and Publishers President's Book Awards for her novels *Ink and Shadows* and *Hanging the Stars*. She is published by Dreamspinner Press and DSP Publications.

She shares the house with Harley, a gray tuxedo with a flower on her face, Badger, a disgruntled alley cat who isn't sure living inside is a step up the social ladder, as well as a ginger cairn terrorist named Gus. Rhys is also enslaved to the upkeep of a 1979 Pontiac Firebird and enjoys murdering make-believe people.

Rhys can be found at the following locations:
Blog: www.rhysford.com
Facebook: www.facebook.com/rhys.ford.author
Twitter: @Rhys_Ford

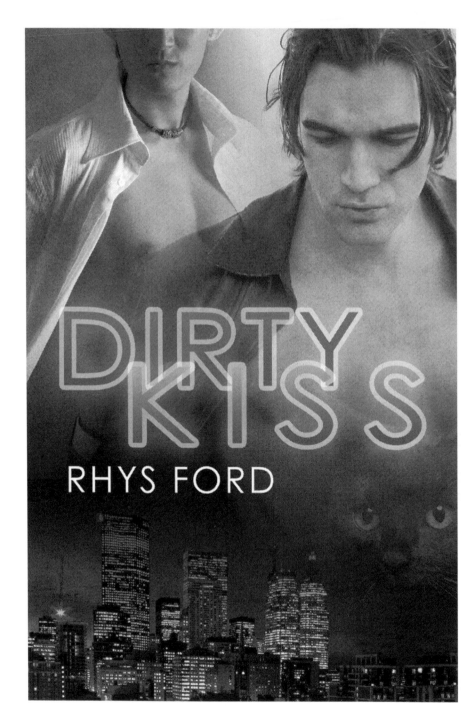

DIRTY KISS

RHYS FORD

A Cole McGinnis Mystery

Cole Kenjiro McGinnis, ex-cop and PI, is trying to get over the shooting death of his lover when a supposedly routine investigation lands in his lap. Investigating the apparent suicide of a prominent Korean businessman's son proves to be anything but ordinary, especially when it introduces Cole to the dead man's handsome cousin, Kim Jae-Min.

Jae-Min's cousin had a dirty little secret, the kind that Cole has been familiar with all his life and that Jae-Min is still hiding from his family. The investigation leads Cole from tasteful mansions to seedy lover's trysts to Dirty Kiss, the place where the rich and discreet go to indulge in desires their traditional-minded families would rather know nothing about.

It also leads Cole McGinnis into Jae-Min's arms, and that could be a problem. Jae-Min's cousin's death is looking less and less like a suicide, and Jae-Min is looking more and more like a target. Cole has already lost one lover to violence—he's not about to lose Jae-Min too.

www.dreamspinnerpress.com

DIRTY SECRET

RHYS FORD

A COLE McGINNIS MYSTERY

A Cole McGinnis Mystery
Sequel to *Dirty Kiss*

Loving Kim Jae-Min isn't always easy: Jae is gun-shy about being openly homosexual. Ex-cop turned private investigator Cole McGinnis doesn't know any other way to be. Still, he understands where Jae is coming from. Traditional Korean men aren't gay—at least not usually where people can see them.

But Cole can't spend too much time unraveling his boyfriend's issues. He has a job to do. When a singer named Scarlet asks him to help find Park Dae-Hoon, a gay Korean man who disappeared nearly two decades ago, Cole finds himself submerged in the tangled world of rich Korean families, where obligation and politics mean sacrificing happiness to preserve corporate empires. Soon the bodies start piling up without rhyme or reason. With every step Cole takes toward locating Park Dae-Hoon, another person meets their demise—and someone Cole loves could be next on the murderer's list.

www.dreamspinnerpress.com

A COLE McGINNIS MYSTERY

RHYS FORD

DIRTY
LAUNDRY

A Cole McGinnis Mystery
Sequel to *Dirty Secret*

For ex-cop turned private investigator Cole McGinnis, each day brings a new challenge. Too bad most of them involve pain and death. Claudia, his office manager and surrogate mother, is still recovering from a gunshot, and Cole's closeted boyfriend, Kim Jae-Min, suddenly finds his teenaged sister dumped in his lap. Meanwhile, Cole has his own sibling problems—most notably, a mysterious half brother from Japan whom his older brother, Mike, is determined they welcome with open arms.

As if his own personal dramas weren't enough, Cole is approached by Madame Sun, a fortune-teller whose clients have been dying at an alarming rate. Convinced someone is after her customers, she wants the matter investigated, but the police think she's imagining things. Hoping to put Sun's mind at ease, Cole takes the case and finds himself plunged into a Gordian knot of lies and betrayal where no one is who they are supposed to be and Death seems to be the only card in Madame Sun's deck.

www.dreamspinnerpress.com

A COLE McGINNIS MYSTERY

RHYS FORD

DIRTY
DEEDS

A Cole McGinnis Mystery
Sequel to *Dirty Laundry*

Sheila Pinelli needed to be taken out.

Former cop turned private investigator Cole McGinnis never considered committing murder. But six months ago, when Jae-Min's blood filled his hands and death came knocking at his lover's door, killing Sheila Pinelli became a definite possibility.

While Sheila lurks in some hidden corner of Los Angeles, Jae and Cole share a bed, a home, and most of all, happiness. They'd survived Jae's traditional Korean family disowning him and plan on building a new life—preferably one without the threat of Sheila's return hanging over them.

Thanks to the Santa Monica police mistakenly releasing Sheila following a loitering arrest, Cole finally gets a lead on Sheila's whereabouts. That is, until the trail goes crazy and he's thrown into a tangle of drugs, exotic women, and more death. Regardless of the case going sideways, Cole is determined to find the woman he once loved as a sister and get her out of their lives once and for all.

www.dreamspinnerpress.com

A DAWSON-TOKUGAWA ROMANCE

RHYS FORD

DOWN AND DIRTY

A COLE McGINNIS SERIES NOVEL

A Cole McGinnis Mystery

From the moment former LAPD detective Bobby Dawson spots Ichiro Tokugawa, he knows the man is trouble. And not just because the much younger Japanese inker is hot, complicated, and pushes every one of Bobby's buttons. No, Ichi is trouble because he's Cole McGinnis's younger brother and off-limits in every possible way. And Bobby knows that even before Cole threatens to kill him for looking Ichi's way. But despite his gut telling him Ichi is bad news, Bobby can't stop looking… or wanting.

Ichi was never one to play by the rules. Growing up in Japan as his father's heir, he'd been bound by every rule imaginable until he had enough and walked away from everything to become his own man. Los Angeles was supposed to be a brief pitstop before he moved on, but after connecting with his American half-brothers, it looks like a good city to call home for a while—if it weren't for Bobby Dawson.

Bobby is definitely a love-them-and-leave-them type, a philosophy Ichi whole-heartedly agrees with. Family was as much of a relationship as Ichi was looking for, but something about the gruff and handsome Bobby Dawson makes Ichi want more.

www.dreamspinnerpress.com